PRAISE FOR *Follow the Angels, Follow the Doves:*
The Bass Reeves Trilogy, Book One

2022 National Indie Excellence Awards
Finalist for Western Fiction

2021 International Afro-American
Historical & Genealogical Society Book Award
for Historical Fiction in Event/Era

2021 Oklahoma Book Award Finalist for Fiction

2021 Will Rogers Medallion Book Award
Finalist for Western Fiction

2021 Spur Award Finalist for Historical Novel

2021 Next Generation Indie Book Award Finalist
for Historical Fiction (Pre 1900s)

2021 Peacemaker Award Finalist for
Best First Novel

2020 Arkansas Gem from the Arkansas
Center for the Book

"A fascinating look at life in northwest Arkansas in the years
before and during the Civil War, when the future lawman came
of age and ultimately made his break for freedom. The rest of
the trilogy is likely to be just as intriguing, especially because
that's the way the real Bass Reeves lived his life."

—GLEN SEEBER, *The Oklahoman*

"Reeves shines. . . . Many a good novel has at its core a spiritual crisis, and readers will experience a great one here. . . . [A] masterful trilogy."

—JOHN MORT, *The Clarion-Ledger*

"Fearless and unflinching, *Follow the Angels, Follow the Doves* is a magnificent work of historical fiction. The characters and the times in which they lived are intensely and beautifully realized, and every line rings with authenticity. . . . Its truths are ever so urgent."

—STEVE YARBROUGH, author of
The Unmade World: A Novel

"Sidney Thompson has the ability to pull you into the narrative and give you a glimpse of the antebellum life of a young slave destined for greatness as a lawman. . . . Highly recommended."

—ART T. BURTON, author of *Black Gun, Silver Star:*
The Life and Legend of Frontier Marshal Bass Reeves

"This novel, like all the best historical fiction, reminds us that the most memorable events in our history happened in specific minutes, hours, and days to individuals every bit as complicated and contradictory as you or me."

—SUSAN PERABO, author of
The Fall of Lisa Bellow: A Novel

"Thompson's historical novel delivers an unforgettable character based on a true American hero. . . . A believable coming-of-age story that echoes *Huckleberry Finn* in its realism and social observation."

—MICHAEL RAY TAYLOR, *Commercial Appeal*

PRAISE FOR *Hell on the Border: The Bass Reeves Trilogy, Book Two*

2022 Oklahoma Book Award
Finalist for Fiction

2021 National Indie Excellence Award
Finalist for Western Fiction

2021 American Book Fest Award
Finalist for Historical Fiction

"If you've read and enjoyed *Follow the Angels, Follow the Doves*, you won't want to miss *Hell on the Border*. And if you haven't read them yet, this is a good time to start. . . . [Thompson] writes with a folksy feel, as if the story is being told by one of the people of the day, perhaps by the light of a campfire as cicadas sing from surrounding trees and a horse nickers nearby."

—GLEN SEEBER, *The Oklahoman*

"Western action and justice certainly figure in *Hell on the Border*, but they are relayed here with a nuanced lyricism, more Larry McMurtry than dime novel. . . . Bass Reeves, as Thompson portrays him, is a complex, compelling character, a fully evolved hero."

—MICHAEL RAY TAYLOR, Chapter16.org

"Gripping, hard-to-put-down."

—SEAN CLANCY, *Arkansas Democrat Gazette*

"A finely calibrated trilogy about a subject who couldn't be more necessary to our moment. The voice with which Thompson pursues Bass Reeves, at once austere and ornamented by its historical circumstances, is just one of the book's many enviable achievements."

—KEVIN BROCKMEIER, author of
The Brief History of the Dead

"*Hell on the Border* imaginatively reclaims the life of pioneering African American U.S. Marshal Bass Reeves. . . . This may be a book set in the historical past, but it contains stories and lessons we should contemplate today."

—W. RALPH EUBANKS, author of *The House at the End of the Road*

"In Sidney Thompson's hands, this story of a remarkable life shows us that Oklahoma was always indigenous land, Black lives have always mattered, and the white supremacy that seeks to squash Black brilliance still must be destroyed. With masterful structure, pacing, and language, this historical fiction reveals the truth of our present moment. . . . If you finished the first book desperate to see Bass Reeves free, in this book you will watch him become legendary, and you'll end this novel dying to know what happens next."

—ERIN STALCUP, author of *Every Living Species*

THE BASS REEVES TRILOGY

Book One
Follow the Angels, Follow the Doves

Book Two
Hell on the Border

Book Three
The Forsaken and the Dead

THE FORSAKEN
AND THE DEAD

The Bass Reeves Trilogy, Book Three

SIDNEY THOMPSON

University of Nebraska Press
Lincoln

The University of Nebraska Press is part of a land-
grant institution with campuses and programs on the
past, present, and future homelands of the Pawnee,
Ponca, Otoe-Missouria, Omaha, Dakota, Lakota, Kaw,
Cheyenne, and Arapaho Peoples, as well as those of the
relocated Ho-Chunk, Sac and Fox, and Iowa Peoples.

∞

Library of Congress Cataloging-in-Publication Data
Names: Thompson, Sidney, 1965– author.
Title: The forsaken and the dead / Sidney Thompson.
Description: Lincoln: University of Nebraska Press,
[2023] | Series: The Bass Reeves trilogy; book 3
Identifiers: LCCN 2023006018
ISBN 9781496220325 (paperback)
ISBN 9781496238184 (epub)
ISBN 9781496238191 (pdf)
Subjects: LCSH: Reeves, Bass—Fiction. | United States
marshals—Indian Territory—Fiction. | BISAC: FICTION /
African American & Black / Historical | HISTORY /
African American & Black | LCGFT: Novels.
Classification: LCC PS3620.H688 F67 2023 | DDC
813/.6—dc23/eng/20230306
LC record available at https://lccn.loc.gov/2023006018

Set in Minion Pro by A. Shahan.

For Bass,
always for Bass

Am I a sea, or a whale, that thou settest a
watch over me? . . . Oh that one would hear
me! behold, my desire is, that the Almighty
would answer me, and that mine adversary
had written a book. Surely I would take it upon
my shoulder, and bind it as a crown to me.

JOB 7:12, 31:35–36

This is not fiction, and I did not make the
characters which the book reveals. I present to
you a history of events as they occurred without
"fixing over," as a writer of fiction might do.

S. W. HARMAN, *Hell on the Border*

The discoloration of ages had been great.

EDGAR ALLAN POE, "The Fall of the
House of Usher"

Contents

Note on Language

A note about the use of the word n——: The policy of the University of Nebraska Press is not to print it because the press "values a thoughtful and ethical use of language." I abhor its casual and slanderous use as well, but my ethical responsibility as a writer of historical fiction is to re-create the past as I honestly see and feel it. Because I want readers to experience the violence, repression, inhumanity, and hate of nineteenth- and early twentieth-century America for its teachable lessons, I have chosen to include this word, even if it appears in a compromised manner, as "n——" or "n——s." Neither the press nor I intend to suggest at any time that the characters using the implied epithet are supplying the blanks themselves out of cultural sensitivity. Sensitivity to the contemporary reader is the only concern.

THE FORSAKEN
AND THE DEAD

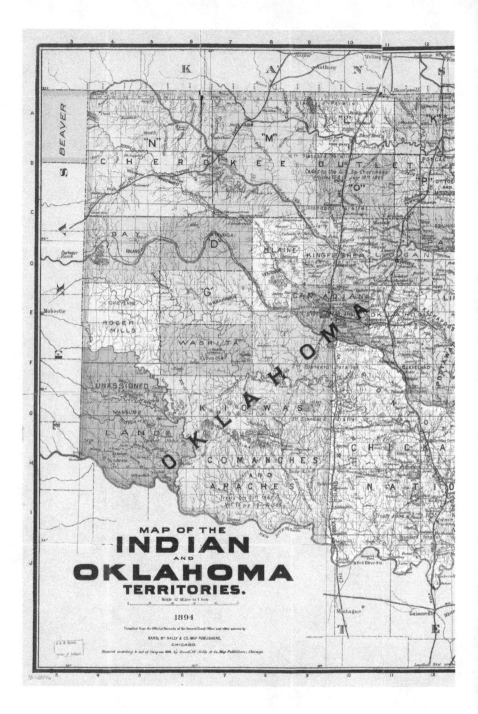

MAP OF THE
INDIAN
AND
OKLAHOMA
TERRITORIES.

Scale 12 Miles to 1 Inch

1894

Compiled from the Official Records of the General Land Office and other sources by

RAND, McNALLY & CO. MAP PUBLISHERS,
CHICAGO.

Entered according to act of Congress 1894 by Rand, McNally & Co., Map Publishers, Chicago.

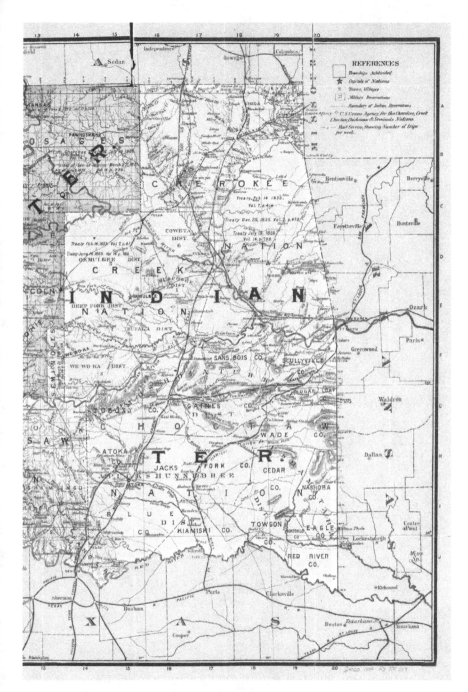

1. Map of the Indian and Oklahoma Territories, 1894. Compiled from the official records of the General Land Office and other sources. Published by Rand McNally and Company, Chicago, 1894. Courtesy Library of Congress, Geography and Map Division, Washington DC 20540-4650 USA dcu.

PART ONE

1895

1

Thatch

Indian Territory was in a dry season in May of 1895, leaving Rock Creek in the Creek Nation especially shallow in its broad bed, the water steepled with rocks where turtles sunned. The three buzzards that the three men had waved away from the bank floated directly above them as if the men's halos had loosed from their moorings from transpiration and in their haste to rise heavenward had collided to form a circling, circling chain that bound these chance souls to this moment and place, their lives to their inevitable long home—starting now.

"He was there, face down in it." The white man who'd introduced himself as Lee nearly two hours earlier in Keokuk Falls pointed with a thrusting action of his rigid coat sleeve to help Bass Reeves sight the spot. "Where it's smooth there, betwixt the froth and them two chicken turtles stacked, that's where I drug him up from to keep him from drifting." He spat the color of wet rocks and let his arm hang at his side. "He weren't that heavy. He might look big but really ain't."

Bass let his chin drop, and he eyed the clothed hump buzzing with flies. It was crisscrossed with ropes that were tied to tree branches and rocks. Eddie Reed, a young deputy Bass was mentoring, wore his neckerchief bandit-like as he stood on the slope of the bank at an angle near the water's edge. He checked the dead man's pockets, but a wadded handkerchief was all he found.

"He smelled better this morning," Lee offered.

"I reckon so," Bass said. The buzzards had flayed the back of the man's head, ears, and neck. Surprisingly there were no signs the buzzards had pecked his hands, despite the exposed flesh of two missing fingers severed at the second joint on his right hand. The man's skin had begun to marble pink and white all over. He looked to be a white man. Bass strained to bend down but hesitated from the sting in his thigh.

"Want him rolled over?" Eddie asked, standing over the dead man's feet. A sock still remained where one of his boots was missing. It was a rich man's sock.

Bass nodded. "Sure could use the help today." He took hold of one of the ropes that wrapped around the man's back and tugged, testing if the rope was taut enough. It was. "Come on," he said, and he and Eddie rolled the man over.

The center of the man's forehead was both concave and swollen, imprinted with a fist-shaped blow, and purple-black with a gash across the top that had long stopped bleeding and opened to redness. The skin around the gash, among the whiskers on his face, and down on his neck seemed to slide away like wet paper.

Bass shifted his eyes to Lee, who was hitching up his trousers, but Lee's gut instantly weighed them down again. "You positive this Thatch?" Bass asked.

Up on his toes, Lee leaned over the body, then rocked back on his heels. "That's who he told me last night he was." He spat and wiped his chin and beard on his sleeve. "I was setting my traps when I come up on him in the evening time. He was stirring up something to eat for him and some sidekicker he had with him, and he say for me to join them. He introduced himself as Zachariah Thatch from Washington County, and the one who ain't here was Jimmy Cash or something, from Arkansas, too, but from Faulkner County, he say."

"If Thatch was the one cooking," Bass said, "what makes you think the one with him was working for him and not the other way?"

Lee hunched his shoulders. "I don't know, 'cause Thatch was twice as old as him and dressed and talked like he had money. I mean, Thatch was white while the younger one, Jimmy, shore wasn't. I mean, he was white-looking but mixed with dark. What kind a dark I couldn't tell you. And while Thatch talked big about inspecting some land about to open for settlement in the Kickapoos, Jimmy was quiet on it. Course, I got family in Washington County, so me and this dead man here did most of the talking about some apple growers we knowed in Georgetown. I guess you know it by Lincoln."

Bass gazed blankly. "Know it by the apples."

"Best anywheres," Lee said.

Bass nodded. "Anything else you recall?"

Lee's eyes seemed to fix on the handkerchief wad on a patch of grass. "His friend say he just got back from Keokuk Falls. His head was bobbing like a cork he was so sour, while this one here didn't act like he drank a drop. Didn't smell like he did, anyhow."

Eddie took a step closer as if to join the conversation, but Bass had never known him to be much of a talker in the company of others.

"Which saloon did he say?" Bass asked.

"Red Dog. He talked about a shooting there. That a man died dueling a colored lawman. He was laughing about it."

Bass turned to Thatch and studied his milky, bloodshot eyes. He eased down on his good knee and waved flies away with his hat, then pressed his fingertips against the man's forehead, around the gash, feeling the give and listening to the bits of skull crackle. "That was in the evening you saw 'em, you say?"

"That's right," Lee said as Bass lifted a branch off of Thatch's chest to look for holes in his clothes. "Weren't dark yet but getting there. The two shots I heard come later. I was in my own camp by then."

Bass tipped one of the rocks on its side as if he were hunting underneath for worms in the man's heart. "Like *pow pow*?" he asked.

"No," Lee said. "Like *pow . . . pow*. Like enough time for a bad shot to jump up closer, you know?"

Bass lowered the rock back down, and with his Sheffield Bowie knife, he began cutting rope. Eddie freed the weights from the rope and tossed them aside. A rock tumbled into the water while Bass unbuttoned the man's shirt. Not until Bass had unfastened the man's trousers did he find what appeared to be a .38 entry hole, like a new navel, a few inches below his original one. Bass squinted up at the dark silhouette of Lee's head, like a hole itself in that sunny sky— the buzzards so slow around that hole to almost be flies crawling.

"Guessing you was that colored lawman," Lee said.

Bass nodded. "I ain't the white one that died."

"But he got you, I see."

Bass shut his eyes and took a deep breath despite what the air over this decaying dead man smelt like. Getting shot for the first time in his life was not something he was proud of. He took up his knife. "God allows the devil to have his luck."

Lee chuckled. "The other one drawed first, didn't he? Don't that make you the lucky one?"

Bass rested the point of the six-inch blade on Thatch's entry wound. "Fear'll make a body move quick, sure true." He pressed the blade down and wiggled it back and forth as it sank and as he felt for the slug in that bloated belly flesh, soft as curd. "But quick ain't the whole of it, you know?" Bass said. "I tried to warn the boy. Sure he was real fast, just like he said, uh-huh. But like a lot of 'em, he couldn't shoot both fast and straight." Once the blade disappeared up to the brass cross guard, Bass eased up on the pressure, and the blade rose back out almost on its own accord. Then he tried again by going perpendicular to the previous puncture mark.

"Jesus," Lee said. "You gotta have it?"

"Maybe, maybe not," Bass said. "But I want it." He wiggled the knife back and forth again as he continued to press it down deep, still not feeling that hard button of lead, so he pulled the blade out just a little, until he had good leverage with it, then pried the belly fat out of the body, spilling it in chunks, like a congealed flower of head cheese. He laid the knife on the ground beside him and searched through the fat with his fingers until he found it: a .38 slug of lead the size of a pearl. He reached for his knife, stood upright, and limped to the water's edge to rinse his hands, knife, and the bullet that might or might not prove that the young man Zachariah Thatch had invited to accompany him on his travels had murdered him in cold blood.

Pow. Thatch hadn't seen it coming. With no time to reach for a weapon, he could only throw up his hands to shield himself. Maybe that was how it happened, first losing the two middle fingers on his right hand, but there was no telling where that slug went. Then came the second *pow* once the shooter had moved closer to his target— this one striking Thatch in the gut to slow him even more so that either Jimmy Cash or someone else with high nerves or a poor aim could finally step all the way up to him, right to his head, and finish him off with something as solid as it was blunt.

Bass stared at the water, clear as glass at the surface but golden as a picture frame at the bottom, then at the belly slime stringing away from his hands like some enormous spiderweb that fell apart as the wind blew. "Can you point out where they camped?"

Lee didn't say a word. He spat as if that were enough of an answer, and indeed it was. When Bass heard him step away, he knew to push on up to begin loading the corpse into the wagon so he and Eddie could follow.

2

Keokuk Falls

Bass had leaned on that barroom table all night as if in a dream. He sort of sat on it with his left leg resting level, but he was standing, too, and pressing a handkerchief to the wound above his knee, below a tight length of rope that Eddie had cut for him, while he watched hands, so many hands moving to straighten chairs after the initial scramble. That, or they raised or lowered glasses or bottles or held cigars or fanned or flicked cards or simply quivered, showing they touched or reached only for the freedom of air to tug a beard, to fix a hat, but inching nowhere near the threat of their weapons. Or the hands were new ones, mostly gloved and appearing from outside as they grasped the top side of the batwing doors. Hands first, then Bass's attention went to faces for intent, the sunburned white man with the pork pie hat and horseshoe mustache . . . the dark-skinned white man with the small, smiling mustache . . . the freckled, dusty white man with near mutton chops, in case there was something akin to loyalty among the drovers and stragglers of Keokuk Falls.

The town sat on the banks of the North Canadian River, one mile north of the Seminole Nation, and though named in honor of Chief Moses Keokuk of the Fox and Sac tribe, it was little more than a whiskey town of ill repute. From Bass's point of view, it had become a baited trap for the worst outlaws hiding in dry Indian Territory, which was the reason Bass had come to play cards and drink: to fit in and collect information from the tales about crimes they told of until a feller recognized him. That was a new pestering way of life Bass had to grow accustomed to. The exposure of his much-delayed murder trial and acquittal in 1887, along with the ongoing accumulation of years—twenty of them now—as a deputy, his reputation as an invincible lawman was a shadow he couldn't shake. It followed him into every corner and hollow of his massive jurisdiction, including both Indian and Oklahoma Territories.

Even as he prayed for the gunslinger's soul, he held a Colt calmly in front of him in case the gunslinger had friends or kin who might take issue with him. Despite the occasional gap between the floorboards, the blood never stopped spreading. Bass had that to gauge the passage of time. And what a dark, hellish rain there must have been in the crawlspace below the saloon. Bass's own had streamed off the table, like rain joining rain, before the flow finally quit. He'd sent Eddie through the Pottawatomie land to cross into the Chickasaw Nation to fetch Doctor Jesse Mooney, the first and only licensed doctor in Indian Territory, who fortunately lived only ten miles away in McGee.

Bass had first met Doctor Jesse seven years earlier when he stopped by Younger's Bend in the Cherokee Nation to see Belle Starr about a stagecoach bandit possibly hiding in the area. She knew most of the outlaws coming and going or knew of them. She usually sheltered prostitutes, so of course the outlaws found her, and in time she had found the doctor for her girls. Bass thought of him as a handsome and polite man with wavy black hair and a clean face and eyes that didn't quite look like eyes—more like the gray-black beads the Seminoles made from the shell of a stinkpot turtle. His diminutive stature therefore became an afterthought. Standing barefoot at five foot five, Doctor Jesse was shorter than the average man, but at the same time he never seemed short even to six-foot-two Bass.

Doctor Jesse was a close friend to Belle and, as a consequence, to her son. *It would almost be worth getting shot*, thought Bass, *if Eddie got to see the doctor tonight and feel close to his mother again.* Eddie had his demons. Who wouldn't with an unmotherly mother the likes of Belle Starr, with her years of lawlessness and then her murder in 1890 and the persistent rumors that Eddie had been the one to ambush her himself, despite having a solid alibi? Eddie was a good, young man, though. He did thoughtful things, but he was awfully quiet and sad-like, with deep-set eyes and a thin, down-pointing mustache that bestowed on him the appearance of a perpetual frown. On the rare occasions he did smile, a circular scar on his right cheek by his nose resembled a dimple, and if his smile stretched far enough, another dimple appeared near his right ear—entry and exit wounds from when Eddie's partner in a horse theft had turned on him, shooting him in his sleep with a .22 rifle. That near-death experience had weighed on Judge Parker, and he took pity, despite sentencing the boy to a federal penitentiary in Ohio. Eventually the judge petitioned President Cleveland to pardon him, asked the marshal to appoint Eddie as a deputy, and then asked Bass to mentor him.

The doctor was a lot like Eddie, Bass realized as he waited, as he remembered. Doctor Jesse was much kinder than his stoic countenance suggested, but he didn't brood, and nothing about him seemed lost or shot as it did with Eddie. It was as if Doctor Jesse had simply decided that playing possum before the forsaken of the territory was the polite thing to do.

When the black homburg hat with an intense crown crease appeared like a crow in slow flight just above the saloon doors, Bass moved to tuck away his Colt. Then the rest of the doctor pushed through—the suit and necktie and watch chain. He strolled in like a banker first thing in the morning, clutching his hat and doctor's bag against his chest as if it were a cash bag. When his unreal stinkpot eyes found Bass across the room, they lowered until he was close enough to greet him.

"Bass," he said, pumping his hand with a vigor that suggested he was happy to help even in the middle of the night.

"You a sight for sore eyes, Doc."

"Well," Doctor Jesse started to say as he glanced at the gunslinger sprawled on his back, then at Bass's injured leg, "sore something." He pinched the blood-soaked edge of the torn trouser leg and pulled it back as if it were a heavy curtain or the flap of a wet tent. Bass had split his trouser leg open about a cubit, a good, rough measurement for checking his wound and dabbing and doctoring it, he had reckoned. Sometimes Bass would go weeks or months thinking in terms of cubits—or windows in cubit squares—ever since his wife, Jennie, had read to him and the young'uns about Noah and his ark and its dimensions. Eventually he'd go back to using feet and then one day he'd size something up and out of a clear sky see forearms everywhere, and that would be the measurement he'd use for a while.

Doctor Jesse let go of the trouser leg, and it fell flat like a dead thing. He eyed Bass without blinking. "Just when I was starting to believe you weren't human."

Bass shrugged. "Bound to happen, I guess. Dang it!"

"I was trying to remember on my ride when the last time I saw you was. It's been a year, right? When we went out to check on Geronimo? Hard to believe it's been a year."

Bass shook his head. "Forgetting Tecumseh. In February."

"Tecumseh!" Doctor Jesse nodded. "When you took the Wewoka Six in on foot? That *was* February, wasn't it? I did see you at the jail then for a quick how-do. I guess that counts. Sure, it does."

Bass reached for the bottle of forty-rod on the table nudged against his left holster. "The Wewoka Six was a fun time."

"You tracked them to a cabin near here, didn't you say?"

"About a mile east." Bass tipped the bottle up, then took a breath that burned.

The doctor relaxed with hardly a smile, but it gave Bass a fleeting glimpse of what he must have looked like as a sweet boy. "I heard others tell it, but not from you. Do you mind?"

"I might be persuaded. I'm pretty sure you don't need to, but I wish you'd check the hot-tempered gunslinger first."

"Of course." Doctor Jesse raised his black bag high into the air as if he were preparing to ford a river, then stretched a long step over the pool of blood and the 1890 Remington revolver still clenched in the dead man's right hand. "Another one to doubt you?" he asked. He turned in his small space that was clear of table and chairs and blood and stood like a soldier with his leather soles touching as he eyed Bass.

"Accused me a cheating."

"Looking to pick a fight, huh?"

"And the whole time he was shaking, Doc. Didn't even allow himself to get his pistol over the table and aim at me good. They think I'm too old to lose to their nonsense, I reckon. I may be fifty-six, but that's God's gift."

"Belle would've set them straight."

Bass's eyes bloomed wide to agree with that. Belle had loved him, and when she loved, she loved fiercely.

"She'd tell them to swallow their pride if they don't want their medicine," Doctor Jesse said.

"She wanted no part of my wagon." Bass grinned. "I do miss that horse thief."

"She wouldn't have turned herself in for nobody else. She really liked you. Respected you. *Feared* you, really, Bass, if truth be told." He gave a nod, and his head gradually tipped toward the body on the floor between them.

Bass realized the table of hushed, late-night, low-stakes poker players had gone quieter. All four of them had stopped their game and were perfectly still and attentive to what Doctor Jesse was doing. As he sifted his memory of that night, Bass ignored their faces because, by then, Jimmy Cash would've already left the saloon, would've already killed Thatch, and might even have already dropped the weighted body in Rock Creek.

Squatting, Doctor Jesse pinched the rounded crown of the gun-slinger's hat and lifted it. The man's face and eyes were pale as beef fat.

"Who is it?" Doctor Jesse asked. "Anybody I might've heard of?" He continued to gaze down, and so did Bass, but in hindsight he only saw beef fat.

"Nobody nobody know, or would say."

Doctor Jesse rested the bowler back over the man's face, stood up, and crossed back onto Bass's side of the blood spill but turned first to the vacant table beside him. He laid his hand on the table, inspected his hand, then set his bag and hat down on it.

Bass cleared his throat. "Well, I tracked them boys from Wewoka to a abandoned cabin they were holed up at in a woody spot, sorta hidden behind some cedars. I do like to dress up, you know. Really tickles me, so I got the idea to come on to Keokuk Falls where I bought a real flea-bitten ox team and ramshackle wagon to go along with my old tramp duds. You know, a pair a patched overalls, some tattered shoes, and a felt hat that looks more like a drunk skunk flip-flopping."

Doctor Jesse grinned and crossed his arms.

"I made myself out to be a hapless farmer riding down the road," Bass said with his hands in front of him as if he were holding the reins to the oxen, "and I see this good stump right close to the cabin I seen before when I was just on my mare. So I decide to hang the wagon up on it, and I mean I get hung up on it good, Doc. That wagon damn near come apart and throwed me off, and those oxes commenced to moo-moaning something awful."

Doctor Jesse laughed, and some others in the saloon laughed with him, all at once. The poker players covered their cards and were listening and looking his way.

"Well," Bass continued, "I got down and started working on trying to free the wagon or something close to it. The front wheels were plumb off the ground. So I'm in and outta the wagon for a shovel first and then a axe. I'm prying and chopping. I'm groaning and cussing. Then two of them Wewoka boys come sneaking outta the cabin as if there ain't smoke coming out the chimney to give 'em away. Gotta see what all my carrying-on was about. They're looking up and down the road and really fit to be tied. Then one says to the other, 'Leave it to a old n—— to get her hung.'"

Doctor Jesse shook his head but was grinning all the same.

"Boy, Doc, hearing that made me sing inside."

"I bet," Doctor Jesse said.

"So I decide to really play the fool. 'Sorry, massas!' I say, and to really goad them I stop fighting with the stump and shut my eyes and ask them to shut theirs, and I start praying." Bass clasped his hands together and shut his eyes, and Doctor Jesse snickered. "'Lordy,' I say, 'will you send a angel to help these here wheels grow some feet so I can run again on down the road far away from this lost spot, or maybe, Lord, you can turn this stout stump to sand or something like it. Maybe a loaf a bread or a string a catfish, fine with me. A bottle of whiskey maybe? Or, better still, a new change a clothes for my young'uns 'cause they shore need 'em. Anything but this here stout stump in the middle a the road in the middle a . . . I don't even know. I just needing a small miracle to free not so much me, Lord. No, not this lowly old n—— alone, but these decent white folk mainly so they can go back about they important sooner or later business.'"

Bass peaked and then opened his eyes wide. "I couldn't wait to spring my surprise 'cause, well, I knew they'd love it, wouldn't see it coming, you know? People love a good surprise. Need it, really. Especially outlaws." Bass eyed the poker players, either chuckling or nodding, if not both. "Y'all know it's true!" He turned to the doctor. "You see, you gotta find a way to break they spirit. You ain't gotta kill 'em, not usually. Once they see how foolish they been when all they been thinking is how big and smart they are and how dumb you is, shit, Doc, they just crumble to nothing."

The doctor smiled as he attempted to remove the handkerchief from Bass's wound, but it clung. He stopped and reached for the bottle of forty-rod but stopped himself again and looked up at Bass.

"Help yourself, Doc. Don't want you having the shakes on me."

Doctor Jesse playfully humped his eyebrows, then took hold of the bottle. "So what happened next?"

"Before you know it," Bass said, "all six of them trading post robbers were out on the road trying to get me gone, and that's when I dipped my hands into my pockets." He motioned as if he were to dip his hands into his pockets now. "My overalls got these nice big pockets you can stuff a chicken in. Well, that's when I showed 'em what for." He moved his hands from his pockets to his holstered Colts and patted them. "Oh, it was a sight, Doc. They never saw it coming. Not a one put up a fight. They throwed down their weapons without a word, I'm telling you, and I marched them to Tecumseh like we was all just making our way to a swimming hole."

The doctor took a swig from the bottle but held the whiskey in his mouth as if to really savor the moment. He closed his eyes as if he might be imagining that day.

"It was perfect weather for a swim, really," Bass said.

The doctor swallowed, then opened his gray-black eyes. They were as dark and mysterious as tiny caves. "Bass, that's thirty miles about."

"Thirty-two."

"With no help?"

"Just me."

Doctor Jesse shook his head. "Bass Reeves, you ain't human." He lowered his eyes to the wound and doused another swallow on the handkerchief. He patted the handkerchief, then passed the bottle back to Bass. "But even if you ain't, this is gonna still bite. You ready?"

"That's all right. You got the badge in these proceedings." Bass clenched his teeth, and the doctor peeled and tugged until the handkerchief finally pulled free.

Bass pulled from the bottle and then sucked a deep breath as the whiskey snuffed the pain. Eddie walked up then, telling Doctor Jesse where he'd taken his horse for food and water.

3

Before, During, and After

"I won't take your silver," said Doctor Jesse, collecting the bloody cloths into a pile beside a tangle of instruments on the saloon table. "You'd think I could extract a .44–40, was hoping I could, but truly best I leave it be. Sorry about that, Bass."

Bass swung his doctored leg off the table and favored it as he stood. He patted Doctor Jesse's shoulder. "No, I appreciate you trying, Doc." He collected his Stetson from a nail on the wall, where other hats and coats hung. He scanned the saloon for Red Dog, the Creek who owned the place. Bass wanted to thank him for the whiskey he'd used to clean his wound and tame the pain, but Red Dog must have stepped into the storeroom or outside again to relieve himself. A lone man stood at the bar and spat into a spittoon at his feet. The table of card players were all scratching their dirty faces with either their fingernails or a card or match. Eddie was outside helping the coroner load the corpse in his low-lying corpse wagon.

Doctor Jesse wiped his probers. "How's your protégé coming along?"

Bass thought the doctor was a good man to care about a young man like Eddie. "Oh, he'll make a fine deputy, I expect." He leaned on his right leg, which brought him closer to the doctor. "If he can get past the past. Weighs on him when he don't know it does."

Doctor Jesse stopped his busy hands and looked at Bass without blinking. "That right?"

"I see it," Bass said. He arched his back to stretch out the stiffness and stifled a yawn. "Well, Doc, I think I'm gonna head next door to get some shut-eye before the sun won't let me."

Doctor Jesse tossed the last of his instruments into his black bag and brushed his right hand up and down his coat before offering it to Bass. "I'm glad you called on me. It was real good to see you and Eddie both."

"Yep." Bass nodded.

"And Mrs. Reeves? Tell me, how's she faring?"

Bass stepped away but slowly, easily, and Doctor Jesse followed with a light hand bracing Bass's back. "Still not good, Doc. Some days she can't bear to get outta bed."

"It's not her appendix, is it?"

"Doctor said it wasn't."

"Sorry to hear it, Bass. Peritonitis tends to cling. You let me know if I can be of any use."

"Thank you, Doc. Sure will."

"She's getting the best care there in Fort Smith. I'll keep her in my prayers, though. Tell her that for me."

Bass didn't know when he'd see Jennie next. Once he filled his prisoner wagon, turned the prisoners over to the jails in the districts wanting them, and collected his per diem plus rewards was all he knew, which could take him a month or more because he hadn't collected his first prisoner this time around yet. He'd been spending less time at home in recent years—ever since 1893, when President Cleveland had appointed former Confederate George Crump, another Democrat, as the new marshal for the Western District of Arkansas. Crump's first action had been to call all the deputies together for a meeting at the federal courthouse in Fort Smith to explain the new plan to divide the jurisdiction of Indian Territory. Fort Smith's court would continue overseeing the Cherokee, Creek, and Seminole Nations, though the Eastern District of Texas in Paris would begin overseeing the Chickasaw and Choctaw Nations. U.S. Marshal Crump then recommissioned those deputies he wished to retain and transferred the others to Paris, including the only two who were colored.

Jennie hadn't wanted to move and refused to ever live in Texas again, not after growing up on a plantation so close to Paris. The family had already moved in 1887 from their showplace in Van Buren to a much more modest house on North Twelfth Street in Fort Smith to allow them to pay off the extensive lawyer fees Bass still owed for his trial. Jennie had tried to convince him to retire as a deputy to prevent their previous master, George Reeves, now the Speaker of the Texas House of Representatives, from being able to provide undue political pressure over his work, but Bass couldn't see doing any other job. When he and Eddie had no other option but to stay the night in Paris, they rented a room. Otherwise they lived together in a rented shack in Calvin on the south bank of the Canadian River in the Choctaw Nation, a short walk from where Bass's twenty-two-year-old son Bennie lived since marrying a Negro girl native to the community once known as Riverview. That was before the Choctaw, Oklahoma and Gulf Railway decided to connect McAlester to Oklahoma City and rename one of the many stops in between. When Bass was fortunate enough to round up outlaws that he was obligated to transport to Fort Smith, Bass usually got to see everyone in the family, while Eddie put up downtown at one of the hotels or brothels.

Now that Bass was injured, perhaps he'd need to return sooner. This was a new test the Lord was presenting him. Bass would have to track his own body this time, measure his strength against the heat of the day, against so many factors.

Bass thought again of the doctor's stinkpot turtle eyes as he remembered shaking his small doctor-soft hand. He thought of how Doctor Jesse's hard leather shoes never scraped or pounded a floor, and how as he and the doctor were leaving Red Dog Saloon, Bass had turned around to be certain no one behind them betrayed a notion of shooting him in the back.

◆ ◆ ◆

As Bass and Eddie followed Lee on a beautiful bay dun to Zachariah Thatch's campsite, Bass continued to search his memory for faces, the whole ghost parade. One of them in the saloon had to be Thatch's friend, and to be on the run, that friend would be the chief suspect. He'd felt lucky, hadn't he, to witness a duel and then chose, as some will, to interpret the tragedy as a miracle and just had to hurry back to his camp to reenact it?

The trail Lee took from the creek wound through a forest for about a hundred yards to a small meadow of dead grass with a solitary tree, a silver maple, which stood as the only object for a body to sit against. And there they were, above the tree, floating with the clouds—the three buzzards, omnipresent as hell.

Lee aimed for the maple but stopped his dun well before it as he approached an obvious campsite. It was an ancient one, sunken with packed earth, worn from use like stair steps. Lee gazed from the saddle at the fire pit's gray, black, and ribbed remains. "This was where I saw them last." He pointed. "Thatch was here and the other was here. Then I left the way we just come."

Bass climbed down from the wagon and stepped up to the fire pit. He slid his Bowie knife from its sheath and raked through the ashes, turning over charred branches, like the cubits of a dead child. He stirred the shards of a once-clear whiskey bottle, though he saw nothing unusual. Not like that time in the Cherokee Nation when he'd found the remnants of a man's boots, the nails a clear giveaway. He walked around the pit, scanning the baked earth, the cracked ground, and the dead grass. Fire ants crawled in and out of the cracks, over clumps of used coffee grounds, and random leaves lay scattered from the nearby maple, bur oak, and red mulberry. Eddie climbed off his mount and joined Bass.

Lee backed up his dun to give them space. "Whatcha looking for?" he asked. "Them fingers Thatch lost?"

Bass searched in silence, enjoying the peace nature provided.

"I don't think you'll find them fingers," Lee said.

Bass continued to orbit the old fire pit, and Eddie followed his counterclockwise rotation on the other side. Together, gradually, their circles and the grasshoppers within them spiraled outward. "Anything, my friend, we're looking for anything," Bass finally said, knowing if he didn't say something Lee would soon again.

When Bass reached the shade of the maple, he removed his hat and wiped his brow on his sleeve, relieved to be standing even in splotchy shade. Then he lowered his head and rubbed his neck, and that was when he discovered the site of another fire. It wasn't as big or old as the other one, but it wasn't small, and it was close to the trunk. Too close. "Eddie," he said and looked up at the tree limbs, coated with soot. He waited until Eddie was standing beside him before pointing down. "What do you make of this?"

Eddie buried his hands in his trouser pockets. He studied the ground, glanced up at Bass, then turned. He stayed twisted like that for a full breath, in and out, then straightened, his head angled upward at the sooted branches. "Think they started here, got smoked out, then started another over yonder where it makes sense?"

"Could be. But ever known anybody to start a fire this close to a tree that wasn't a child or some halfwit?"

Eddie grew still.

"Whatcha find?" Lee called.

Eddie shook his head. "Don't know, boss."

"Y'all find anything?" Lee asked.

Bass turned and walked a few steps toward Lee. "Where they tie their horses at?"

Lee looked away and pointed. "Tied them to a little wagon. Not as big as your'n."

Bass wiped his mustache from the corners of his mouth. "Could you describe the team?"

Lee hunched his shoulders. "A black'un and a chestnut."

"Did you see a fire burning under the tree?"

Lee sat up straight and squinted toward the maple. "Under?" He shook his head and nodded at the fire pit closer to him. "Here is all. Right here."

A sudden thrashing in the silver maple made Lee and his bay dun jump. Bass and Eddie watched the buzzards settle down for a rest.

"I don't like them things," Lee said.

Bass walked to the gray mare hitched to the prisoner wagon. He unbuckled a saddle rider and reached for his coin purse. "You've been mighty helpful." Bass walked up to Lee and now held out a silver dollar. "You married, Lee?"

Lee took the dollar and turned it over in the sun, nodding as he watched it flash.

"Deputy Reed will take you and your wife's name and get directions where we can reach you if need be. We appreciate you."

"Shore, uh-huh, and a dollar's mighty nice," Lee said, "but one'll get lonely without a second to rub against."

Bass pushed his hat back so they could fully see eye to eye. "Is that right?"

"I did do the right thing and ride to town to tell the law, and when I heard you was around, I hunted you up and waited for y'all to wake up good and for you to purchase yourself another pair of britches before leading y'all here and all. I did spend all morning—"

"All right, all right," Bass said, opening his purse.

◆ ◆ ◆

If wheel marks stopped but hooves continued or if wheel marks switched from a wobbly left wheel to a wobbly right wheel or if shod prints vanished into unshod, then Bass could guess something close to knowing when it was a ruse. Tracking Greenleaf, Ned Christie, Tom Story, and Bob Dozier over the years had taught Bass nearly every elusive trick there was. Jimmy Casharago, though, didn't seem to know a single one. The suspect simply rode a straightaway path from the murder scene as any innocent man would.

"To survive," Bass explained, sitting shotgun to Eddie, "a body's got to stay alert to the idea that the living world is God's way of shutting the past outta your head in order to show you the future. To do that, a body needs a silent mind. He's a quiet one, God. If your head ain't quiet, too, you ain't gonna hear him. You ain't gonna reach heaven 'cause you ain't ever gonna leave hell behind."

"You think my head's a beehive?" Eddie asked. "That what you telling me?" He was driving west along the north bank of the North Canadian River after stopping again in Keokuk Falls to send and receive telegrams about the identity of Zachariah W. Thatch, forty-six, and his companion, James W. Casharago, twenty-six, who had a record of being an incorrigible swindler. Thatch had taken him into his home months earlier as a favor to Jimmy's uncle, a family friend. Thatch had given the boy work and made every effort to groom the delinquent into a man. It had taken three transmissions to complete the summary of Casharago's criminal past, consisting mostly of bur-glary, larceny, and fraud, which led to a three-year sentence in a Tennessee prison. His most recent crime had been his most creative. First Casharago mortgaged a mule because he claimed he needed seed to farm. But he bought another mule instead. At another bank he mortgaged the two mules and bought a wagon with the money. At a third bank he mortgaged the two mules and the wagon, then purchased a wagonload of merchandise from a dry goods store in Harrison, Arkansas, which he peddled throughout the Ozarks.

"Eddie, I'm thinking your head might be louder than you know. Or your eyes are remembering sometimes more than they're seeing. A body in this line a work needs eyes to be like dog ears, you know?"

Eddie drove with the reins wrapped around his wrists. His con-trol of the team was improving. He was judging better when to read the road or the team and when he could look away at Bass or just to work the stiffness from his neck. He smirked this time without looking away and formed pistols with his fingers, aimed at their team eating up Casharago's tracks, which were so clearly marked on this less-traveled, dusty, baked road that Bass didn't need to get on his mare to scout ahead of the wagon. Even Eddie could read them from this perch. "I reckon you right," Eddie said. "Wanna know what I was thinking?"

"What's that?"

"A tale about three buzzards."

"Pardon, Eddie." Bass stretched out his wounded leg so that his boot rested on the footboard in front of Eddie, and that relieved some of the throbbing.

"They was called," Eddie went on, "well, I don't remember what they was called in Cherokee, but their names in English was Before, During, and After."

"I was expecting Father, Son, and Holy Ghost."

Eddie shook his head. "This a Cherokee tale."

"Oh, okay. Let's hear it." Bass reached into his coat pocket for his brick of tobacco.

"Well, these three buzzards was in search of carrion and they was really carrying on about it."

"Good start," Bass said. "I like it already."

"One said to the other two, 'We need a plan.'"

"That was Before speaking up, right?"

"I don't know," Eddie said. "Coulda been. Yeah, I guess so. I see what you saying."

Bass bit a plug off the brick and offered the brick to Eddie, who reached short because of the reins. Bass placed it in his hand, and then Eddie craned his head to take a bite.

"So what did During and After say?"

Eddie worked the stiff chew into his cheek. "During said for them to follow the next animal they saw, whether crippled or stinking or not."

"Dang, they was hungry then."

"So the first one, Before, said, 'That sounds like a plan all right. What you think, After?' After was quiet like he usually was. Once a little time wore on, After said, 'What do we do after we see one and follow him?'"

"That's what I was wondering." Bass tucked the brick into his pocket.

"'If you wanna find out,' says During, 'follow me.' So the buzzards stop soaring on the breeze, and Before and After follow During to a tree below."

"A silver maple?"

Eddie gave Bass a side glance. "You hear this before?"

Bass shook his head. "Lucky, I guess."

"Except the leaves on this silver maple grow in the other way so the tree actually looks silver."

Bass's eyes landed on his gray mare, Hammer. "Nice, I like Cherokee tales."

"Exactly," said Eddie. "So they perched there on this *silver* silver maple, then Before said, 'Do y'all see anything?' After said, 'Not yet.' But During said, 'Hold on, follow me.'"

"I'm liking this buzzard, During."

"So Before and After follow During even though, to them, it appears During is only following a flame running through the dry underbrush and not an animal at all."

Bass pointed ahead of them. "Still watching the road, ain't you?" He didn't see anything changing, but a body shouldn't assume.

Eddie nodded. He glanced at the road, then again at Bass. "So this flame During was chasing was actually a fox sniffing up a trail, so During was onto something, all right. In fact During begins to catch up to him because the fox stopped to try to figure out which way the trail went, left or right, or if the thing he was tracking some-how went straight up into the air. During is meanwhile thinking to himself how hungry he is. He's thinking, 'How come I gotta wait till after a thing dies before I can eat? I ain't a child without a mind of my own! How come I gotta be the same thing today as I was yes-terday?' During, meanwhile, is getting closer and closer to that fox so he all of a sudden decides he ought to just kill that fox, and he gets his buzzard claws ready."

"This is some story," Bass cut in.

"Hold on, gets better," Eddie said with his mouth brimming, so he turned and spat, and so did Bass. "During's about to grab the fox around his throat to carry him off to the *silver* silver maple to share his bounty with his buzzard friends when that fox looks up and sees what he was beginning to wonder was only a thing buzzing in his head but was a real turkey buzzard, for sure! And that bald, bloody-red head and neck was like a flaming arrow sailing right for him, with his deadly claws stretched out and about to sink!"

"Uh-oh."

"Well, that fox didn't think about nothing then except maybe how hungry he was and that's all, so he was quick-acting, Bass, let me tell you. He opened his jaws like a trap and snapped down on that bald buzzard neck and held on. He had to because there was quite a tussle at first, but that fox sawed with his teeth like he was cutting timber—like he was a dang beaver—and before he knew it, that fox was having himself a feast. And in due time, so did Before and After."

Bass chuckled and then was quiet. Eddie was quiet, too, but he was also smirking at the road signs that told them they were still heading right.

"Maybe I need to preach a little less," Bass admitted. He paused to let Eddie respond, but Eddie remained silent. "I don't want nothing happening to you, you know. You like a son to me now."

"I'm grateful," Eddie said.

It pained Bass to reflect on his eldest son, Robert, who had died far too young, crushed while coupling cars on a Friday in July two years ago as a brakeman for the Central Arkansas & Houston Railway, and to reflect on his old posseman and son-like good friend Floyd Wilson, killed in his first commission as a deputy three years ago in a gunfight with Belle's nephew, Henry Starr, of all people.

It was too easy to bounce on a wagon seat from heartache to heartache, so Bass stopped reflecting and twisted to look past his brim to gaze at the sky. He nudged Eddie with his elbow. "Two more's joined them. Must be Might Could and Shoulda Done."

"Hey, now." Eddie laughed, displaying his dimples. "Don't be trying to tell my story your way. That's *my* heritage."

"Hold on, I thought you was a white man?" Bass snickered.

"Shit, anybody can see I ain't."

"I never met Jim Reed, but I heard stories, and none of them was about him being a Cherokee."

"Shit." Eddie turned and spat. "I know you bull-mudding me, boss, but it's shore-fire crazy how folks believed whatever my mama said. I'm telling you, she never went to bed with the same man twice in a row that I ever knew, so I don't see how she could ever know who my daddy was—or Pearl's daddy neither. That don't make her badder than she was. I'm just saying she didn't have a bit of a loyal dog about her. She hated routine and preached against it. She couldn't even be a Democrat through and through. Had to go be friends with you. Crazy."

"I admit she did seem to have a taste for Cherokee."

"Come on, boss, admit something else." Eddie lingered in the pause as if the horses trotting hard had decided to eat his thoughts with the road. He finally whipped his head toward Bass and then did it a second time, maybe to check if Bass was paying attention, so Bass looked his way to let him know he was. "Ain't I the splitting image of Blue Duck?"

"Ha, you noticed that?"

"Shit, down to my mustache and every hair on my head. Just keep mine shorter."

Bass nudged him. "You put your finger on what I liked best about your mama. Some's got notions that freedom is always going against the law, but that ain't it. Freedom's about not having a certain way you gotta always be. That's what your mama was," Bass said. "*Freedom*, through and through. Like how she hated a wall if it didn't have a door or window in it."

"Yep, yep," Eddie said.

"That dime novel tried to put into words who she was but couldn't quite do it. *Bella Starr, the Bandit Queen!*"

"*The Female Jesse James!*" Eddie and Bass chimed in unison. They guffawed at the coincidence, which reminded Bass of when Jennie would read the book to him after dinner before she fell ill. How they laughed and laughed like this.

"More like Jesse was the male Belle Starr."

"Hell, he was a downright puppy compared to Mama."

Bass felt a fly crawling into his ear and caught it between his fingers. A black onion fly. "Belle shore never had to hide out at his place."

"It was like that book was describing a totally different person."

Bass mashed the fly and wiped his hand on his trousers. "A totally different world."

Bass and Eddie nodded almost in rhythm with the horses. The bend of the North Canadian that Bass had been on the lookout for finally came into view with the sun shining upon it. He pointed ahead, and Eddie pulled on the reins to slow the team.

4

The Kickapoos

They stopped at the river bend to let the horses drink, but when Eddie spotted a diamondback water snake, he had to catch it by its tail and play with it first. He was twenty-four years old, but snakes always brought the kid out in him. Bass wanted to stretch his legs and distance himself from the wagon even if he had to limp, and he walked a little farther up the road until he reached the fork. One path followed the river as it turned south, toward Shawnee and Tecumseh, while the other continued west for McLoud. The Kickapoo reservation was north of McLoud.

Bass hobbled back to the stench of the wagon and watched Eddie play cat and mouse with the striking snake. The flock of buzzards wheeled above like cogs to a clock. He stepped to Hammer. "Looks like he's headed for the Kickapoos."

Eddie laughed at the snake but was otherwise unresponsive.

Bass stroked Hammer's nose and cooed to her, asking her if she was thirsty. He liked that she had freckles to mirror his. He liked that his son, Robert, had been fond of the mare, naming her Mama after witnessing the birth of her one and only foal, who was hitched behind her. But Bass was never going to call his horse Mama. He remembered being home with his family in Fort Smith and cleaning his Colts the time he found himself realizing, after so many years of carrying Colts and cleaning them, that their hammers resembled little silver saddles. Seeing a thing where he'd never seen it before, even if it was hardly a thing, more a secret than a fact, could perk him up with what felt like hope for better times, even if the times demanded he replace his dear old sorrel, Strawberry, who'd been as true as a disciple. He'd intended to find another sorrel, but the Lord had pre-sented him with the gray mare, as smart and special in her own way as any horse he'd ever owned. Bass had been free enough in his heart to accept God's blessing and sure enough had been rewarded.

After unhitching her, he unhitched her sorrel son, marked almost identically to Strawberry, including even the river-winding blaze, so Bass was thinking of naming the stallion Strawberry too. He'd have to see. "Get you some water," he said, letting him loose to fol-low his mother. As they drank, Bass went to his saddle on Hammer and untied his gourd. He leaned over the river's edge to rinse it and scoop it full, then eased himself down on the bank.

He spat his tobacco, raked his tongue along his gums for the dregs, and spat again, then sipped from his gourd. He watched the horses drink and whisk their tails, while the other two horses blew impatiently for their turn at the river.

"Wish I could find a cottonmouth basking," Eddie said, stepping to the water's edge. He lowered and released the diamondback into the murk, then walked along the river, scything the dry grass with his boots.

When Bass finished his water, he set the gourd beside him and cupped his hands to whistle how an old Kickapoo friend had taught him one cold night many years ago while they drank coffee and told stories around a fire. That was back during his years as a scout. Usually bounty hunters had hired him, but he'd also worked for marshals, Pinkerton agents, Lighthorsemen, and various trappers and treasure hunters. He once led an expedition organized by the Treasury Department to locate the lost Spanish gold mines in the Washita Mountains. When that proved fruitless, they hired Bass to help locate four barrels of gold coins that outlaws had stolen during the Civil War and had supposedly hidden in a cave near the Blue River northeast of Brown. The government was always wasting money to find money.

Bass folded his thumbs over his index finger and made sure the chamber inside his hands was as airtight as he could make it and the width of the space between his thumbs was no greater than a blade of grass. With his lips against the dusty knuckles of his thumbs, he gently blew down into the flute-like tone hole to sing like a dove.

Young Kickapoo lovers would court this way over the distance of a village, letting their hand flutes speak for them in the night, the notes mimicking the sounds of the words they wanted to say: *I'm thinking of you. Let's go away. Come to me.* It had taken Bass an hour or longer to make a note that first time, but now whistling was as easy as speaking. If he flattened his hands, he produced a higher pitch, or if he fluttered his fingers at the back of the chamber, the notes warbled.

He whistled until Eddie returned empty-handed, then Bass lowered his hands and watched his flute break apart in his lap into two halves of a bird, his fingers like feathered wings. "Well," he said and seized his gourd, "we best water the other pair now."

Eddie made a face. The buzzards were lighting on the ground on the far side of the wagon. He offered Bass a hand up, and Bass clicked his tongue for Hammer to come.

◆ ◆ ◆

Bass and Eddie passed the time as they traveled west by counting the buzzards their tether of stench was accumulating. By midday— not noon but the most stifling time, between two and three—there were as many as a dozen. It wasn't long after that, while gazing at the ground's heat shimmers, Bass sighted a cloud of dust at the top of the hill far ahead of them at the end of the road. The cloud wasn't from a horse but a wagon coming in their direction. Eventually Bass could make out horse or mule heads, and neither was black, so it wasn't Cash sitting high on a seat being tricky to double-back. Bass couldn't hear anything over the noise of his own outfit until the dark Indian in work clothes and his two-mule team were almost beside them with a load of rye tied in sheaves.

Bass greeted first, and the farmer nodded, keeping his small, intense eyes on Bass, which reminded him that his badge was on his lapel.

"I'm Deputy Reeves, and this here's Deputy Reed."

"King," the farmer said, who hadn't yet acknowledged Eddie with his eyes.

"King," Bass said, "we're looking for someone who traveled this way yesterday. He was in a wagon driven by black and chestnut horses. You seen him?"

"Yessir," King said.

"Did you speak with him?"

"Yessir, he stopped at my house yonder way." He pointed behind him. "He asked if I was in want a clothes. He had some to sell."

"Did he tell you his name?"

"George. George Wilson, he said."

"Did you buy any clothes from him?"

"No. I looked, but he didn't have clothes for me."

"What do you mean?"

"I don't need no clothes to wear to town. I need work clothes."

Bass nodded. "How would you describe his manner?"

"Manner?"

"Yeah, like happy, tired, nervous?"

King gazed at Bass, then blinked with a shrug. "Like a fellow who minded his manners and how he look. Like a salesman, a store-keep, I reckon."

"Beard? Mustache?"

"Mustache. A neat one."

"So not like mine then?" Bass said, stroking the left side, then the right. "I like something I can paint with and use to sweep a mess off the floor."

Eddie smirked, but King gazed solemnly at Bass.

"Did he say where he was going?"

"No, sir. I fed him and give him drink, and he give me a shirt, but I don't know what I'll do with it." He clapped a hand over his nose and mouth, and his eyes trailed to the back of the prisoner wagon, at the buzzard settling onto it.

Bass laughed. "Shoo, bird!" he shouted, and the buzzard flapped away to the ground. "King, I appreciate your help, but we best get going."

The farmer's wagon had scrambled Cash's tracks, so after a moment Eddie looked at Bass, and Bass pointed ahead. After another moment Eddie looked again at Bass. "Just keep heading to the Kickapoos?"

"To the Kickapoos. I don't think this fella's got any more big ideas."

After about a mile of scrambled tracks, they approached a half-harvested field of rye, followed by an empty pasture and a one-room shack. In the yard, seated on a barrel under a sycamore tree, a woman waved to them while a naked child waddled around her and two hounds howled, racing to the road. Bass waved. Then Cash's tracks immediately reappeared.

Once the hounds had quit their racket, Eddie turned to Bass. "Why'd you ask the farmer to describe his manner?"

Bass remembered the face in the saloon with the small, smiling mustache—one of the men who'd gone in and out alone. He'd worn town clothes, too, not new or old, fancy ones, but they weren't clothes meant for doing much work in either. Bass repositioned himself on the wagon seat and stretched his legs out over the footboard. "Thought it'd be a good thing to ask so we know how desperate he might feel. You don't?"

"I don't know. Maybe. You the boss."

"I'm feeling like we got a good picture of him."

Eddie nodded. "A heartless son of a bitch, ain't he?"

"Yeah. You right," Bass said, stroking the bushy ends of his mustache. "That and he's in way over his head." He looked around at the world God had made, at the trees and hills and grass, at the red and brown dirt where there wasn't anything else, then at the world man had changed, like this road, like this or that crop of cotton or corn or rye, and thought about how God had changed even that with wind and bugs and no rain.

Bass had an impulse to sing:

Cash, Cash, with your little neat mustache,
Look what you got yourself into!

You killed a good man for what? your blacky and
    chestnut bray,
While I whistle like a flute and you squat in the
    Kickapoos.
You smelled wealth and it's a-coming from old Thatch
    hisself.
Truth even time is still on his side 'cause blood rises and
    cannot hide.
Nor can you, Casharago, behind a name like George.
No no, no no, no no no no no.

Eddie steered the horses onto the road branching north for the Kickapoo reservation. Although the tracks again became scrambled with other tracks, Cash's heavier wagon prints remained clear, like a current in a river. The fish simply flowed on it, like those buzzards floating on Thatch's stink.

"Follow the scramble till it stops," Bass told Eddie, reaching for his brick of tobacco. He offered Eddie a bite, but Eddie shook his head. "Need food."

"Only way we catch him," Bass said, "is we don't stop more than we got and he loafs like he's got all the time in the world."

Eddie grunted. "You right don't mean I ain't hungry."

Bass offered the brick again, and once again Eddie shook his head but then took it.

The other tracks were mostly from human feet and a donkey with curling hooves. Before long they passed the Kickapoos who were making them. A group of children dragged sticks and kicked a dry gourd, and a little later, Bass and Eddie came upon two women— together nearly the size of a donkey—riding a donkey, which was also pulling laundry bundles on a travois. Goat horns appeared to grow from the animal's hooves, making one shameful sight. Bass asked the children and then the women if they'd seen a white man in a wagon, but no one had. Before parting from the women, Bass told them the hooves needed tending to. With their eyes back on the road ahead of them, the women appeared to only hear voices from the future, so Bass stopped them by speaking again. "Tell your men I said for them to tend to them. With a file. You hear? You understand me?" Once the women both looked at him and nodded, he nudged Eddie to commence.

Closer to the reservation, they came upon a man with a gray braid that hung like a rope down his back. He had deep fissures in his face and carried a dead raccoon by its tail. The man said he'd found it in the woods behind him and wanted to make his great-granddaughter a marital headband with the hide, tail, and claws. He claimed he hadn't seen a white man in a wagon, but that morning he'd seen campfire smoke drifting from the hills where he didn't usually. He said it wasn't a Kickapoo's. He pointed west of the evening sun with the hand holding the raccoon and gave directions. Bass told Eddie to fetch his purse. While they waited for Eddie, the old man screwed up his face at Bass and asked what they had found.

◆ ◆ ◆

That Cash could have felt safe enough to stay a second night in one place seemed a gift too blessed for this Bass, making him question if the Lord was testing him this evening. George Wilson could have actually been George Wilson, who just so happened to have a black and chestnut team, but that would also mean Bass and Eddie had been tracking an innocent man all day, one who just so happened to leave the murder scene around the time Cash had left it. The other Bass had grown to expect intercessions on his behalf. This Bass instead had learned to doubt himself even when appearances told him he shouldn't. Because this Bass had killed one of his own hired hands—a fact that had followed him on a tether of stench too. Bass had only intended to wound him, to stop him from shooting horses, including his own, who had been equal to the best horse he'd ever ridden, and to avenge a dog his cook had killed in the worst way, all on top of trying to teach Willy Leach a lesson about bulling his weight around—a mistake atop another for Bass to believe he could teach Willy anything. So this Bass sailed a river of misfortune he sometimes looked to steer free of but never quite could.

So this Bass had been charged with murder and not manslaughter or negligent homicide. The acquittal came as a win, but, going nearly bankrupt defending himself, Bass couldn't afford to wait until his head cleared to return to work. Almost immediately upon the return of his badge, the Bruner gang ambushed him. There were four of them—Frank Buck and brothers John, Perry, and Ransom Bruner. In the winter of 1884–1885, that gang terrorized the Seminole Nation with every conceivable crime as if they were hell-bent to prove who among them was the freest Negro. After learning that the gang was likely hiding in the borderland on the Chickasaw Nation side of the Canadian River, Bass and his posseman, Floyd, split up for a search, and it was Bass who found seventeen-year-old Ransom Bruner, the youngest of the four, fishing under a tree.

Bass had begun making small talk with Ransom when the three others emerged from high grass with drawn weapons. John, the oldest of the brothers—who were all dark with the common shade of a Seminole freedman—was the talker, and he told Bass to dismount. Then he said, "We know you got writs to give, you so fast to turn us in. But you are just ready to turn in now yourself." Bass shook his head, denying that was true. He held his hands up as he backed away to his horse, explaining that he'd prove it. He withdrew the writs from his saddle rider and returned easily, offering them to John. The three others closed in as John flipped through the writs. Maybe John could read; maybe he couldn't. Frank Buck, darker than Bass but lighter than the brothers and bigger about the arms and chest, grew impatient and snatched the writs out of John's hands. "Let me see," he snarled, and when Bass saw that all eyes had shifted to Frank, Bass drew with his right hand and shot Frank in the buttons while he grabbed John's pistol with his left and shot Perry next and then Ransom as he wildly fired his rifle into the dirt at Bass's boots.

A month later Bass turned over the wrong man to the Fort Smith jail, a hilarious first to some, after hearing him tell how he'd given

$100 to two Texas Rangers, who had tricked him into believing they were holding the prisoner he was searching for, with a $500 bounty. One of the Rangers was the son of the great gun John Armstrong, no less.

This Bass had been sailing, hadn't he? And then he'd allowed a man as dangerous as Bob Dozier to take a shot at him while he slept. The outlaw would've killed him if he hadn't been too drunk to maintain an aim. Bass returned fire and ran him off, but that night Dozier had the last laugh as he circled Bass's camp, laughing and slurring taunts, his feral throat making sounds that swam and hung in the blind air like bats.

Lowest of his lows, though, had been this Bass's long succession of heartache. What he was certain he could have prevented with better advice, greater attention, and longer presence. Within a year he'd lost his best buddy on the trail and his firstborn son, and only months ago two of his sons, Newland and Edgar, had turned to thieving, fortunate now to be awaiting trial for the reduced charge of perjury. There was always more a body could say or do. Now this Bass awaited the loss of his wife, who was a mere shadow of a thing, a husk a body couldn't much talk to, no matter the attempt. *How-do, baby girl? What can I get you? More a the laud? Sure, baby, huh—the good laud coming. Just know in your dreams, baby girl, Bass love you.* Jennie was a shadow of a shadow, if that was a thing. It was how this Bass was dying, slowly peeling apart from the seed himself, he was afraid.

Now the latest upon the latest, he'd let a gunslinger beat him to the draw. There was a heavy price to pay for being away from home to build a safer nation *for* the home, for believing he was equal to any man—could get rich and stay rich in all ways that mattered, here and in heaven.

Bass paused to thank the Lord that at least he didn't have to worry about his son Bennie anymore, the one child of all ten who'd seemed most destined for trouble. Bennie had grown into a man making a respectable living as a barber. By firmly staking his claim on middle ground, safe from high and low waters, he appeared most like Bass himself but potentially better because he chose to surround himself with law-abiders and not breakers, with fresh faces and heads like flowers.

Yet God appeared to be steering Bass free this twilight. Smoke signaled the way as surely and fairly as the buzzards signaled where he and Eddie were.

When they arrived at the Kickapoo village at the foot of the hill bearing smoke as if from a permanent fire, children ran to greet them. Bass promised to give them silver if they kept the buzzards away from the wagon; he'd known of buzzards getting smart enough to pull away or eat through canvas to get at sour flesh. After he and Eddie collected their Winchesters, they hiked out of the village and up the woody hill to that smoking camp that smelled of bacon.

Actually finding Cash's camp, if this was Cash, and laying eyes on those black and chestnut horses and finding him idle in it, whistling with a plate and a fork in his hands instead of weapons, and recognizing the dark skin of an Italian and that small smiling mustache Bass remembered from the Red Dog Saloon, and now appreciating the added shock on his face upon learning he had company filled Bass's gut with the hope that maybe some of the tracks to his past were vanishing. Time, at last, was changing, not so much *tock tock* directing his life anymore but *tick tock*, like normal, and if that were true, maybe he could eventually return to *tick tick*, when every step moved him forward, where there was never an instant of retreat or regret or surrender.

To prevent them from shooting each other, Bass and Eddie strode into the firelight at the clock position of 12:45, with Eddie emerging from the north and Bass from the southwest. Cash looked from one to the other, then offered up a nervous laugh.

"Fellas, howdy. Come join me," he said and turned to the two pots on his fire. "Got beans and bacon. Come help yourself." He looked back and forth between Bass and Eddie, but his eyes lingered on Bass.

"See these badges?" Bass asked. "What's your name?"

Cash startled. "Me?" He seemed taken aback by the question or the familiarity of Bass's voice. "I'm George Wilson. And you men?"

"George Wilson, I'm Deputy Bass Reeves and this here's Deputy Eddie Reed."

George Wilson, or Cash, looked to the north and back to the southwest. "Y'all don't need your rifles out like that. I ain't a threat to nobody. Y'all looking for someone?"

"Somebody missing you know of?" Bass asked.

Cash set his fork on the plate and the plate on the ground. "No, that's not what I mean. I'm just waiting it out for the land to open up to make my claim."

"So you're out here alone?" Bass asked.

"No, no," said Cash. He wiped his mouth on his sleeve and then smoothed his mustache with his fingertips, each side with a flourish. "My uncle is with me. Well, *was*, but he got a hankering to hunt buffalo and rode west today. He said he'd be back in a couple days or so."

"What's his name?"

"Zachariah Thatch."

"You funning me." Bass chuckled. "Zachariah Thatch from Washington County?"

"Why, you know him?" Cash repositioned his hat so that it sat lower and shaded his eyes.

"I'm from Crawford County," Bass said. "You know how Arkansas is. We're all family there."

Cash laughed, or tried to. It sounded as if he were laughing through a stomachache.

"Open your coat," Bass told him.

"My what?" Cash looked down at himself. Was he seeing how slight he was? Was he seeing the dark spots on his trousers that could have come from bubbling beans or popping grease or some other way? Was he seeing in all that the shape of his heart? He hardly seemed to fill the clothes.

"We will shoot you dead," Bass said, "if you reach for anything but your coat. I told you to open your coat, and we won't wait."

Cash's hands shook as he reached for the quarters of his unbuttoned coat. He opened it while still looking down at the slight naked onion of himself.

Bass stepped closer, so Eddie stepped closer.

"Keep it open," Bass ordered, spotting a holster belt lying across Cash's laid-out blanket, but he wasn't taking any chances. He stepped closer and told Eddie to check him, so Eddie laid his rifle on the ground next to Cash's plate and took a strip of bacon from it before straightening up and patting Cash's chest and trouser pockets. "Lift your coat up in the back now," Bass said.

"I ain't armed." Cash lifted the tails of his coat, and Eddie patted his back. "No need. I ain't done nothing."

Eddie stepped aside and picked up the plate. "Much obliged," he told the suspect and rapidly forked beans into his mouth.

"My pistol's right there." Cash pointed, but Bass ignored him. "Look at it. I ain't fired it in a long time. Clean as a whistle."

"I'll look in due time. Eddie, hurry up with them beans and check out the wagon."

"I ain't stole nothing," Cash insisted. "That's my uncle's wagon. The team too. He left it all in my care. He'll be back in a couple days or so if you wanna come back and ask him yourself what it is you need to know." He laughed, like *ha ha*. "As soon as he gets him a buffalo and has the hide, he'll mosey on back." He nodded and pushed his hat back on his head so that Bass could see his full face. Cash looked much older than twenty-six. "We staying right here till the land run starts. We ain't going nowhere."

Bass caught a slight light out of the corner of his eye, so he turned and raised his face to admire the hoof-shaped moon. "God's winking at us."

Eddie set the plate down. "Okay, I'm done." He reached for his Winchester and paused to pluck a stick from the fire and walked toward the wagon with only a fat firefly of light.

"Bring me any tools you find. Anything with blood on it."

"Blood?" Cash laughed. "Lordy, you deputies got the wrong idea about me. I'm a simple country boy from Faulkner County myself."

"That ain't too far from the state penitentiary, is it?" Bass turned to see Eddie climbing into the back of the wagon.

"My daddy was a farmer, salt of the earth," Cash said, but neither Bass nor Eddie made a show of hearing him. "One cold morning when I was little, he went up in the loft of the barn and was pulling on hay he'd tied up for the winter, and one way or other he flew out and landed practically in front of me. Landed right on his head and snapped his neck. I saw it and heard it."

Eddie clanked things in the dark that Bass couldn't see.

Bass turned to Cash. "I'm sorry about your daddy. I know it's tough on a boy not to have one around. You and me's in the same boat there, but we make decisions, don't we?"

Cash's shoulders seemed to sink all the way to the ground. He was revealing himself. He was this slight soul trying to escape the jail of a sinking coat, which the horses could near blow to the next world with one hot breath.

"Well, boss," Eddie said, jumping down from the wagon, "I got something you should look at." His rifle clattered with a shovel and an axe that he balanced in one arm while he carried the fire stick with the other. He laid the tools at Bass's feet and held his rifle on Cash while Bass crouched, inspecting the shovel.

The fire showed nothing unusual about the shovel. Some dirt, some ash, but no blood. Then Bass inspected the axe. He stood up with it.

"George," he said, stepping to him. He held the head of the axe out for Cash to see. "What can you tell me about the blood here?"

"Oh," Cash stuttered, "my uncle and me killed and dressed a prairie chicken yesterday. No, maybe day before. Before we got here." He crossed his arms and nodded.

Bass rolled the axe over. "But the blood dried running from the blunt side, not the blade."

Cash hunched his shoulders. "I don't know. I used the blade on the chicken. I don't know how come the blood's dried like that. Maybe 'cause I wiped the blade side and didn't the other. That's probably it."

Bass nodded and looked Cash in the eyes. "Is that how you got them blood stains on your trousers? Killing and dressing that chicken?"

Cash uncrossed his arms and looked down at himself. "I don't know." He brushed his trousers. "Maybe. I guess. Ain't noticed."

"I wouldn't want anybody to hit me with a axe. It might hurt." Bass held still while Cash's eyes fluttered.

"You ain't gonna hit me with that axe, are you, deputy?"

Bass smiled. He took a step back and lowered the axe. "I ain't gonna harm you none unless you gimme reason to. That a deal?"

"Yessir," Cash said. "I ain't looking for trouble."

Bass motioned to the woods behind him. "George Wilson, I got some things to show you at our wagon. Eddie, why don't you lead the way with your paltry fire stick? George, you follow him, and I'll limp along in the rear."

Eddie walked ahead and Cash followed without a word.

"You know, George," Bass said, "I got shot a couple days ago when we was at Red Dog in Keokuk Falls. You been there recently? You sure do look familiar."

Whatever Cash spoke, he spoke in a whisper, sounding as though he might float away at any moment.

The three wove through trees as the ground sloped and then sloped the other way. Eddie found the hardened trail they had taken, and they returned to the village. A bonfire lit up the doorways of all the shacks. The women busied themselves preparing food while the men sat on the ground behind them, smoking and passing bottles. The children were gathered around a tree and throwing rocks into it while the buzzards cried at them to stop.

The air smelled of Thatch and burning wood. The canvas covering the wagon was how they'd left it.

Eddie leaned his rifle against the wagon and heaved himself into the back of it. He drew back the canvas. "Come on," Eddie said.

Cash consulted Bass.

"Tell us if you recognize him."

Cash's eyes said it all. He turned and stepped to the wagon with the same dragging pace that nearly every man found on his climb onto the gallows. He was sinking all over even as he ascended. He craned his head at the corpse, and after a silence, Bass heard him suck in a breath. Cash wagged his head. "Oh, no."

"Who is it?" Bass asked. "Tell us."

Eddie tucked the canvas back over the corpse.

Cash climbed down but didn't look at Bass, his eyes minding only the ground. "That's Zachariah Thatch. Don't know how, but that's him."

"Don't know how your uncle found himself dead in my wagon?"

Cash stood flat-footed as he crossed his arms and shook his head. "He ain't my uncle."

"He ain't?"

"No." He raised his hanging face. "I didn't know what you was after, so I said it. Law and me never got along. I was scared, I guess. Name's not George Wilson either but Jimmy Casharago. I was working for him. I ain't killed him though. I don't know nothing about this. Mr. Thatch said he was gonna hunt buffalo and for me to stay put. Where you find him?"

"Did you see his forehead?" Bass asked.

Cash didn't budge. He was playing possum.

"Plumb stove in. He was knocked good with something."

Cash's eyes returned to the ground as Eddie stepped up, his rifle resting in the crook of his arm.

"Course he was shot too," Bass said. "You think the .38-caliber bullets in Mr. Thatch will match the ones in your pistol?"

"I don't know how any of this coulda happened."

"Now I agree with you on that, son." Bass eyed Eddie, who looked sad. It was getting to the boy how long this was taking. Bass turned his attention back to Cash. "I got one more question for you."

When Cash didn't look at him, Bass told him to look. "I got one more question for you, and I want you to give me the truth."

"Yessir, I'm being honest to God."

"I want you to think about your daddy when you answer. I want you to make his name mean something. He was salt of the earth, you say. Well, tell me this, son: Why did you build a fire up under a tree when you had a perfect one going under the sky?"

Cash hung his arms at his sides and stretched his lips apart in a terrible grimace—how a child who hadn't yet learned to smile would. "I ain't got a fire going up under a tree up there. You saw I didn't." His hands trembled out of his coat sleeves, and his knees appeared to buckle.

"Want me to get it?" Eddie asked.

Bass gave a nod, and Eddie walked to the team. Bass was almost tired of talking for the night, so he remained as silent as Cash, as silent now as the buzzards, who maybe finally had had enough of this hide-and-seek cross-country game and were tucking their beaks into their wings to get some sleep. Eddie was silent, too, then Eddie returned from Hammer with Bass's saddle rider.

Bass indicated for Eddie to set his rifle on the ground in front of him and Cash, so he did. Then Eddie kneeled on one knee and unbuckled the saddle rider. He blew on the fire stick once and then twice to keep it glowing above the saddle rider.

"Go on, Jimmy Casharago," Bass said, lowering his own rifle. "Look in and tell me what you see."

PART TWO

1896

5

Living God

Bass usually celebrated his birthday on whichever day Jennie decided, and that depended on what days in July he happened to be home. No one, not even Pearlalee, his mother, remembered the exact day. Those who were slaves at that time remembered events differently, in relation to seasons or other events. For a slave—with neither ink nor paper—to remember in days would have been a burden heaped upon other burdens, like counting the cotton bolls a body picked or the meals a body missed. So all anyone remembered was that Bass had been born on a day in July that had felt in Van Buren like a day in April, as it had followed the great hailstorm of 1838. Newspapers in print then had gone out of print. Determined to pinpoint the day, Jennie had once located a book collector in town who had saved every copy of the *Farmers' Almanac* that he'd ever bought, including the 1838 issue, but it had failed to predict any storm for the month of July. It was as if history had forsaken the people of Van Buren by robbing them of their only momentous occasion.

At other times Bass claimed the timing of his birthday celebration himself. He'd be feeling thankful to the Lord for his life and bounty and decide, wherever he was, alone or not, to treat himself impulsively to a hotel dinner or fudge squares or ginger cakes from a boardwalk or train station vendor, or he'd simply light up a cigar as he was doing now, in his fifty-eighth year, while riding Hammer to a hanging. Bass hoped it would be the last one he'd ever attend. He wasn't feeling particularly thankful for his life and bounty today, not after his worrisome talk last night with his son Bennie, but he thought if he lit a cigar, which he didn't often do, and held some

47

warm smoke in his mouth, the uneasy feeling would either melt away or get covered up.

He hadn't ridden this far in many years, across the Dead Line from Calvin in Indian Territory to Fort Smith, Arkansas, without performing the duty either to make an arrest or turn a prisoner over. He'd heard a few white men in his life use the term "vacation." He guessed that's what this was since he was purely making time to celebrate Judge Isaac Parker's twenty-one-year career at what was looking more and more to be the last hanging of his court given that Congress had decided to close his court's jurisdiction of Indian Territory on September 1, 1896. Owing to the recent decline of the judge's health, it was everyone's conjecture that he would be retiring soon. For years newspapers had called him "the Hanging Judge" and his court "the Court of the Damned," but Parker detested romanti-cized violence, and so did Bass unless he was singing and then he couldn't resist the fun:

> Cash will make the seventy-ninth noose to hang,
>   Though he stops to ask don't seventy-eight sound a whole
>   lot sweeter, dang!
> But the Hanging Judge can't care, Cash, he can't care,
> 'Cause the Court of the Damned, I swear, gotta always be
>   square.

But as Eddie didn't feel like talking, Bass didn't feel like singing. He composed silently as he smoked, something to block his mind, like an idle wagon, from rolling backward on his vacation.

Once they crossed the Dead Line and the smiling telegraph lines that followed every railroad, they could afford to allow their minds to wander beyond their immediate vicinity. Bass remained mind-ful of desperate rogues in the hills since the towns that had sprung up like mushrooms east of the Katy line fed the trails with sparse, yet regular, traffic, making an ambush of two men riding together highly unlikely.

As they skirted the soft south end of the Canadian River wetland,

Tucker Knob appeared for the first time, a mountain that mounted closer mountains.

"Be good to see Judge again, won't it?" asked Eddie.

"Sure will," Bass said.

"Be a nice thing to take him something, I was thinking."

"You right. Like what was you thinking?"

Eddie balled down on his saddle and reached for his saddle rider. "Something I been holding onto." He unbuckled his rider strap and reached in. His hand studied the things it held until, at last, he withdrew a fist. He slowed his horse, so Bass slowed his. Eddie turned his fist over and uncurled his fingers enough to expose yellowed cloth.

"A handkerchief?"

Eddie nodded. "Thatch's."

Bass thought back to a year ago when Eddie searched Zachariah Thatch's pockets and found only that handkerchief and tossed it onto the creek's bank, though Bass didn't recall seeing him pick it up.

"You been holding onto it as a good luck charm?"

Eddie stared without expression at the road as if he were lost in the melody of horse music. "It was all he had on him," he said with despair. "All he had."

"It's a nice thought."

Eddie lowered his head to the rocking neck of his buckskin quarter horse and thrust his hand back into his saddle rider. "Thatch is probably the last man Judge gets to stand up for, you know. Thought he might want it. Guess it's all I got to give."

"Thatch did by all accounts appear to be a good man."

Eddie stared ahead, maybe at the valley among them or in the distance at Tucker Knob. The Choctaw, upon their arrival from the South, had spoken of the mountain's teat shape as a sign that the land here would always feed them. "It was wet like the man cried on it," he said. "Like maybe the creek cried on it."

Bennie, Bass's son, had tipped his hat when he walked up the previous night and had joined Bass on the porch without a word. While Bass shot the bull and rocked in his rocker, Bennie leaned on a post as if he wanted to weigh it down. He may have said two short strings of nothing before he took a seat on the old nail keg that Bass often used in the morning as a table to set his cup of coffee on. Bennie looked close to crying.

"Does it bother you some people still think you murdered your cook?" Eddie asked.

That's how Eddie was. Quiet for so long and then loud as a bee in your ear.

"Sure," Bass admitted. "Best we can do, Eddie, is show 'em what they don't wanna see."

Eddie clenched his jaws. "You know who started them rumors about me, don'tcha?"

Bass nodded. "I know what I heard is all."

Judge Parker had always made Bass feel welcome whenever he stopped by the courtroom between trials to chat. Bass would usually find him at his massive oak desk reading a newspaper or leafing through one of the law books he kept stacked around him. Regardless of how foul-smelling Bass was from being out in the territory, Judge Parker would say, "Pullerup," and wheel his index finger, an invitation for Bass to move the witness chair up on the platform closer to him.

"Well?" Eddie said.

"It was your sister, right?"

"*Half* sister."

Bass waved away a cloud of gnats, and so did Eddie. "Heard you got tired a taking beatings."

"Tired of taking Mama's mouth too. Who wants your mama cussing and beating on you when you're seventeen? So I moved out. Didn't have to kill her."

"Never thought you did."

"Judge didn't either."

Bass nodded. "He told me. Judge been a good father to many a us."

"Pearl don't even believe her own nonsense anymore, you know."

"A good deed makes up for a lot," Bass said. This was the very sort of thing he couldn't or shouldn't say to most people. Without his experience, others would simply find themselves at a loss to understand how Pearl Younger's work as a prostitute to pay her brother's legal defense could be a good deed. Sometimes, like last night, when he wasn't working and on guard, Bass slipped and said something he regretted.

Bennie was sitting on that old keg Bass had bought and emptied in Van Buren to build his showplace. It had gone with them when they moved to Fort Smith, and Bass had filled the barrel with dried butter beans for his move from Fort Smith to Calvin. Over the years he'd cooked all but a couple of cups, which rattled against the wood when Bennie inched the keg closer to Bass's rocker with the edge of his boot.

"Work still keeping you running?" Bass asked, deciding to get at what was eating him.

Bennie bit his bottom lip and nodded. "Gotta provide, you know." He removed his porkpie hat, a thing that was in fashion with young people like Bennie and Casharago. It didn't make a lick of sense to Bass, not with a brim too short to keep the sun out of a boy's eyes. Casharago's had been mushroom colored. Bennie's was black, like Bass's Stetson. Bennie was holding it by its brim, nothing more than a rim, and gradually turning it in circles.

"Make sure to spend time with your pretty wife." Bass winked. "Without children yet, she'll get lonely. Bring her with you next time, Bennie."

Bennie's eyes were as pink and swollen as the clouds in the sunset.

Bass patted his son on the leg and stood up. "Back in two shakes." He walked inside, past Eddie sitting in lamplight and cleaning his guns in preparation for their ride today. In the kitchen Bass broke open a crate of contraband and grasped the necks of two bottles of forty-rod. "Huh," he told Eddie, leaving one beside the lamp and making it flicker. "Huh," he told Bennie and eased back into rocking. "Want you to get a good swallow or two, then tell me what's eating you."

A cork popped inside the house and then one popped outside. There was such a whirl of sound that night from the insects and birds that the Canadian River attracted so close by, and from the creaking of the rocker on the porch boards and the porch boards from the rocker and the rickety table bearing Eddie's weight as he rubbed steel, and from Eddie snoring later that night like a growling dog as if he couldn't wait for their ride to commence. The nervous energy of Bennie's boots scuffing the porch boards, though, seemed to lord over it all, then and now.

"Can't just taste it, son. You're licking it!" Bass leaned forward with his elbows on his knees—on his "high cricket-leg knees" Jennie had playfully called them back when she had been playful. Sure, Bennie pressed the bottle to his lips and held it there, but Bass didn't hear the bubbles and slosh or the swallowing heartbeat. "Come on, chug the jug, boy. Kick it to get relief. Gotta kick it!"

Bennie didn't like the taste of whisky yet, but he tipped the bottle quickly as if from agitation.

"That's it," Bass said.

Bennie's face contorted, and he shivered even though his face was turning dark from a rush of blood.

"Let it set. Catch your breath." Bass patted his son's leg. "Sometimes you gotta swallow your pride. You gotta feel something before you dull it, understand?"

Bennie nodded and tipped the bottle as before, then passed it. Bass took his time holding the bottle before lifting it, and when he did tip it up, he did it easily and sipped without a hurry because he didn't have anything he had to let loose.

Bennie took a deep breath and began wheeling his hat faster. "I know I'm gone too much," he said. "That's my job. Gotta go where people need me. You know how that is."

So cutting heads now was like hunting outlaws? Maybe it was.

"That's why I quit being a porter. I'm not gone like how I was before. That's why I decided to come home early the other day. You know, to surprise her. I even stopped and gathered some Indian paintbrush by the road." The wheel of his hat slowed and he looked off toward the river beyond the darkening tree line. "I heard laughter before I walked in. I was thinking she heard me coming up and was excited to see me, but when I walked in, there was Dell Weems sitting in my chair, and Castella was cooking up hash."

Bass leaned back off his elbows. "What the hell, son!"

"Castella dropped a spoon or something, then Dell jumps up, and I ask what he's doing there. He does nothing but stutter."

"What'd Castella say?"

"She run over for the flowers and carried on about what a surprise it was to see me, saying Dell come by looking for me and they got to talking and realized they both were hungry, had a hankering for hash."

"Dell Weems playing house with your wife?" Jennie had had a routine for years whenever Bass got mad. She would frown a silly frown and touch the downturned corners of her lips with the tips of two fingers to remind Bass that his mouth had disappeared under his mustache and that his mustache looked like a long, bushy frown. That's how it must have looked to Bennie, but Bennie didn't find it amusing and neither did Bass. He was shaking his head to keep from saying more while Bennie continued to look hurt when he needed to get mad too. Bass kicked it, taking two great back-to-back swallows just to show the boy how.

"I don't know what to believe," Bennie said, placing his hat on his head and angling it low as if he could hide his youthful face with a porkpie. He was twenty-one and had never shaved.

Bass wiped his mustache on the back of his hand, then offered him the bottle, but Bennie instead just swatted away a bee.

"She swore up and down they didn't do nothing but talk. Dell maybe wanted more, she didn't know, so she got busy in the kitchen to be polite."

"Did he stay?"

Bennie shook his head. "Whatcha mean?"

"Did he leave right away? After you showed up?"

Bennie nodded with the delayed motion of a drunk.

Bass stiffened. "Son, you telling me that he came looking for you in the middle of the day but left soon as you showed?" He found his boy a lost vessel posing as a man, as though he'd never had a father.

"*What*, Pop? What are you thinking I should've done? Tell me."

"I'd have shot hell out of the man and whipped the living God out of her." Bass's raised voice surprised even him. "What should you a done?" he asked. "*Something*, son. Damn." He choked the bottle's neck and leaned back and kicked it once more, then stared ahead at nothing, at the very nothing his boy had done.

In the face of time and truth, at their very meeting, with the very essence of life swimming and jumping before Bennie's eyes, at his very fingertips, the moments Bass had lived his entire life chasing to behold and hold on to for as long as he could milk them, all his boy could do was nothing—*nothing*! As if the boy had never really been born and God had never known him.

The rocker and boards returned to their tired song, but at least Bennie's boots had quit their infernal racket for a spell until he made like to leave. Then, without another word, he did.

◆ ◆ ◆

"Go on, Jimmy Casharago," Bass had said, recalling how he'd lowered his Winchester in the glow of Eddie's fire stick. "Look in," he'd said, "and tell me what you see."

Cash leaned over the saddle rider that Eddie had set at Bass's feet. It looked dark and empty from Bass's height, so he told Cash to get down, get closer.

Cash knelt on the ground and peered inside. Then he looked up. "Dirt?"

"Look again."

Cash craned closer to the rider, then faced Bass again with no emotion and hunched his shoulders. Only his eyes told the story. "Dirt?"

"And?"

Cash silently shook his head.

"You don't recognize those seeds with angel wings?"

"Dog, boss," Eddie said, "you starting to sound like Judge."

Bass glanced at Eddie to acknowledge the compliment. Nobody used words quite as Judge Parker did in his sentences. The only person Bass thought had come close to his rank of eloquence had been Bass's former master—not the first, William Reeves, but the last, his son, George Reeves—who had strung words together on a line of greed and hate, never love and truth the way Judge Parker always had.

Bass crouched down to see Cash better and so Cash could see him better. "I found this dirt," he said, "under the silver maple you built a fire under." He waited for Cash to blink, but Cash outwaited him. Bass rested the butt of his rifle on the ground as if he were holding the shaft of a shovel. "Maybe in the day you'll see what we saw—and I ain't talking about the ash mixed with that dirt and those seeds, son. You know what I'm talking about now, don't you?"

Cash shook his head.

"We got you," Bass said, straightening and taking a step back. He leveled the rifle a cubit from the empty barrels of Cash's eyes. "We got you."

David Gavin, the bailiff for the trial, would carry the sugar sack with the rider's contents into the courtroom and waggle the chunks and clods onto the exhibit table in front of Judge Parker's desk for him and the jurors to rise up and inspect.

The coagulated dirt was unmistakable—nothing like how clay-rich soil looked and broke apart. The color too was darker, rustier, a bold sorrel, as if the dirt, with all those tiny wings firmly attached to it, were alive and would breathe and soon attempt to fly.

"Even nature revolted against your crime," Parker would say at the sentencing, reading from his many notes. "The parched earth cracked open and drank up the blood, held it in a fast embrace until the time it should appear against you." Cash meanwhile sat untouched, back to pretending that his name was George Wilson, that he didn't know who James W. Casharago was, had never met him, and that there was a purely innocent explanation for his possession of Thatch's belongings, including those stained with blood. "Sadly," his attorney had told the courtroom in his closing statement, "innocence sometimes has no easy or even consistent explanation. Lamblike, the defendant misspoke. Confused and scared by the accusations of the arresting lawmen, he did what lambs do when cornered. Incomprehensibly he bleated." He eyed the jury as Bass eyed them, yet incomprehensibly not a single one of them joined Bass to crack a smile.

That was eight months ago, on December 15, 1895. Father Time could really tumble and jumble. The trial, despite these vivid parts, had gradually become less vivid to Bass. It seemed instead to have ensued earlier in his life, before the crime even, unlike his own trial that had occurred, inconceivably, many years ago.

6

Home

Bass was always riding through the city of Fort Smith. Whenever he wasn't, his thoughts were never far from a previous visit or an upcoming one—as if he were a lifelong prisoner to a maze that included the city's roads. This ride on Hammer, with Eddie on Fly-catcher, was his destiny.

Only in Fort Smith would white people, according to their upbringing, see through him as if he were no more substantive than smoke, but then, as nowhere else, their eyes would—by accident or curiosity—rove over him again, and, a miracle, they would catch sight of his height or badge or mustache, which would then hatch a curiosity that told them he couldn't be just a n—— on a horse. He'd witness every step of that registration and, another miracle, feel almost reformed by it. Feel, good heavens, that he had returned home, at last, the home of being Bass.

Well, Bass had to laugh to himself, he felt as at home as a head could feel in a noose. The courthouse was there at the knot of the Arkansas and Poteau Rivers, which nearly encircled the entire city, because a knot didn't care what the head saw or heard tell of. A knot's promise was simply to hold tight, and there was never a body who visited Fort Smith who wasn't always hustling to stay clear of that knot's pinch. Over the course of his life, he'd watched men and women from every American region and race strut like the sun along Garrison Avenue as if the east-west rows of stores and saloons would never end and a body would never need sleep and a purse would forever remain full, but he came to believe that no one strutted the avenue more earnestly and recklessly than gray-haired white men.

Their long history of favor before the law had apparently instilled a deep-seated belief in their own inferiority and, as a consequence, the view that their favor was necessary for survival. Without it they would find themselves banished like Adam and Eve to the meadows of mediocrity, lucky on a winter night to find food and shelter. It was natural for those who had the most to lose to fear the most. Lord, how he knew that.

Passing City Hotel reminded Bass of the blistering August day in 1886 when A.J. Boyd had accosted him on the boardwalk—there between the hotel and Bolinger's Store. Bass had met his friends John Williams and Dave Pompey in the saloon below their hotel room. Bass was telling them a story when A.J. broke into their circle at the bar to announce what they already knew: that the drunken banker would be a juryman in Bass's upcoming murder trial. A.J. kept rapping the brass tip of his walking cane on the floor to interrupt the men's laughter and goad Bass into explaining how he happened to kill his cook, until Bass, John, and Dave settled up with the barkeeper and walked out.

The story Bass had been telling his friends had been a good one, or it had been going so well that Bass was getting eager to know how it would turn out himself. It had started out true enough, about the time a prisoner woke to find a mouse in one of his boots and then, low and behold, a rattler in the other, but A.J. was determined to snap the spell of it.

Between City Hotel and Bolinger's, Bass felt the tap of the old man's cane on his right shoulder.

Bass turned and the sun lit A.J.'s gray whiskers bright as snow. "A.J., it ain't proper for us to be talking. You know that."

"Listen," A.J. said, and where his face wasn't covered with snow and the muddy tracks of black whiskers, it was berry red from forty-rod, "if you want to save your neck, you had better make a statement to me."

"Go home, A.J. Won't be any statement today." Bass tipped his hat, and A.J. caught Bass by the coat, then reared back his cane.

"You damned Black son of a bitch, I am just as certain to break your neck as I have this cane in my hand." He'd said it just that way, and Bass would never forget it. As if Bass weren't really a deputy with a badge. As if he weren't a man either, with a Colt on each hip, or even a human capable of speaking or understanding English. As if Bass were no more than an aggravating shadow of some vague notion that could be beaten with mere light.

John Williams stepped between them. "Whoa, easy does it, A.J.!" he exclaimed, but A.J. persisted, waving his cane.

"Me and three others have got it in for you!" A.J. snarled and spat on the boardwalk.

"Well, that is all right," Bass said calmly.

John pulled Bass aside while Dave Pompey attempted to reason with A.J. Eventually Dave would escort A.J. back to the saloon, and at A.J.'s hearing the following week, charged with contempt of court, Bass would begin his testimony by saying that he was standing on the boardwalk between City Hotel and Bolinger's Store and that he thought the incident happened the previous Monday. He had purposefully avoided any mention of the saloon and knew the incident had not occurred on Monday but the previous Saturday, a day of leisure and excess. Words mattered to a picture. Every experience of Bass's life had taught him to be mindful of how a body received his words, to let a party's likes and dislikes inform his choice of details. To tell a story the way a good cook cooked, by tasting and doctoring along, not the way a bad cook like Willy Leach cooked, by trusting a list.

More sky appeared once they passed the broad side of Bolinger's. Eddie reined in Flycatcher, so Bass reined in Hammer.

"You sure you don't want to come to the house?" Bass asked. "We can make room for you."

Eddie nodded. "Thanks, but I might want to lean up against a bar all night."

"I might too." Bass smirked without humor. It was sadly true. "See you at the hanging then."

Eddie trotted Flycatcher onto the lane for the livery stable. A bird with long tail feathers, a flycatcher, happened to then flutter out of the open stable loft window and swoop low, just above Eddie's and Bass's heads, as if to scout the traffic of horses and wagons and mud-caked men walking along the manure that cobbled the avenue. Bass followed the pretty thing with his eyes until he lost sight of it among other birds flitting between perches.

He'd never admired flycatchers for their buckskin tail feathers until Eddie had mentioned them. Bass had instead always been attracted to their beaver-brown crowns and ashy throats. He guessed a body was inclined to neglect something when he stopped to admire something else. He'd have to watch that about himself.

"Bazz!" a man's voice called from a passing buggy.

"Oh, it is! Bass Reeves!" the man's companion said, her face shaded by her hat piled with pink roses.

Bass raised a hand and suddenly found himself surrounded by white townspeople he knew and considered friends from the court and the church and the neighborhood. All were saying his name, greeting him as they passed or stopped, none with a lick of judgment or any lingering suspicion, saying with love, "Where have you been? How have you been? Tell us what in the world you have gotten yourself into!" As soon as he parted one cluster, he found himself in another. "You must be here for the hanging!"

"I am," he said to them.

"That prisoner's his, you know," one of them grinned with pride.

"Come over afterward if you don't have other plans!"

"Tomorrow is gonna be something!"

It was as if they believed God would never in a million years conceive a body like him to be capable of conceiving, in the heat of the moment, the unusual notion—the miracle notion—of putting a body down by aiming for the meat of the neck. Not even what happened last year near Gibson Station could swerve them from those thoughts. Deputy Bud Ledbetter and every man in his outfit had been firing at an outlaw who had escaped them on foot down a ravine. Bass had been on his way to Muskogee and heard the commotion for half an hour, so he rode out to investigate. Bud immediately called to him, "Get him, Bass!" So Bass dismounted in a flourish and crouched at the cliff to level his rifle. "See him? See him?" Bud asked as Bass stilled his aim. The outlaw was a quarter mile away by then and running as well as he could over rocks. "I'll break his neck," Bass had said, and he did with one shot, just to prove he could. Hell, to confess he had.

Yet these people believed something entirely different. They loved him too much to believe the truth. They believed he'd shot Willy by accident, that the event unfolded from an accursed set of unfortunate odds, and for that reason, they believed Judge Parker and the jury had bestowed upon him their grace of unwarranted favor. Bass must have appeased some sense of guilt these white people had been carrying, heavy as a cross, ever since Jesus had carried his, and for that, upon seeing him free—generous evidence that their favor was real, a gift as much for them as for him—they rejoiced.

◆ ◆ ◆

Bass had nearly reached the end of town when he reached North Twelfth Street and turned left, giving his neck a little relief from the sun before it began to dissolve as quickly as sugar between the houses and then, like seed, sprout autumn prairie grass among the clouds

"Howdy, deputy! Bass!" He was so close to home now, at the corner of Twelfth and Park Place, that he tipped his hat without stopping and said with more joy than he felt, "Almost there!"

"Send our best to the missus!"

"Will do. Good to see you."

He and Jennie had painted the old showplace in Van Buren buttercup yellow because that had been the color she had most wanted to see everywhere she turned, whether inside or out. This four-room house, half the size of the other, had never exceeded a single expectation. Well, Jennie liked the linoleum flooring in the kitchen, how it was easy to clean and shone like ice afterward. Otherwise the house had simply been what they could afford after moving to clear Bass's debt. The house had been gray at the end of the road when he first laid eyes on it, and that's the color it remained—as gray as a dry goods store. Most of the young'uns were either grown or dead or in jail, which had a way of depleting the color from a place anyway.

Bass dismounted behind the house and the motherless black kittens leaped and pranced from the dark space under the porch to greet him. He tied Hammer to the pump because the only grass in the yard was what grew around it from spilled water. Then he removed the bucket hanging on the spout and set it on the ground out of the way. There wasn't even space on the lot for a little one-horse stable. After a few pumps of the handle, Bass rubbed his hands and drank from them, the warm water tasting how his hands smelled—of leather, horse, dust. He removed his hat and rinsed his face, then swallowed two more handfuls before filling the bucket and setting it on the dirt in front of Hammer. He paused to watch the kittens nuzzle his boots and watch Hammer lap the water as greedily as a pup.

He hadn't meant to kill Willy. He had pulled the trigger but only to nick the stump of his neck. To get his attention and back him down. They were camping northwest of Cherokee Town in the Chickasaw Nation to pick up Chub Moore, a murderer known to be hiding nearby. Bass was sitting on his bedroll and emptying his Winchester to clean it, and whenever he threw a cartridge, the bull pup he and Floyd had taken in the day before would try to catch it in her mouth. That had tickled Bass. Willy had pork and beans on the fire and his silver-plated Smith and Wesson holstered on his waist, and he was ornery about Bass telling him to make corn pone. And he was ornery about the pup because he detested varmints and was fretting that Bass would give the varmint some of that corn pone. Floyd had just finished checking on the prisoners, so all three—or four—were together again.

And then Willy did his hateful thing, and Bass hated nothing worse than a hateful thing. Willy teased the pup by holding the frying pan above her nose as if suddenly he was growing a heart for a varmint and would feed her himself, so she got up on her hind legs and danced for a savory bite. She was wagging her tail, just being cute, just being pure and sweet, just being a hungry thing, as Willy was saying, "Open up. Come on, pup, open up." And then Willy had to be Willy—sizzling her head into a cloud.

Willy had bowed his shoulders as if he were preparing to fight Bass and Floyd both. Bass could hear him as if Willy were now shouting at him in the yard: "Don't push me off my space, or I'll commence to killing horses next." Looking inspired by the notion, Willy had reached for his pistol.

Equally surprising was how Bass had made the same mistake. A host of reasonable solutions simply had never occurred to him. Only the singular challenge of nicking a neck that was hardly a neck as if he couldn't miss. The notion coalesced in his mind, so he was certain it was something he could do and should do as the quickest, most definite way to stop Willy from doing one more hateful thing.

Bass stroked the mare's flank and reached for his cane tucked into the scabbard with his rifle. His thoughts drifted ahead of him, skipping over this moment, the cautious walk to the door to avoid kicking a kitten, to the next moment, when he'd be sitting inside with the women, catching up. Later he'd get a bite to eat, and when the women were turning in, he'd ride Hammer back to the livery to have her fed and cooled properly. He'd also check on Hammer's stallion and then on Strawberry, loose in the lot behind the stables like a horse ghost. Bass missed his old, slumped sorrel who was no longer sorrel but as gray now as Hammer. He missed him especially on a night like tonight, when he was pressed to think of times when he was riding Strawberry and when Strawberry was carrying him.

If the groomsmen were shorthanded or too busy to bring him back, Bass would find someone along the avenue to do it. That would be the story of his life, he guessed—making do. In his bid to free the territory of its demons, and he was freeing it, all right, a demon or two kept following his tired butt back across the border, like how those orange hay rays, like a carotid blood spill, traveled far and deep from its source as if to prove to him they were as free as ever to haunt and hound, so he better live on the ready.

◆ ◆ ◆

The back door opened with a long, thin yawn, and the muslin curtains rippled before the open windows in the unlit kitchen. The sitting room beyond it glowed yellow from the kerosene lamp beside his mother, who looked up from her knitting.

"Mama," Bass said as he shut the door and took off his hat.

"Son, that you?" Exuberance was slow to alter the neutral features of her face. "I was praying I'd see you tonight. Come here."

"Yes, ma'am." His boots stuck to the linoleum, a reminder for him to take a seat in the nearest chair at the round table to his right. He hung his hat and cane on one of the mule ears of the chairback, then sat down to begin removing his boots. Ever since the shooting at Red Dog Saloon in Keokuk Falls, he'd gotten in the habit of reaching for the easier boot, the right boot, first. That would give his children, if they were home, or Eddie, if he was in the territory, enough time to hear him and come help. Like a board, his left leg just didn't have much bend.

"Need help?" Pearlalee asked.

"No, Mama," he said. "You stay right there."

She laughed. "That's what I'm doing."

He peeled the wet sock off his right foot, and he could feel the rain of dirt and sand. "Making a mess over here."

"Pay it no never mind," she said. "You sure you got it?"

Bass chuckled. "I'll get the rascal." He bent his left leg at the knee all he could, maybe the length of his pinky, then used his right foot to work the boot loose.

"You getting it, Bass?"

The floor in the sitting room creaked, but Pearlalee hadn't moved.

"Huh, see if you can help him," she called, pointing her crooked pointing finger in Bass's direction, and from the hallway to the two bedrooms, Winnie appeared on soft feet.

"Evening, Winnie," he said.

"Bass." Smiling, she passed in and out of the lamplight but also bore her own natural glow of sorghum butter into the shade of the kitchen. Jennie's cousin was pretty. He'd always thought so.

She touched his shoulder. "Let me help you."

"No, I'm too filthy for that," he said, but she pulled out a chair and sat down in front of him nevertheless.

"I know how to wash." Winnie leaned down and grabbed his boot at the heel and toe. "Ready?" she asked, and when she tugged, he tugged and then grunted from the mounting pressure on the bullet that would forever remain lodged in his leg. Maybe in time the bullet would become a pearl, but right now it was a seed stuck between two teeth.

"We budged it." She took a breath. "Again," she said, and they tugged until the boot slid free.

"Get it?" Pearlalee asked.

"Yes'm," Winnie replied. She set the boot standing up next to the other one while Bass stretched his arms and pushed his sock down to his ankle with his fingertips.

"Here," Winnie said, and she hooked her fingers into the folds and peeled the sock off his foot.

Bass sighed and wiggled his toes. "That's better! Thank you, Winnie."

She patted his knee and stood up. "You hungry, I know." She crossed the room and opened the stove door.

"You know right," he said, watching her reach for one of the logs stacked on the floor. He regarded his mother and her working hands, steadily knitting as if she were holding onto the reins of a galloping horse. "I'm coming, Mama." He pushed himself upright.

"I thought you done forgot about old me over here." Pearlalee slowed her hands and watched him teeter into the sitting room without his cane. His good leg was stiffening. Riding all day was starting to do that to him.

Bass peered into the darkened hallway at what was visible in Jennie's bedroom. It was hers more than his and hers. A lamp burned low beside her bed, so he could see the lump of her feet beneath the fringed coverlet but nothing more.

He smiled at his mother and she smiled back, emptying her hands to open her arms. "Mama," he said and leaned down into them.

"Son, son," she said, smelling like herself. It was the rose water from the Wakelee's Camelline lotion she rubbed into her skin each night before bed. Her embrace was soft everywhere except her hands, where she held him fast by the bones. She hummed. "So good to touch you, son."

"Yes, indeed."

"I'm gonna boil you some water for a bath too," Winnie called from the kitchen.

He pulled halfway out of Pearlalee's grasp. "Thank you, Winnie!"

The brown of Pearlalee's eyes had faded over the years, and the whites were redder, but she was strong and healthy yet in every way. She'd outlived her sister. He guessed she would outlive him too. He hoped so.

Auntie Totty had been living with them for years—first in Van Buren and then here because the sisters had refused to live apart. Three years ago, the same year he and Jennie had lost their oldest son, a stroke left Auntie Totty paralyzed on one side of her body, rendering her like two people—one dead and the other half-dead. She hung on for about eight months like that, able only to quarter-talk, quarter-eat, until she was a quarter of her normal size and then died without a sound one night during a peaceful rain. But not before Jennie had called on her cousin to move in to help tend to her, along with the home, her aging mother-in-law, and the last of the children. But Jennie took cancer then, leaving Winnie to care for everyone for a while. After Auntie Totty passed, Winnie didn't hesitate to stay on to care for her cousin. What a gift from God Negro women were. All of them. Not a one ever failed, which probably explained why Bennie's story had struck such an angry chord with him: because it made no sense. Something didn't. Maybe Bennie just needed to give his young wife time, or better time, to help her see what she could do on her feet and not just on her back. Because Negro women were strongest on their feet, as strong as God's feet—every one of them.

"You been getting along all right, Mama?" Bass asked.

"Yes, son. Winnie gets her hands full, but Sallie and Georgia and Alice, they real good about pitching in and taking turns to watch Lula and Homer some. That's where they be, at Alice's tonight." Pearlalee tilted her head and took up her needles and black yarn. A yard of purl stitches covered her lap. "No child need to watch their mama go all the way down."

"No," he said, watching her hog-tie her needles. She didn't often knit with black yarn. "Who this for?"

"For your wife, son," she said.

"A shawl?"

Pearlalee nodded.

Winnie opened the front door and went out, and Jennie groaned from her bed.

"How's Bennie and his wife?" Pearlalee asked. "She with child yet?"

"No, ma'am."

"What they waiting for?"

"A sign, I guess, that they should stick being married."

Pearlalee grunted, and Jennie groaned again, longer this time, like a barn door closing.

He turned from his mother and gazed toward the hallway, at the rectangle of nothing he had to walk through. "You wanna sit with me, Mama?"

"No, you go. I got a few more rows to make yet."

Jennie's groaning was persistent.

"Go on, son. She talking to you."

"I'm coming, baby!" he called. He limped forward, and the front door opened. Winnie carried a bucket of water, the sky behind her a deep-dark blue.

"If pain's getting too much," Winnie told him, "it be close enough to time you can give her more."

Bass nodded. "Seven drops still?"

"Nah, ten now," Winnie said.

"Ten?"

Winnie nodded as she shut the door. Bass shook his head and looked away.

The lump of Jennie's feet under the white coverlet was as still as a flat iron, so she wasn't squirming yet. That was good. Her chest didn't appear to raise the smooth surface of the coverlet, and that wasn't good. As he stepped into the bedroom, she began to groan her shallow groan as if stirred by nightmares. When she quit and breathed in, her groggy, faded eyes pulled open. They found the direction of the door and then found him moving away from it before they dropped heavily down.

"Hi, Jennie, baby," he murmured, almost beside her. He didn't want to dirty her, but he had to. He needed to touch her. He gave her arm, spindly as a buttermilk racer, a gentle squeeze. "Got here quick as I could," he said. "You making it, honey?"

She remained still, which had been her way lately. As if it took her a few minutes to summon enough energy to talk and think and feel things. She had fallen ill a lifetime ago—the time he'd stopped to visit her before escaping the plantation in Texas. He'd had no choice then, in 1862, but to leave her behind, and on the short side of two days, after Casharago's hanging, he would need to leave her behind again, not knowing what the future would hold for them but knowing it would be much less than ever before.

He just didn't understand why the Lord would make her life a sideways picture. She used to make him see standing trees, with her dark bark skin and strong limbs. It wasn't, of course, impossible for a body to see a tree sideways. All trees eventually got sideways, as floating timber or tables and floors or fire logs or pianos or boats, and then they stayed that way. But sideways trees were always dead trees. He just didn't want to see her that way yet.

"Before I ever saw you, I heard you," he spoke easy and low. "'Member that?"

A sound issued more from her nose than her closed mouth—a moan more than a groan that was as dispiriting as a purr was comforting. A cry that barely reached his ears as if from below water or from far away, from beyond trees or walls. Then the moan fell silent in her throat and she breathed in, slowly, and slowly her eyes pulled open.

He smiled. "'Member that, Jennie?"

Her cheeks pulled her lips into a subtle but certain smile. Then her eyes drifted shut, but not suddenly and heavily, and she began to moan again—no, *hum* a familiar melody. She was remembering, of course. She was singing without words the old song she and Winnie had sung—as if to him alone, to serve as his salve and prayer—when he'd first arrived at George Reeves's plantation and for two nights had been shackled to the sticks in front of the overseer's cabin.

Bass shut his own eyes and joined her, humming the words he could still clearly hear:

Jesus a-coming and I's a-going,
Praying for that Heaven place,
It's a place I'd die to taste,
Praying for that Heaven place,
Where it be can you guess?

The floor seesawed beneath him from the padding of feet in the next room, and then Winnie joined them from the kitchen, singing, "Praying for that Heaven place." Bass kept his eyes closed, preferring to remember the past. Even the sticks. Even the awful hacking pain he'd endured in the meat and bones of his shoulders. Even the tart smell of the blackjacks, which could hide those beautiful faces, but not their voices, sifting through the latticed trees from the stream where the women labored with the wash. Winnie was voicing the words Jennie could only hum:

Smack dab twix east and west,
Praying for that Heaven place,
Follow the angels, follow the doves,
Praying for that Heaven place,
We'll nest in the one safe home above,
Praying for that Heaven place.

In the reverberating silence, he reached blindly for Jennie's arm to squeeze it again. "I got good news to share about Edgar," he spoke of their sixteen-year-old son. "Governor gonna be pardoning him for testifying against Newland. Ain't that good?" He opened his eyes, expecting to see her smile, but Jennie was eyeing him instead, with no smile beneath her gaze.

"Ain't that good? I mean, it ain't good that Newland's still locked up and that Edgar had to testify against him, but that's on Newland, you know? And if Newland do right, Lord'll look after him too. Maybe nudge the governor on his behalf, you know, baby? We'll see." But Jennie's mouth never budged. He thought about opening up about Bennie's troubles, just for something to share, but he decided to keep the burden his.

Jennie eyed him a long while without blinking. Her lips parted, and she took a breath. "How's Bennie?" she asked from her throat, her voice weaker than a whisper. Her eyes drooped as if suddenly exhausted by the effort.

"He's okay, baby." He patted her arm. "Don't you worry; I'm looking after him."

"He always looked up to you." She breathed in. "We all did." Her eyes drooped again and then drifted shut as she breathed in again. "Bennie was different, wasn't he?"

Her shoulders and neck squirmed, and she moaned like before.

"He a little lost, baby, but he's a good boy. I'm watching out. I got him on my mind." He nodded and patted her arm again.

"He sure dreamed of being you."

Bass smiled, but she appeared to shake her head. "Lord," she whispered and shut her eyes. "Please, Lord," she said, and he watched her closed eyes cry.

"Sorry, baby," Bass said. He let the line of his vision trail away to the pillow and the cross-stitched flowers along the pillowcase's hem—Auntie Totty's handiwork—to the cast-iron bed frame he'd forged for Jennie within days of their wedding, then to the table beside him. He wasn't thinking about where he'd bought the table or the lamp sitting on a doily that Auntie Totty had also made for the newlyweds. He was thinking about the tin spoon and the corked bottle of laudanum in the lamp's light, about what ten drops would look like.

"Lord, Lord," she repeated as if she were speaking to the Lord himself.

7

Geronimo

What Bass knew about Geronimo before he'd ever met him was that the white world appeared to be closing in on him with a vengeance for the very last time too. The same week A.J. Boyd had accosted Bass on Garrison Avenue was when he heard the news of Geronimo's capture shouted throughout town. First by the *Fort Smith Weekly Elevator* newsboy, then by everyone else. Five months earlier Geronimo had surrendered to General George Crook in the Sierra Madre Mountains of Mexico, but at the eleventh hour—suspecting betrayal—he instead escaped in the night. General Nelson Miles's reinvigorated manhunt, with five thousand U.S. troops, twenty-seven heliograph signal stations, and three thousand Mexican soldiers, eventually forced the last great Indian war chief to surrender at Skeleton Canyon in Arizona.

By the time Bass's murder trial had begun in October of 1887, Geronimo and a small band of Chiricahua Apaches had already been transported by train to two prisoner-of-war camps—first to Fort Pickens on a spear-shaped island near Pensacola, Florida, and then again a year later to Mount Vernon, Alabama, since so many had been succumbing on the coast to yellow fever, malaria, and tuberculosis. By the fall of 1894, Geronimo had become a national curiosity and was transported yet again, this time to Fort Sill in the Kiowa-Comanche-Apache Indian lands of Oklahoma Territory, approximately eighteen miles west of the Chickasaw Nation border.

Whenever Bass and Eddie were at home in Calvin and a new edition of the *Indian Citizen* was in print, Bennie would drop by their place in the evening and read the paper to them on the porch while they sipped rye or ate from a dinner plate on their laps. One story reported how Geronimo had sold the buttons off his clothes at train station stops along the way from Alabama for a quarter apiece. One mentioned Geronimo had a family at Fort Sill and was farming squash and pumpkins. Then in December of 1894, news of Geronimo reached Bass by messenger.

Bass happened to be in McGee the day two buffalo soldiers from the Tenth Cavalry rode into town to request that Doctor Jesse return with them to Fort Sill. Bass was waiting on a saddler to finish mending a stirrup strap when he walked to the road and offered to help the Negroes in blue locate the doctor, who was away from his store, Mooney Drugs, to assist with a childbirth. The news from Fort Sill was that Geronimo and two of his children had fallen ill with a high fever, and Geronimo had refused to take the military doctor's medicine. He said he would trust only the good doctor he'd heard was living among the Indians in the Chickasaw Nation.

The Tenth Cavalry had built Fort Sill, so Bass was happy to have the opportunity, at last, to see it and meet Geronimo, and Doctor Jesse welcomed the company. By the time Doctor Jesse had packed and was ready to leave town, the soldiers' horses had been groomed and fed, and Hammer was saddled and itching to ride even in the cold.

For two days the four men rode hunched against a bearing-down, frigid wind that seemed to shear the clothes right off them, so they wrapped their bedroll blankets like mourning shawls over their hats and around their shoulders and faces. Bass sometimes closed his eyes and imagined the slog to Fort Sill was something akin to seafaring—with Hammer's rocking and that buffeting wind, like ocean wind. He hoped to ask Geronimo, once he was well, if in Florida he'd ever spotted a whale.

Fort Sill appeared small on approach, a well-fortified citadel on a squat bluff as flat as a milking stool. But once Bass was standing inside the stone walls, he could see the fort stretched farther than he'd anticipated, spanning nearly twice the acreage of Fort Smith, with a commander's house, officers' quarters, supply buildings, barracks, stables, training fields, and a hospital, which sat on the northwest corner of the fort, facing Medicine Bluff Creek.

Geronimo lay still and hard as a corpse the first time Bass's eyes fell on him. Doctor Jesse felt his forehead and took his pulse. He spoke to Geronimo but received no answer. "Tell him I need to place a thermometer under his tongue for five minutes," Doctor Jesse told Geronimo's English-speaking wife, Zi-yeh, who was sitting on the floor on the opposite side of the bed but was now rising to her feet. Her upper lip curled in a perpetual snarl from a cleft palate, or perhaps she'd been sliced with a knife. "I need to know how bad his fever is," he said. "Tell him not to bite it."

While Zi-yeh spoke in Apache to Geronimo, the doctor uncapped a paper tube, slid the thermometer out, and shook it. Geronimo groaned and parted his lips. The doctor consulted Zi-yeh, but her stoic face offered no response. Her hair fanned down her back, long and thick as a broom.

"Here." Doctor Jesse tucked the end of the thermometer with the silver tip under Geronimo's tongue. Geronimo's dry, cracked lips closed and puckered, then remained as motionless as the rest of him. Neither the bed nor bedcovers moved, and neither his eyes nor closed eyelids. After five minutes, the doctor snapped his pocket watch shut and read the thermometer. "105," he announced and looked at Zi-yeh. "Tell him I need to give him a febrifuge— medicine—to bring his fever down."

Zi-yeh spoke in translation, and though Geronimo must have groaned in agreement, it sounded to Bass much more like disagreement.

While the children showed signs of improvement the next day, Geronimo lapsed into a coma. Bass attended each visit with the doctor throughout the day. He watched as Doctor Jesse listened to Geronimo's heartbeat and his breathing, and as he inspected the Apache's scarred hands, arms, and chest, counting over fifty old bullet and buckshot wounds. On Geronimo's right shoulder, Doctor Jesse found a lump. The doctor pressed on it, then asked Bass to take the lantern from the table and bring it closer. When he did, they could see what was beneath his skin was gray.

"That's a .44-caliber," Bass said.

Doctor Jesse reached into his bag and produced a scalpel. "Lift that, will you, Bass?" he asked, so Bass raised the lantern's chimney. The doctor held the scalpel in the flame until Bass could see soot begin to swirl on the steel. Then the doctor held the blade in the flame another moment longer before removing and wiping it on a white cloth from his bag. When he lanced the skin, the bullet bobbed up like a bloody cork.

"The chick that's in him pecks the shell," Bass muttered.

"Do what?" Doctor Jesse asked.

"You mean you ain't read *Moby-Dick* yet?"

Doctor Jesse smirked. "Yeah, there's no quit in him."

Bass admired the man lying like a corpse with his dark pitted face like baked ground that could soak up so much water, so much blood. There would never be enough spilled to right the wrongs in his life.

Geronimo's body bottled up a vastly different spirit from Jennie's, Bass considered now in hindsight. Jennie looked so much like love dying and not hate surviving. Bass was riding Hammer in a death procession of horses and bodies and buggies and wagons. Dogs trailed behind, and children laughed. No one on the avenue traveled away from the gallows along the river. In a way, no one showed a face.

But Geronimo had roused more than Jennie could anymore. After three days in a coma, his pulse strengthened, his fever broke, and his eyes crept open. He looked at Doctor Jesse, who was nearest, then at Bass, then at his wife, then at Bass again. His eyes kept returning to Bass. He lifted his head from his pillow to swallow water, then after a few deep breaths, resting from that effort, he raised a limp hand and curled a finger, summoning Bass, it seemed, to step closer.

Geronimo's finger curled again and then he raised his hand higher, palm outward as if to touch Bass's face, but as Bass leaned over the bed, he could see Geronimo was looking at the top of his head, at his hair. So Bass lowered his head and waited as Geronimo touched it with his fingertips. They lingered on his curls before gently pressing them as if he were testing the ripeness of a tomato. Once his finger-tips stopped testing and pressing, they slowly roved in circles over Bass's scalp of sheared-short hair. When Geronimo removed his hand, Bass raised his head and stood straight, watching Geronimo carry his limp hand to his nose. Geronimo took two short breaths and then one long inhalation. Then Geronimo's eyes drifted shut, his hand fell away, and he resumed his sleep.

The next morning Geronimo had the strength to chew food and later to speak. The children were already well enough to play across the room. They were making up a game with the deck of cards Bass had given them the previous day, but Doctor Jesse stepped aside to check on them once more before he and Bass left to return home. Geronimo watched the doctor put his stethoscope to his ears, then spoke to Zi-yeh, bundled by shirts over dresses. Geronimo con-tinued to look at his wife as she asked Bass to explain who he was. Only after she had spoken did Geronimo regard Bass as if to watch the words scroll onto his breath in the cold room.

"I may look like a buffalo soldier, but I'm a deputy," Bass said. While Zi-yeh translated his English, Bass unbuttoned his coat and showed Geronimo the badge pinned on his vest.

Geronimo's eyes remained small as a bird's. He spoke and then Zi-yeh spoke for him.

"You are no buffalo," she said.

"That's right, no buffalo. I'm a deputy marshal for the Western District of Arkansas."

"No, he says you are no buffalo."

Bass waited for more.

"Buffalo were born as I was born, where there were no enclo-sures," Zi-yeh said for Geronimo.

Bass nodded. He thought he understood him. "Yes, I was born a slave. There were enclosures everywhere I went, all the time." Listen-ing to the music of Zi-yeh's Apache translation, Bass recalled George

Reeves reading poems like songs to him from a book by Longfel-
low. That had been before the war, the time they'd gone hunting in
the Ozarks and killed every animal they saw. He suddenly remembered what he'd nearly forgotten to ask. "Chief Geronimo," he said,
and Zi-yeh turned to Bass. Geronimo was already turned to him.
"I wonder," he paused but continued, "if when you were down in
Florida you ever saw a whale?"

"Whale?" Zi-yeh asked.

"Whale?" Doctor Jesse laughed from across the room.

"It's a big fish that lives in the ocean, a very big one," Bass
explained, stretching his arms out wide and looking to the rafters.
"A whale's as big as this room—bigger even."

Zi-yeh spoke many words, but Geronimo spoke only one.

"He says no."

Geronimo muttered a few more words and crossed his arms.
Bass believed him to be angry.

"Apaches don't eat fish."

Bass nodded.

Geronimo continued to speak, chopping his words. "I should
have never surrendered."

Bass listened without reaction the way Geronimo listened, as
they steadily watched each other speak.

"I never understood enclosures," Geronimo said. "You do.
Remember."

Bass nodded to show he'd heard him, but he didn't understand.
"Remember?"

"Don't forget." Geronimo uncrossed his arms and searched his
shirt with his left hand. When he found the top button, he grasped
it as if to unbutton his shirt, but he pulled the button instead until
it pulled the shirt with it and then snapped free. He held his fist
toward Bass, and Bass placed a hand beneath Geronimo's so that
he could give him the button if he wanted. "Don't forget," Geronimo repeated and opened his fist, the button falling and rolling into
Bass's palm—a black button knotted with a kinked thread.

"Thank you, Chief Geronimo," Bass said.

Geronimo held out his hand again, but this time it was open and empty—palm up.

Bass looked Geronimo in the eyes, and Geronimo looked in his. Bass nodded. "Of course," he said, closing his fist around the button and displaying his fist.

8

The Court of the Damned

More and more people were gathering on the avenue than could ever squeeze inside the gallows' privacy fence to view the hanging, but their city was making history today and everyone wanted to lay claim that they were present when it happened. There was always a chance they could position themselves close enough to witness some part of the ceremony by standing on a wagon or sitting on someone's shoulders. Bass had once seen a young woman perched on a man's shoulders who was himself sitting on a horse. Even if they saw none of what transpired on the gallows' platform, they might hear the rector pray or the prisoner protest his innocence or, better yet, confess or the trap doors bang open or, during the crowd's hush, the rope creak as Casharago dangled. And they could always eat a tamale or a sack of boiled peanuts and pass the time with friends. Only the old executioner had felt no pull to attend.

The door to Maledon Groceries & Provisions stood open, so Bass turned Hammer out of the current of traffic to tie her up at the rail.

"Hey hey, Bass Reeves!"

Bass knew who was calling him before he'd dismounted and turned.

"I thought that was you ahead of me!" Deputy James Mershon said. He grinned beneath a graying red mustache as his dark bay quarter horse trotted past. His hat stood tall and stiff like the man beneath it. "I'll take a peach or something while you're at it, and tell George we'll miss him today!"

Bass waved and grabbed a storefront post to heave himself onto the boardwalk. The pungent odor of cheese was immediate, unlike the grocery's increasingly fecund and fuggy shade. Then George Maledon greeted him himself, seated on a stool beside a scale on a safe at the far end of the vacant store. Bass surveyed the bins of dusty vegetables and fruits and shelves above them stacked with canned goods, cheese wheels, jars of candy, pairs of spermaceti candles, and bars of glycerin or beef tallow soap.

Bass removed his hat and smiled, surprised to see George wearing a white apron because in his old life he'd always worn black, even the time in 1881 when, deputized for the occasion, he helped Bass and four other deputies guard a rail transport of twenty-one prisoners from the Fort Smith jail to the Detroit House of Correction. "George, my friend," Bass said fondly. "How are you?"

He couldn't pass George's store today without checking on the man who'd been the executioner for Judge Isaac Parker for twenty-two years. When George retired in 1894, he'd had the distinction of executing more men than anyone in U.S. history by hanging sixty-one and shooting two more attempting to escape. Bass had never seen anyone else tie or tighten the noose or pull the lever, not even after George retired two years ago to open this store to enjoy a different side of life. In spite of his dream, his eighteen-year-old daughter, Annie, had gotten into an argument last year with her boyfriend after learning he was actually married, and at some point he'd heard enough words and shot and killed her. Bass worried about George.

George shrugged. "Will be busier and better after the hanging, I reckon." His wiry white beard looked a little longer; his eyes were set a little deeper. "Couldn't see going and not being up there, you know?"

"Yeah," Bass said, nodding, scanning the bins of fruit. There were peaches, plums, blackberries, huckleberries, black cherries, figs. "What's sweetest right now?"

"Everything, but I'm partial to those." George pointed low, almost to the floor.

Bass looked beneath the figs to find three oblong watermelons as thick as his thighs. He smiled. "Perfect, but I never was good at picking one. Would you do me the honor?"

George slid off his stool, and he seemed shorter than Bass remembered, with a back more curved. He leaned down and thumped each melon. They all sounded full of water to Bass. George then rolled each one to inspect their bellies, which were all yellow, but the middle one had the darkest shade of yellow, almost orange. George rolled that one out. It was also the biggest, as long as Bass was broad.

"Take this'un," George said.

"That watermelon's something, all right." Bass lowered and shouldered it.

"How much for it, George?"

"Oh, stop," George said, returning to his stool.

"But it's for Mershon."

"Shit, that'll be a dollar then for that son of a bitch."

Bass laughed. "He told me to tell you it won't be the same without you."

George smiled. Bass hadn't seen George smile many times in his life outside that trip to Detroit. George had smiled every time he got to hold Arena Howe's baby, who had been born in the Fort Smith jail. Now George's own baby was dead. Bass hated to think of dead babies.

"You're a good man, George." Bass reached out and shook his hand. George had fought for the Union with the First Arkansas Light Artillery. He looked like the devil, but looks could be so deceiving.

George's hand was small and without much meat, but his grip was firm and lingered as if he didn't want Bass to leave. "Shore glad you never had to stand over my trap."

Bass smirked even though he could see George was sincere. They withdrew their hands, and Bass patted his plaid bow tie. "Stay away, Prince of the Hangmen."

George grinned, displaying too many old teeth.

"You're scaring me, George," Bass said, turning to leave, his boots rasping the gritty floor. "Smile, but don't be grinning. Gonna scarecrow your customers away."

"Come back and see me, Bass Reeves."

"I will, George Maledon."

◆ ◆ ◆

Hangings had always attracted crowds but never the size of what Bass witnessed congregating that day. Wagons continued to line South Third Street and Rogers Avenue, emptying death watchers toting picnic baskets, parasols, guitars, fiddles, flutes, whisky bottles and jugs, and blankets to throw on the rolling courthouse grounds. Bass seemed alone, though, lugging a fruit the dead weight of a toddler.

Bass greeted everyone he passed with a tip of his hat, a handshake, or a how-de-do, even those who scowled at him and looked the other way. He joked about being a granddaddy again while patting his melon, but he kept moving to avoid a conversation that would slow him. According to the bell at Saint John's Episcopal, the hanging was only a half hour away.

On the backside of the courthouse, Bass found his buddy James Mershon holding court at the base of the steps as if he'd never been relieved as a deputy for overstating his fees. Deputies Bud Ledbetter, Heck Thomas, Clemer Large, and Sonny Fair were hanging onto every word, along with Samuel Harman, a savvy, young defense attorney who was scribbling away in the leather-bound book of blank pages he carried everywhere he went because he was working on a book about Judge Parker's court. James was the best storyteller of that group by far, and James was taking full advantage of it, so no one had seen Bass coming.

"Excuse me, fellas," Bass said, bumping shoulders as he broke between James and Samuel. He held the watermelon up by both ends. "Something sweet from the prince!" he bellowed, then thrust it straight down on the ground in the middle of their circle, splitting it open into three glorious parts.

James guffawed, and his blue eyes grew bigger and rounder, not smaller, glinting in the sun like Churchill dinnerware. He slapped Bass on the back, so Clemer followed suit and knocked Samuel back a step, along with the pencil out of his hand. Clemer was a damn fool, though Bass hadn't known the extent of it a year ago when he'd asked Clemer to sign his name on Casharago's arresting paperwork as a favor, and the fool Clemer signed his own.

But Sonny grunted. "What the hell?" he grumbled, brushing his trousers of watermelon splatter. The old Democrat perpetually looked for reasons to sneer at Bass. He'd probably never been kind to a Negro in his life, especially one who could beat the court. Especially one Sonny himself had arrested.

"Loosen your collar, Sonny." Bass produced a six-inch Bowie knife from his coat pocket. "Sabers up, boys!"

"Heck, yeah," Heck said, as always.

"Anybody got salt?" Bud asked with a laugh, already stooping with his own knife to carve a bite.

Ever eager to laugh and laugh about laughing, James struck up again as Bass—wielding a succulent wedge of seedless heart—strode away to find Eddie or a turnkey, whoever came first. A good sign of Eddie's experience as a deputy was that Bass found him outside the jails, in the shade of the courthouse steps, talking to Lester, Bass's favorite turnkey.

"Eddie, Lester!" Bass called, wiping his blade on his trousers before sheathing his knife. The three shook hands, and Bass and Lester asked about each other's children. Bass kept his side short. "Well, I'm their daddy, so I guess I gotta love 'em!"

That made Lester smile. So many treated a hanging as if it were Christmas and every prisoner was Jesus Christ reminding them of the blessing of life. Bass had to admit that was a pretty nice way to think about the day.

Bass finally gave Lester a friendly pat on the shoulder, and Lester, understanding, reached for the key ring hanging from his belt.

"Ready?"

Bass nodded, and Lester led the way.

Bass glanced at Eddie following behind, appearing alert and content, with his hands in his pockets but eyes up.

The keys jangled as Lester turned the lock and shoved the jail door open—the door on the left, not the one on the right. Then Lester stood back as if he vainly hoped to avoid carrying home on his clothes that heavy, hot stench of the prisoners' urine, which moved at them like a boulder as slow as a sunset.

"I'll leave the door open for you," Lester said. "Hell on the border today, no joke."

Bass nodded as he gazed inside at the shaft of sunlight, only that. Against his instincts he took a deep breath because for the moment he was lost in his memory of 1884, when Sonny, James, and Lester had ushered him to this same left-side jail—not to the other—as a prisoner and not a lawman. Yet congruent with his instincts, Bass removed his hat and stooped as he stepped in to keep his head from striking the ceiling's low planks.

Jimmy Casharago sat in the suffocating heat on a blanket spread across the flagstone floor of the foyerlike lawyer box while shining, brooding faces huffed through the bars of the gate on the cell side of the box. "Bazz Reeves, Bass Reeves," the congregation of felons said in lazy, raspy whispers to him and about him.

Jimmy Casharago raised his eyes then lowered them again. Perhaps the sun was too bright for him, or, like some on the outside who believed Bass to be a cold-blooded killer who should've been hanged for murder, he feared looking Bass in the eyes would invite the devil into his heart. Cash's thin, dark hair, which was longer now than when Bass had seen him last, at the trial, lay flat on his head as if he'd just walked out of the Arkansas or Poteau River and put on those filthy clothes.

"Cash," Bass said, "we've come to pay our respects."

"Boy!" Cash raised his face and eyes but again refused to look at Bass or anyone else as if electing to gaze only at that trespassing sunlight. "How about respecting who I am and calling me by my name? You know what it is. I done told you and told you, told everybody."

"*George*, was it, did you say?" Bass asked.

"George something," Eddie said.

"George Maledon?" Bass asked.

"No, George Crump," Eddie said.

"George Wilson!" Cash screeched as if he was losing his voice box in this heat.

"No, that don't sound right." Bass crossed his arms. "George Reeves, is it?"

"I know it ain't George Washington," Eddie said.

"I said *George Wilson*, and you know it!" Cash screeched again, now eyeing Bass with terrified eyes; Bass was glad to see them that way.

"Are you sure?" Bass continued to goad. He brushed his coat open and rested a hand on his hip. Cash's eyes slowly trailed down to Bass's uncovered Colt as if magnetized. "Are you sure, Cash, or *Jimmy*, you wanna belong to a group a George? That's a tough group, that George group. They killers, every one."

Cash dropped his head so that all of his face but the tip of his nose was hidden. He squeezed one hand with the other. Bass wondered if this strange fellow was shaking his own hand, making a promise. Then Cash pressed the heels of his hands against his eyes.

"I ain't convinced," Bass said, taking a step forward, and Eddie followed, their boots scraping the floor. "Nobody convinced. That's a problem. *Your* problem. Nobody else's, son." Bass clasped his hands and hat together in front of him and shut his eyes. "Lord," he started, "you led me to this here Jimmy Casharago—"

"Stop calling me that!" Cash spat into his hands.

"—so I'm gonna try to lead him to you," Bass said calmly as if Cash hadn't interrupted him. "I pray if he hadn't started to open up to you yet, and I'm guessing he hadn't if he won't even own up to who he is, then maybe he will here, directly on his walk out to the gallows. I pray that as Jimmy Casharago climbs those white steps of the platform, it's like Jimmy climbing up to you, Lord. And I pray Jimmy takes his knot and your love and everlasting hope like a choke of cold water. There's quite a drove out there, so I pray Jimmy will admit he ain't no George, that he a killer all the same and will show them people gathering something beautiful, something amazing, something they ain't never seen and won't never see in Fort Smith never ever again. Amen."

Bass had plowed on through his usual hanging day sermon despite Cash's repeated objections, then abruptly turned amidst the chorus of amens among the prisoners and walked out after Eddie. Though Bass had been gladder in the past to be free of that box, he was mighty glad today all the same.

"Seen Judge?" he asked Lester, but when Lester shook his head, Bass asked James Mershon.

"Not yet," James said. "Maybe inside?"

Bass checked his pocket watch as he climbed the steps. George Winston, who had served as Judge Parker's private bailiff for all but the last three years, was chatting under the portico with another of the old Negro bailiffs who had been relieved under Marshal Crump's Democratic leadership.

Bass gripped George's arm as he squeezed past. George had the stoutest arms of any man he'd ever known and one of the smartest minds for books. Jennie could read anything and understand it, but George Winston could refer to what he'd read in great detail, a lot like a preacher or teacher, but not by reciting—by referring—and he referred often to Twain, Douglass, Lincoln, and Stowe by using his own words to capture theirs, which reminded Bass of George Reeves, who often referred and recited. But George Winston didn't do it to show off, it was just his way, while Bass's old master always did it to show off because it, too, was just his way. "George," Bass said, noticing George's mutton chops were now white as wool, "I was just thinking of you."

"My friend, how are you?" George's baritone voice always verged on song.

"Pretty fair. My wife's dying of cancer, and I got two sons in prison, though the governor's about to pardon one because he testified against his brother, but I been worse. How about you?"

It was as if Judge Parker's court demeanor all those years had rubbed off on George Winston, who would go to his grave too dignified to laugh. He only smiled, no matter what Bass had ever thought to say.

"Well, good to see you," Bass said and turned to the other old bailiff. "You, too, Goose."

Bass reached for the brass doorknob and opened the courthouse door. This—this mellow, wood-scented silence—was what he thought he would miss most about the courthouse. Even when it bustled, it retained an undeniable stillness that he had only heard or felt here and in one other place. There had been a two-hour wait for the train in Chicago to take the prisoner transport to Detroit, so the deputies were all taking turns getting a bite to eat and stretching their legs. Bass had seen a rectangular stone tower when arriving on the train from Memphis, and after sitting in the station and admiring how the tower rose above shops and boardinghouses, he decided to inquire about the fort that looked too beautiful to be one. He approached a dark-skinned Pullman porter and asked what it was. He pointed at the tower, but the porter refused to look away and instead gawked at Bass as if he believed he'd been the only Negro in the world allowed to walk and talk and couldn't trust his eyes. As though Bass were a ghost or a dream. The porter scrutinized Bass's badge, leaned closer to it as if to read it, and maybe he could read. Then he looked back at Bass's eyes, his mustache, his Stetson hat, and then he looked at Bass's pistols and maybe his boots, then back at his eyes, hat, and eyes. "You're the law?" the porter asked incredulously. "Where?"

Bass answered him and pointed again, and the porter leaned in for one last inspection of the badge as Bass gave the porter's round, flat-topped hat another look—like a tin can—before he turned and followed Bass's arm and pointing finger.

"That St. James Church," the porter finally answered. "Uncle Abraham worshipped there."

"Honest Abe?" Bass asked.

The porter nodded. "The Great Emancipator hisself, God bless him. That's right."

As soon as Bass's turn came for a break, he made a beeline to St. James Church. He had to see for himself what the fort was protecting, what Uncle Abraham had seen for himself, and it stopped him dead in his tracks and took his breath. The ceiling was as high up as the sky but painted gold, with a pattern of diamonds, so that it could've been God's ascot. He beheld crisscrossing beams, like ribs—God's ribs—and the pipe organ, what could have been sugarcane, his granddaddy's heavenly stand, and everywhere else were those blue-and-red-and-green windows—not so a body like Uncle Abraham or Bass could look out but so only God and his angels could look in. Whenever a body used the word "miracle," this was what Bass remembered. Maybe a pine box felt the same way to a soul. Not so much protecting it or even enclosing it as announcing it, like a line in the sand, like a border marker. He hoped that was so.

The courthouse was much more modest yet grand in its own way, with an announcement just as clear from the worn-smooth floorboards and banisters and cave-like courtroom that God's work—a lot of it—had taken place here.

"Judge?" Bass asked the cave, and the cave swiftly countered by repeating for the record precisely what he'd said. Bass and Eddie spun around and took turns calling for the judge while checking the corners and chairs and pews for a judge reluctant to be celebrated. Those who worked for the court were all aware that Judge Parker valued solitude and would demand it if you didn't give it to him.

"Got your handkerchief?" Bass asked, and Eddie patted his coat pocket.

Bass climbed onto the judge's platform and craned low to peek under the desk stacked with the judge's books as though he'd never retire, never die. It wasn't like the judge to do a young'un thing like hide, but Bass wanted to look everywhere to be certain, maybe to see it all one last time.

Bass stepped down and took the witness chair by the arms to set it on the platform, just as he'd done numerous times, but he thought better of moving it. He should experience the chair one last time where it was, where it usually rested as the witness chair, so he sat down in it and looked straight ahead into the gallery. Not as a friend or deputy under the judge but as a witness, a defendant. Eddie was walking along the last row of pews in the gallery, but, noticing Bass, he decided to sit too.

Bass took a deep breath of that silence. He looked past the first row of pews to regard Eddie, who looked half-bored and half-glad to be sitting. "I testified at more trials than I can count. At more trials than I imagine the court even know about. They get sloppy with the bookkeeping like they can't help it when it come to Negroes."

Eddie nodded his head at Bass's words but remained quiet as if the judge were behind the desk and might fine him for disrupting the peace of his court.

"Did you know I was charged with murder in '75? Hadn't been a deputy two full months before some drunken hayseed wanted to prove he wasn't a drunken hayseed."

"No, I ain't heard about that time."

"Brought up on state charges. The old boy put up a good fight. Not even a outlaw, just another anguished old boy, disgruntled I was a deputy and he wasn't. Came up and walloped me from behind with a billhook. God's grace he got me with the handle and not the blade, or he woulda taken my head clean off. Before I could stand back up, he jumped on me and tried to choke me out, so I done the same. One of us was gonna choke the other out. It was a race at that point. Most around never believed I done anything wrong, but his family insisted on a trial." Bass stretched out his legs. "The second time was different."

He allowed his eyes to rove the room to the first row of pews again. They remembered the way a horse remembered. The space where George Reeves had sat to be noticed and crossed his legs at the knee, rocking that shined shoe of his and fingering the hat in his lap, caught more shadow. George had darkened that space for all eternity, which would just be another added to a multitude.

"Like somebody in here forgot to wind a clock," Eddie said.

Bass stared across at that dark space in the first pew row. He could hear him again before he could see him—his tiny dark eyes and spearhead of gray whiskers—and what he heard was his profanity.

Bass had knelt on the floor with his Winchester to show the jury how, in camp, he'd laid his rifle across his left arm and worked with his knife to pry .45-caliber cartridges from the chamber.

Just as his attorney Theodore Barnes had told him, it'd be a whole lot easier for a dozen white men to believe that the most experienced and respected n—— deputy simply couldn't avoid making a host of greenhorn errors than to concede Bass could actually come within a hair of measuring up to his reputation as invincible. He'd loaded his Colt .45 bullets into his .44 rifle and gotten them jammed, recklessly aimed his rifle in the direction of a hired hand while working to clear it, and then let either his hand or knife—he didn't know which—unwittingly strike the trigger. Of course, that's what a n—— deputy would think to do.

The prosecutor had asked, "Did you intend to shoot him?"

"No, sir," Bass had stated, rising from the floor. He handed the rifle to the prosecutor and returned to the witness chair.

The prosecutor laid the rifle on his table and walked away a step as if he had no more questions and was about to take a seat, too, but Bass knew by how slowly the prosecutor stepped away, how he tapped his bottom lip, that he wasn't finished. He was just starting up. And then he turned back to Bass and asked it. "There was something said about a dog—what was it?"

Bass tilted his head and shrugged, performing himself. "He was running around there, and I said, 'You had better kill that dog.' We didn't need no pup among us with no rabies. That was where my mind was at, so I grabbed a skillet a hot grease and doused her good."

"Goddamn hogwash!" George Reeves erupted.

Remembering, Bass glanced at the space darkened first by the man, no longer a stylish dresser as he was in his younger years. In old age he dressed only in black. George had been stewing over Bass's previous lies, but this one had been too much for him to suffer through silently.

Judge Parker rapped his gavel until the murmuring in the courtroom had subsided. "No more of that, you hear me? I want order in my court."

Bass recalled the jury's looks of confusion and irritation with his old master, how absurd his outburst about a dog's death must have seemed to them in context of a man's, even a Negro's.

Bass couldn't let Willy kill the pup. He was still working to explain it to himself. He'd always told the truth and wanted to, that was true, but admitting he intended to shoot Willy would have convinced jurors of a falsehood, that he had intended to kill Willy. And what kind of truth would a truth be if it motivated the regrouping Democrats to lynch one more Negro like Henry Smith, who three years ago had been burned all over his body with hot irons up on a scaffold in Paris before ten thousand spectators? An hour of his screams had been recorded on a graphophone and played again and again for pennies. That was before he'd been burned alive with kerosene oil. Those people had had enough reason already in their hooped and scalloped hearts to do what they did to a seventeen-year-old, to sell Henry's ashes and bones as souvenirs. With one more reason, what more could they have imagined doing?

"'Be of good cheer. It's me. Don't be afraid,' Jesus told his disciples when they were on a ship tossing in a tempest and saw him walking out on the water to reach them. They saw him as a man, not recognizing him. Peter stayed afraid and demanded evidence, miracles. You hear how fucked up that is?"

"Uh-huh," Eddie said from across the courtroom, from up over that blighted space.

"None of those disciples deserved to be disciples. Like how masters never deserved a jot of the riches they got. That's why I don't need to read a lick to know the Bible to be the Word of God. Look around. The world it tells about is the selfsame one we got."

Eddie silently nodded, and Bass took a breath. He hadn't been to church in a while. He hadn't wanted to arrest his preacher, but Reverend Hobson had left him no choice.

Bass noted the jail smell of urine seeping through the floorboards. He stomped his boots, and the bell at Saint John's Episcopal on North Sixth began to toll, and the crowd outside started to count in the hour.

"Well," Bass said.

"Shore wish that was our dinner bell," Eddie said, rising as Bass was rising. They walked outside and followed the procession of the rector, marshal, prisoner, and turnkeys into the gallows, then another joined their rear guard as though a dove had flown up beside Bass and wrapped a wing around him.

"Bass," Judge Parker said, his hair and beard as white as the gallows had once been. His eyes nearly closed as he smiled.

Bass could feel the ends of his mustache hitch up, which meant he was smiling big. "Judge, how are you, sir?"

The judge's nose and cheeks appeared swollen, puffier than normal, and ruddy. Maybe he was coming down with something, or maybe he was simply getting older and couldn't take the heat.

"Give us some ground, folks," Lester said behind them, attempting to close the gate, but the crowd continued to jostle forward. "Ladies and gentlemen! Boys! Please, y'all gonna need to step back, back up, now," he implored, and two other turnkeys joined him, motioning for the crowd to back away. "We can't begin till we close this here gate," Lester shouted over their requests to leave it open.

Bass and Judge Parker turned and eyed the crowd. The judge stepped forward and pointed at them with his short arm and stubby finger, his stance pulling his suit tight across his chest as a stifling breeze ruffled the frayed end of his beard.

The crowd stopped pushing and was now frozen by the imposing sight of the judge.

"Y'all all wanna turn on the gallows or something?" Bass hollered. Two or three in the throng chuckled. "Come on, people. Need to hoof it on back so we can get the gate shut. Part of the proceeding."

Enough of the crowd softened and pressed backward, then the rest followed.

"That's it," Lester told them. "Little more!"

Bass and Judge Parker glanced at each other before turning around and continuing to walk in past the gate. The judge leaned over to be heard. "Good news about your boy's pardon."

Bass leaned over too. "I appreciate you speaking to the governor."

"There's nothing I wouldn't do for you, you know that," Judge Parker said. "Your boys are good boys. Newland, too."

"I know you right." The judge had given Newland work and had allowed him to live in his house. Bass had hoped that seeing goodness up close from another side of life would inspire his son to want not just more but better. What was it about being born with nothing that made a body want everything, but when he was born with everything, he wanted nothing?

The turnkeys closed the gate behind them and locked it, and immediately a few of the boys outside tried to climb it—their boots and shoes kicking and sliding against the boards.

Bass and Judge Parker both preferred to watch a hanging from the fence as the last men standing. "Good men make sacrifices," Judge Parker told him. "You're a good man, Bass. You made sacrifices I didn't have to make." The judge grasped his arm. His eyes opened wider despite the sun. "You know I'm grateful, don't you?"

"Oh, yes, sir." Bass nodded. "It's been a honor, sir."

Once the rector stepped upon the platform, followed by Jimmy Casharago, the crowds inside and outside the gallows hushed.

The hangman wasn't nearly as neat in appearance as George Maledon or as quick to fit a noose. The rector cleared his throat and licked his lips, preparing to speak, while Casharago lost his color as he stared in shock at so many watching. Bass shook his head. It didn't matter what race a boy was. A boy with nothing to strive for was bound to find trouble.

9

A New Moon

Bass stroked Strawberry's gray head where his river blaze no longer showed. His eyes were so like clouds he saw only by nosing, by remembering. "I miss you, Strawberry," Bass whispered. Strawberry had been with him for so many of his better times, some worse, and he wished he'd brought more than one apple. Saying goodbye that morning to Jennie after giving her a spoon and a kiss on her warm, hard brow hadn't blurred his eyes until now. Now it was Strawberry on top of Jennie and that was on top of Cash on top of Willy on top of Robert and Newland and Edgar and Bennie on top of Mama—his never knowing when or how or where—which fell on top of so many other hangings and killings and sorrowful waitings and wonderings.

"Sure was hoping he'd fess up to what he done," Eddie said, leaning against the livery fence with a boot up on a rail.

Bass patted the slope of Strawberry's back and stepped away. The sun was pretending to be a gentle thing, but it was just about to show itself. Bass and Eddie would be sitting on their porch in Calvin and watching it dip back out of sight. The day would be gone before they knew it.

"Maybe, Eddie, instead a hoping, you shoulda been praying."

"Yeah, maybe so." Eddie turned from the fence and collected Flycatcher's reins and a handful of mane. "They say, 'No Sunday west of St. Louis, no God west of Fort Smith,' but guess it can't hurt to try."

"Oh, it'll hurt," Bass said, stepping into a stirrup. "No way around hurt." Hammer jigged beside Flycatcher once Bass had mounted her and until he let her go onto Garrison Avenue.

God had given them clear skies for today's ride, but if Bass and Eddie had planned to track someone instead, it would no doubt be raining. That had never failed to happen for a reason Bass couldn't quite figure. Maybe God liked for Bass to track in the rain because God liked a fair fight, or a good one, a challenge on both sides. Or maybe he liked to give his people a fresh start and considered his rain a baptism. Or maybe God wanted to wash away his own tracks, so no human knew the truth of God's presence west of Fort Smith and wrongly blamed him for all the awful goings-on. Tomorrow Bass and Eddie would ride to Pauls Valley in the Chickasaw Nation to learn who in the Eastern District of Texas for the last few days hadn't been behaving themselves. Maybe then the rain would start.

Bass didn't know when he'd get another vacation, so for a midday meal he agreed to Eddie's suggestion that they veer off the road a few miles to stop at a branch south of Younger's Bend, a place where old Choctaw friends of his and his mother fished and fried all day this time of year. They lived in lean-tos with their dogs. Eddie had lived with them for several months once, which was when he learned to identify and handle snakes.

When Bass and Eddie took the last trail to the branch by riding through a grove of robust sycamore, a pack of mongrel hounds encircled them, barking and howling, before they ran ahead to lead the way. Bass could hear trickling water, and he realized that the dogs were hushing themselves, tucking their tails, some sulking on their bellies, as the branch came into view—likely, from beatings, the dogs had learned better.

Bass had never seen this particular branch, which bloomed with islands of lavender pickerelweed, just where it flowed from too sunny of a stretch to one shaded by a thick canopy of hackberry and catalpa trees—where bass would surely want to hide.

Eddie knew two of the three men but neither of the women in this group of Choctaws. Regardless they all welcomed him and his friend. When Bass introduced himself in their tongue, they respectfully stood erect from the bank but then laughed about his name. They had already caught two dozen or more smallmouth and large-mouth bass by using boxelder bugs for bait. Occasionally the strewn fish would flop along the bank among the Choctaws in an attempt to reach water, and one of the Choctaws would leave for the nearest boxelder to collect another handful of the red-and-black bugs. Then the two women offered Bass and Eddie their poles and began frying the fish in pans while holding them down with sticks.

♦ ♦ ♦

When Bass and Eddie arrived in Calvin, the skies were still clear, and the sun was still a hot iron against their clothes and skin even as it cooled on its slant. They followed the road along the Canadian until the road narrowed to a trail and, at last, they reached their cabin, though a handsome brougham carriage with a solid black hackney sat in front of it.

Bass reined Hammer in and spun to look behind them as far as he could see, fearing an ambush, but there was no one, only their trail dust settling. He eyed Eddie, who asked him whose carriage that was. Bass shook his head and scanned the yard for someone waiting since the driver's seat was empty and the curtains inside the carriage were pulled to. Then he spotted a shadow in the shadow of the porch, a Negro in dark clothes sitting in Bass's rocker. A Negro who looked uncomfortably like Willy Leach. Dark skin, barrel body, no neck.

Bass kept his hands low and walked Hammer into the yard. His eyes flitted between the Negro—whom he assumed was the driver—and the carriage's curtains, which he expected to see draw open any moment, while the hackney calmly watched him and Hammer pass. Bass couldn't think of anyone he knew who would own a hackney with a docked tail or a new carriage, which was black except for dark-green bottom panels and a yellow stripe, with windows and silver door latches.

The Negro smirked from a deep-down place as Bass rode up. His eyes were really eyeballing him like he was stewing over something Bass had done to him long ago. His head had a ring of short gray hair and a pink scar stretched in a straight line across one cheek.

He looked so much like Willy or Willy like him. Bass took in a long breath. "Rub?" he asked. "Rub, that you?"

A shadow suddenly fell over the yard. The sun had dropped past the line of elms on the other side of the trail.

"Be me," the man said.

Bass returned his attention to the carriage, but the curtains still shut out who or what was inside. "You here with George Reeves?"

"Do I hear my good name on your forked tongue?" a voice called from far away, beyond the yard and trail. A thin old white man in a black suit was hobbling up the bluff, between the elms, with his trouser legs rolled up. He carried a pair of shoes shaped like mule ears, and he wore that same black grackle of a hat Bass recalled from years before.

Bass regarded Eddie, who appeared reasonably confused. "It's okay," he said and dismounted. He stepped up to the porch as Rub rose out of the rocker. They stood at about the same height, which must have delighted Rub. "You doing all right?" Bass asked him, offering to shake hands.

"Yep," Rub said, giving him a familiar small, meaty grip, but his eyes refused to meet Bass's. They shifted nervously as if following a fly, but Rub half-smiled nevertheless. "Yep," he repeated.

"Eddie, this here's Rub." Bass pulled his hand away and watched George cross the yard. "We were slaves together down in Texas for that offensive man coming."

Eddie and Rub tipped their hats.

"I hope our stately presence didn't startle y'all," George said.

"You always startle," Bass said bitterly.

George laughed. When he reached the porch, he set his leather shoes down beside a post and sat with a sigh of exhaustion. He looked up at Eddie. "So you're Eddie Reed, Belle Starr's boy?"

"I am," Eddie said, tipping his hat.

George smirked and rested his right leg on his left knee. "There's only a hair's difference between law and lawlessness. Always has been." He took a sock that was tucked inside his shoe and began wiping his dusty foot with it. All three men watched him do it.

Then George shook out the sock and worked to pull it over his pale, crooked toes and bunion. "We've come a long way to share some unfortunate tidings with you, Bass Reeves, some very unfortunate family tidings, I'm afraid." He reached for his shoe and put it on and began tying it. "On such a hot day, I just had to cool off while we waited."

Rub sat back down in the rocker. Bass and Eddie remained standing, watching George roll his trouser leg down, plant his right shoe on the ground, and begin wiping off his left foot.

"Look how things have changed," George said with a glance at Bass. "I'm sure you remember when I wouldn't allow my help to position themselves higher than me." His once-dark goatee formed a silver spearhead in a perpetual kill position. "Now look at Rub and me." He smiled. "We have witnessed tables turn in this world, haven't we, deputy? And I'll admit to you that it was difficult for me to come to terms with our reconstructed nation, but I have. I'll even admit that we're all better off moving on from our savage institution of slavery. I've come to terms with my past, Bass Reeves. I hope you have, too." George smiled again and moved his hand, the hand holding the sock, and patted the space on the porch beside him. "Please, make yourself at home."

"Been sitting all day," Bass countered.

"Suit yourself." George wiped his bare foot again and nodded. "I'll also admit that coercing people like Rub here, for instance, to treat me with respect was unseemly. It's much more dignified and plain easier for both of us if he chooses to see me and treat me as his superior." He turned and regarded Rub by swinging his sock in his direction. "If I give him a wage he wants to keep, then the wage is the overseer, am I right?" He paused as if he believed Bass would answer. "I'm not out any more money than I was before because I don't have to pay an overseer's wage. Sean wasn't much company anyhow. And if I find I need to punish Rub or the house help or whoever, I still don't need Sean and his whip. I simply lower the wage or I raise the price of lodging or food, whatever Rub needs that I used to give him for free. So it all evens out." He stretched the sock over his toes and then stopped and looked at Bass again. "We each get what we want, which is what we already had but under a kinder name, the 'free market,' but I acknowledge it's better. It doesn't threaten, doesn't stir up resentments and vengeful demands. It's why we gave up trying to repeal the thirteenth amendment."

"So what are your tidings, George?"

"Bass Reeves," George said, shaking his head, "if you're going to keep my family name, you need to practice the good manners you were taught." He gave his attention back to his sock and pulled it over his bunion and then heel. "Let me get dressed fully and we'll finish sharing our pleasantries."

"You're gonna be pleasant?" Bass asked.

"Now, I didn't say that, did I? But, of course, I will!" George grinned and slipped his shoe onto his foot and tied it. Then he rolled his trouser leg down, planted his foot in front of him, leaned back against the porch post beside him, and sighed deeper and louder than before. "It's one hot July, Bass Reeves!" Removing his hat revealed thin gray hair, and he closed his eyes while he fanned his face with the brim. After a moment his eyes fluttered open and he laughed. "I do believe I read somewhere among my father's papers that you were born in July. Please forgive him for not recording the day, but those were the times. People didn't record when a horse or pig was born or when a carriage or house or shoe was born, you know? But happy birthday all the same, Ole Bass Reeves!"

Bass nodded, refusing to show the extent to which this sour man irritated him.

"That gives you something in common with Julius Caesar."

"George," Bass said calmly, "that enough pleasantries yet?"

George turned away, in the direction of the bluff, and pointed, maybe at the golden sun sparkling between the trees. "We're inosculated, you and me," he said, "and I guess even old Rub here too. If not family, we're close enough to it to say so, like the two lacebark elms I was admiring a while ago. They're peeling off each other's bark they're rubbing up so close together. Isn't that cute?"

"Good God, mister!" Eddie groaned. "Will you shut up already and state your business?"

George pinched his small dark eyes at Eddie, but Bass took off his hat and laughed and slapped his hat against his leg.

"It takes a lot to rile my man here," Bass said, liking his hat off, so he stretched and set it on the old nail keg. He wiped his forehead on his coat sleeve. "We all know you wouldn't be here with Rub except to rub something in my face. So out with it and be on your way."

George returned his gaze in the direction of the river. The dropping sun no longer sparkled. He fanned his face again with his hat, then stopped and set it on his head. "When I learned what your boy had done, I felt an obligation to come right away to warn you. I knew you wouldn't know a thing about it, being off in Fort Smith celebrating Judge Parker and the righteous execution of a murderer, but I wanted to be the one to tell you. That's what family is for."

Bass glanced at Rub, but Rub was looking down, giving nothing away.

George wove his hands together in his lap and tipped his head up. "Your son Benjamin is in a heap of trouble. He'll most certainly need your help. Go talk to him if you know where he is. Comfort him, Bass. You know how a father does. And tell him to do the right thing, to turn himself in. It'll be the safest option."

Bass grew rigid to contain his concern for Bennie and his rage for George. He bristled with incomplete thoughts.

"That lying hogwash won't work this time," George snapped. "He needs to turn himself in."

Bass consulted Rub once more, but Rub refused to look at him. Bass glanced at his mute hat resting on the keg, then spoke before he knew he would. "Get outta here," he told them, more to George but to both. "Get gone, both of you!"

Rub jumped up, but George didn't budge.

"Men are gathering," George said.

"Faster!" Bass ordered, and Rub hurried to the carriage and unlatched the door, holding it open as George eased onto his feet and took slow steps.

"With a bounty on his head for twenty-five thousand dollars," George said, "every lawman and outlaw, hell, anybody old enough to hold up a gun, will be foraging by morning under every thicket for that no-account murdering Brer Rabbit son of yours. Sorry, *ours*, I mean," he said, turning to Bass and placing a palm over his heart. "What's yours is mine, you know." He climbed inside the carriage. "Bass Reeves," George called from the seat inside, "I hope the Lord accords us enough years to meet again."

Rub moved to shut the door, but Bass blocked it with his arm.

"We'll meet on my terms if we do." Bass dropped his arm and stepped back, wanting George and Rub and that hackney and carriage gone off his property; he wanted to watch George's spearhead grin disappear behind the door and the wash of black curtains.

Rub hurried past him to his high springy seat. He collected the reins and turned to Bass. "God bless," he muttered, looking at him but looking low, then he clicked his tongue and whipped the reins to make the hackney jump.

Bass pivoted to Eddie but then averted his eyes to his hat sitting on the barrel, then to his son, as if he were sitting on the barrel still. Bass remembered what Bennie had said a few days earlier about Castella—what each of them had said. He spun his head to watch the carriage, to see which way it would go. Bass thanked God that Rub steered it right, for town. The curtains parted so Bass remained unhurried, stoic as a tree, until the hackney's proud trot had hauled that sorry load out of sight. Then he ran for his hat.

"Bennie's!" he said.

God, Bass thought to himself again and again like a frantic tolling so that it became what it should have been all along: a singular word with infinite syllables—for Bennie's sake, for Castella's sake, for Jennie's sake, for Pearlalee's sake. He galloped left, away from town, and left again, away from the river and into the black, young night. Bass and Eddie would need fresh horses if they needed to go farther than Bennie's. That was the rare, coherent thought that entered his mind as he continued his ride-long prayer, with Eddie following—*God, God, God*, the word beating the tracks like a train in the open prairie.

◆ ◆ ◆

There was no hope to his ride, just black and more black, so many shades of black overlapping black, when he wanted none of it tonight. And the house was too thick with it—too silent and still, there but not, like the new moon offering nothing. As dead as a mountain while young'uns squealed at the next acre lot and while smoke drifted from a fire there over to Bennie's—or rightly Castella's since she could own the land as a Choctaw Negro and Bennie, as an American, couldn't. The smoke smelled rich with sheep or goat, while this place offered nothing.

"Goddammit," Bass grunted with a leap to the ground. He ran onto the porch and banged on the door. "Bennie! Castella!" He banged again, and each time the only answer was the door's rattle against the frame. Behind him Eddie had caught up and was dismounting. "Son, it's Pop!" Bass shouted. "I'm coming in!" He reached for a Colt in case this was a trick. "Step back," he told Eddie, and Eddie stood aside but drew a pistol too.

Bass threw the door open, letting it bang against the front room wall. He waited to enter, trying to block out the young'un sounds next door and, closer, the barred owl nearly barking like a dog over so many other living things all around them—cicadas and crickets and frogs—but not over anything inside. So he stepped in with his free hand searching his coat pocket for his fire-starter tin. His slow steps mewled the floorboards until he reached the table with the lamp, which was not overturned: a good sign. Eddie remained in the doorway until Bass had fingered a match from the can, struck it off the round lid, and lit the lamp. He turned the wheel for as much light as it would give. Nothing in the room looked out of order. The hall tree held a parasol and two hats that Bennie and Castella rarely wore. The chairs around the table were around the table. The plates and pots and utensils were stacked or hanging from hooks in the hutch.

Where Bass stood had been where he imagined Dell Weems had been sitting when Bennie had come home early to surprise Castella, who would've been standing over by the stove, cooking hash. "I'd have shot hell out of the man and whipped the living God out of her." His words and raised voice shamed him, mocked him, in this empty house.

Bass gripped the lamp by the base, careful not to knock over the jar of dead flowers beside it—the Indian paintbrush his son had told him he picked, which were now the color of dried blood. He glanced at Eddie, whose eyes were scanning the floor—a good idea. Bass proceeded to the back room with his own eyes on the floor.

There was no blood smear, no drops, no spills, *thank you, Lord.* And whose blood would it have been if he'd found any?

The lamp's glow showed him nothing unusual so far, and that was how he wanted it. When he reached the bedroom, he raised the lantern until he bumped the ceiling with his knuckles, but he still saw no blood on the floor and no signs of a struggle, and he thanked the Lord again. Then his attention went to the bed, stripped of its covers, and the lumpy, cotton-stuffed mattress made deep shadows, like valleys, like puddles. He holstered his Colt and stepped to the footboard, but the shadows were stubborn, seemingly impervious to light.

"Dear God." He walked to the side of the bed, and the deep shadows, at the dead center of the bed, appeared from this angle as one dark gourd-shaped stain. He leaned over and ran a fingertip along the stain. The mattress felt dry, and when he turned his hand over in the light, there was nothing on him. But that could mean nothing, so he reached into his pocket, withdrew his handkerchief, and pressed it down in the middlemost part of the gourd, ready to hold it there, but he shut his eyes and immediately let up.

He asked the Lord to forgive him—his son and him both. The cotton deep down was wet, and his hand was wet. Sticky wet. When he opened his eyes, he saw what he knew he would. He turned to Eddie to show him the blood-soaked handkerchief, and Eddie's eyes bulged in the scant light as if the lantern were a forge. Maybe his own bulged that way. "Dear God, Eddie," he said, trembling, "what did my boy do?"

Eddie laid a hand on Bass's shoulder. They breathed in unison, and that was a slight but real comfort. Bass gazed across the room at the mahogany dresser, which he and Jennie had given the couple as a wedding gift. There was a sterling silver comb, brush, and mirror set on it, a wedding gift from Castella's parents. His eyes trailed upward to the wall space above the dresser, to a roofing nail showing its face, and he tried to recall what had hung from it, but a stirring outside disturbed his thoughts.

Bass let the handkerchief fall to the bed. He pointed with his bloody hand to alert Eddie to listen for what was beyond the door and the other room, past the restless stamping of their own horses. Distant voices approached slowly, not on horseback. Bass dropped his head, straining to identify them as he watched the handkerchief gradually bloom open.

Bass spat on his hand to wipe the blood on his trousers. "Let's see what they want." To keep both hands free, he returned the lamp to the table in the front room before stepping outside.

Two men in overalls were walking up to the house carrying Winchester rifles the way of hunters, not outlaws, and the shorter one held a burning log. Bass recognized the taller one as the man who lived next door, also a Choctaw Negro. The shorter one was the man's teenage son. Up at the house, the young'uns had hushed.

"Been an awful tragedy happen here two days ago," the neighbor said.

"I heard. I'm the boy's father," Bass said, stepping onto the porch.

"Yes, sir," the neighbor said. He and his son kept their distance. So did Eddie, who stopped behind Bass in the doorway. Bass would have to remind him how much he hated for a body to stand in a doorway.

"We the law." Bass showed the badge on his vest.

"Yes, sir, I know of you."

"You know anything about what happened?"

The boy looked at his father, and his father nodded and said, "Go on."

"About noon I heard Mr. Reeves walking up, and he was walking up real slow," the boy said. "I thought his horse maybe was hurt or had a loose shoe, why I was watching, but now I'm guessing," and the boy paused, shifting his eyes again to his father, "he was maybe slipping up."

"If my son did wrong," Bass explained to him, "he'll have to pay. You can tell me anything. I don't want you leaving nothing out, okay?"

The boy nodded and motioned to the porch post at the farthest end of the house. "He tied his horse next to another one out here and walked up easy-like again," he said, pointing out the path Bennie had taken to get up on the porch and go to the door. "And when he walked inside he left the door open like he was coming right back out." The boy turned to face his home next door. "I started to go about my business then and looked away, and that's when I heard yelling."

"Who?" Bass asked.

"It was just him, just Mr. Reeves."

"Could you make it out?"

"No, sir," the boy said.

"Then what happened?"

"And then I heard a pistol fire—pretty sure a .38, though hard to tell being inside the house. But it weren't a boom like a .45 and not so small like a .22." He jounced the rifle in the cradle of his arm. "Pretty sure it was a .38, how they whistle or whisper-like, kinda like *pssst*, you know?"

Bass nodded.

"And when it went off, a man run outta the house so fast he fell down in the dirt." The boy pointed at the place in the yard. "He could hardly get up. And then a second round went off, and that man on the ground, he jumped up then and took off up the road. Didn't even take time to get on his horse."

"Tell him about the man," the boy's father said.

The boy half-smiled. "He was naked. Nothing on him but a hat."

Bass looked off at Hammer, nibbling the leaves of a gardenia bush. He stroked his mustache, drawing the stray whiskers out of the corners of his mouth. He thought about his son, how scared he must have been walking out of this house. He looked back at the boy. "When did my son walk out?"

The boy shook his head. "Seem like a long time later. I didn't know what to do. Pa wasn't home. I just watched."

"Did he have anything with him?" Bass asked.

The boy squinched his face, appearing confused in the light of the log's dimming flames.

"Was he carrying a bag or anything?"

"Oh, no, sir. I didn't see him with nothing but his pistol. It was still in his hand. He never put it away. He got on his horse and rode off and was still pointing it."

"Which way?"

The boy turned and pointed toward home.

"Tell him what he took," said the boy's father.

"Oh, he untied the other fella's horse and took it along with him. Rode right by me," he said, pointing toward home again. "He didn't see me. Course, I was hid."

"You did right," Bass said.

The boy smiled.

"Can you tell me what that other fella's horse look like?"

"A dark color, close to brown but with a lick a red in it." The boy patted his belly. "What do you call that? A real pretty brown-red color, mostly brown though?"

"Liver chestnut?" asked Bass.

"That's it!" The boy smiled again. "Knew it wasn't kidney but couldn't think of what it was." He nodded. "Liver chestnut."

"Anything else you remember, son? I appreciate all you telling me. You're a big help."

The boy looked toward the house, the doorway, at Eddie leaning in it. He shook his head.

"You should know somebody come by yesterday," the boy's father said, "and this was after the Lighthorse come by and talked to us and collected Mrs. Reeves' body."

"A deputy?" Bass asked.

"Nope. I walked over thinking he'd wanna talk to my boy about what he saw. I called out to him, and he come out to tell me to go on. Didn't have a badge. Didn't act like no federal lawman to me."

"Bounty hunter?"

"What I'm thinking."

"Did he take anything from the house that you know of?" Bass asked.

The neighbor nodded. "He come out holding a picture of some sort. Don't know what."

Bass nodded. He remembered now. "Oval shaped?"

"That's right. Almost looked like a small ox collar but knew it couldn't be that." He smirked but quickly corrected his demeanor. "I'm sorry for your family."

Again Bass nodded. It occurred to him to go to his saddle rider for silver, but he didn't want to give them anything for what he got. He needed the information; it was good information, but he sure didn't want it.

"Thank you, son," he said, then looked at his father. "Appreciate you coming over, keeping a eye on things."

"Course."

Bass turned to walk back inside the house and eyed Eddie, and Eddie skittered aside to let him pass.

Bass plucked the lamp up on his way by and took it to the hutch. "Come here," he said, opening the cabinets, and he filled Eddie's arms with cans of Underwood deviled ham, Columbia River salmon, and Van Camp's pork and beans. "We might not always have time to hunt a meal."

"Don't forget the can opener."

Eddie was trying to provoke a laugh, but Bass scanned down the row of utensils hanging on hooks by hemp or leather strings below the cabinets. Once he found the can opener, he said, "Huh," and removed it from its slipknot. Bennie had shown it to him a few days before the couple's first Christmas, and he'd been as proud of it as anything else he'd ever bought. He'd spotted it at J.J. McAlester Mercantile Co. and knew Castella would love it, but the day after Christmas, not long after Bass had returned from visiting Jennie in Fort Smith, Bennie rode over to see him and told him how she'd had a fit and not a joyful one.

"You giving me a *can opener*?" Bennie repeated Castella's words. He explained how Castella had accused him of not loving her and slapped him on the ears for it and then shut herself up in the back room for the rest of the day and cried. "I kept telling her to look at it, just look at it, look at the detail," Bennie said. He pulled the can opener out of his pocket and showed it to his father again, holding it out in his palm as he sat on Bass's porch telling him the story— and telling Eddie too—and having the can opener to admire while thinking about Bennie's Choctaw-Negro wife throwing a white-girl tantrum made Bass laugh even harder. Eddie too.

"It's pretty, ain't it, iron shaped like a fish?" his boy had asked him, and he was right. It wasn't just a can opener. The blade cleverly formed the fish's lower jaw, and the pounded rivet holding the blade to the handle was rounded to look like an eyeball. There was even a little fin on top, while scales were furrowed into the handle. Bennie had pouted but eventually swallowed his pride and laughed with Bass and Eddie before leaving.

Eddie carried the cans and can opener outside to his saddle riders while Bass went around to the feed shed. He found one and a half 50-pound sacks of oats, more feed than he'd expected his son to have. Enough to feed two horses for two days would surely help.

"What you make of Bennie taking that fella's horse?" Eddie asked, walking up.

"Well," Bass began, lifting the full sack and laying it on Eddie's shoulder, "tells me my son listens to my stories." He twisted a knot in the half-empty sack. "And if that be true, well," he said, turning the wooden latch on the shed door and tromping through the darker darkness of the side yard, "we'll know where to find him."

Hammer glowed at the edge of the side yard like a mare-shaped moon and was happy as a lark. Flycatcher was, too, seeing or smelling the oats and believing there was time to eat. "Later," Bass told them, but watching their tails swish, he dropped the sack and untied it. He poured a pound onto the ground for each. "Guess y'all want a drink, too." He took out his knife and cut a hole at the top of the sack so he could hang the sack on his saddle horn, then retrieved a bucket of water from the pump.

"Wanna share a can of beans?" Eddie asked.

"Nah, but help yourself," Bass said, preferring to chew. He reached into his coat pocket for his tobacco and sat on the edge of the porch. He bit in half what little remained of his brick and watched Eddie work the can opener beside him.

"Nice," Eddie said. "Cuts right through." He bent the jagged lid back and dug in with the tin spoon he always kept in his saddle rider.

Bass consulted the horses' vanishing oats. "Better eat quick."

"Won't be hard," Eddie spoke around a mouthful.

Bass stood up and paced. He was too nervous to be still. He glanced up and suddenly stopped and leaned back on his heels to pray to the darkness between the stars. Maybe Bennie was looking at it, too, and would receive his prayer if Bass prayed upward to it right now, so he asked the Lord to allow his son to be alert, to make wise choices, to no longer react out of fear or anger or pride, and, above all, to stop killing.

Eddie interrupted his prayer by scraping the can with his spoon to get every drop of pot liquor, and the horses started neighing and blowing, begging for more oats. "Sorry, gotta get," he told them and hiked himself onto his saddle.

Eddie dropped the can but kept the spoon in his mouth like a lollypop as he grabbed the full sack of oats off the ground and laid it across the pommel of his saddle.

"Got Castella's can opener?" Bass asked.

Eddie patted his coat pocket, then took the spoon out of his mouth and pointed toward the house next door. "I guess we're headed that way."

Bass turned aside and spat. "Not yet. Going first to Pauls Valley to pick us up a warrant."

Eddie mounted Flycatcher. "We got time for that? Can't telegraph for one?"

"How you find out if your old master's arranged to have you followed? I'll tell you, Eddie—go one way, then turn back." Bass lifted his hat to cool his head and made it snug again. "Got a couple questions for the commissioner, then we'll sure head that direction," and he nodded to the east and the house next door.

10

Pauls Valley

The bottomland of Pauls Valley was so low that, until this morning, Bass had no recollection of ever setting foot in the town when it wasn't muddy. But a dry wind was bucking, and the dust it stirred lashed like rain. "Beware of dogs," he thought. In Pauls Valley, he always gave his respects to the Apostle Paul.

Only a handful of townspeople braved the dust storm to cross from store to store. Those who did rushed with their coattails and petticoats flying, though one cowboy walked the boardwalk without concerning himself to pull his neckerchief up or clutch the brim of his hat.

Horses at the courthouse sulked under coats of dust. Inside it seemed everyone either whispered Bass's name or reacted with mute surprise to see him as if he were a ghost. By God he prayed he was a ghost for the Lord because there was one lost soul—at least one more—he had to do his best to save.

He removed his hat and nodded or muttered a *howdy* or *how-do* to the clerks and deputies and Lighthorsemen as he walked past them, past the jails and prisoners, to the commissioner's office.

The commissioner, Randolph Darley, was the splitting image of President Cleveland, never more than when he was filling up his chair. Bass usually initiated their conversations with a joke, calling the commissioner the president of Ohio or remarking on his morbid appetite for gold and unwilling girls, but today Bass could see his friend was fretting, so Bass got to the point. "What do you know?" he asked and reached for Darley's outstretched hand.

Darley shook firmly. "Nobody in the district wanted to track him, Bass." Darley slowed their handshake but kept his grip. "You should know that, out of respect for you, not a one." He relaxed his grip and pointed at the empty chair beside his.

As they sat down Bass averted his eyes to find Eddie lingering in the hallway outside the office. Not in the doorway this time, thank goodness. "Give me the writ," Bass said. "I want it."

Darley nodded as if they were in church and he was silently agreeing. "I'm glad for your son you do. You're a good man, Bass. As a father I couldn't sympathize with you more, I really couldn't. You're in a tough position. The toughest."

"Got no choice," Bass admitted. "Sure look like Bennie did it. Witness say so, and he run off." A vein of sadness opened up in his chest for the sweet boy Bennie was and always had been, even if he'd been a little troublesome. Never troublesome with the law, but he'd seemed poised at the line between headache and heartache his entire life—always ready to bolt one way or the other.

Bass sat up straight as if to pinch the vein and he took a breath. He let it out slowly and fumbled with his dusty hat while Darley watched him fatherlike. "I thought his mother and I raised him to do better, be better," Bass said. "He know better for damn sure. So he knows I'm coming for him. I'll make certain he does right, Darley. If I have to drag that boy in by his feet, you know I will."

Darley turned in his chair and rifled through papers on his desk. Eventually he plucked up a wanted poster. "I received this by messenger yesterday evening." He handed it to Bass, and Bass's attention went immediately to the picture of Bennie wearing the suit Castella had insisted he buy specially for their wedding. It was the same picture that had hung until recently in the couple's bedroom, though for the purpose of the poster, Castella and her extravagant hat—as tall and round as a three-layer cake—had been cut out. Above Bennie were the words "Wanted for murder dead or alive," and below the picture and his name was the reward amount. George had told the truth: $25,000. An absurdly high bounty, five times what banks and railroads typically offered for their worst tormentors.

Bass's heavy eyes dropped to the bottom edge of the poster. He looked for the name of the court, which should have looked like the eastern district of texas, but there was no name, no words, only more poster the color of dust. It was as if no one had really posted the reward or printed this poster.

Bass's eyes returned to that underlined word at the top. He traced the line with a fingertip and took note of Darley's pursed red lips.

"Says to me somebody prefers your son brought in dead."

"George Reeves?"

Darley tipped his head as if he were wearing reading glasses and needed to see over them. "What's he hold against you, Bass? That's a mean grudge."

Bass shook his head. He didn't really want to answer. "He can't live with the notion I whupped his ass at poker," he said finally, "and then whupped his ass."

Darley squinted. "Thirty-what years ago? You wanted to be free. Who wouldn't?"

Bass handed the poster back.

"Things are changing quick," Darley said, turning back to his desk. This time he plucked up a sheet of paper the size of a telegram. "This morning I received this." He showed it to Bass, but Bass didn't attempt to make out the words, and neither did Darley. "Says John Armstrong and Bigfoot Wallace have joined the hunt for your son, and more retired Texas Rangers are assembling. That's all I know, Bass. But it don't look good."

"Who sent the telegram?" Bass asked.

Darley slapped the telegram message behind him and smirked. "George Reeves."

Bass leaned forward and rested his arms on his knees. "What's the report say about the caliber a bullet used?"

".38 long."

Bass lowered his head. "I helped him pick it too. A '92 Colt army/navy issue. He was like a young'un about its swing-out cylinder. I told him it weren't no toy. I shoulda known better."

"Not your fault."

"Maybe is."

"Not like you pulled the trigger."

Bass smiled at him. "Might did, Darley."

Darley interlocked his short, thick fingers in his lap. Like Rub's sausage fingers. He remained silent.

"Peaceable fruit." Bass sat up straight, then decided to stand. "Won't do me no good to grieve. We walk by faith, not by sight."

Darley hiked his eyebrows and offered him his hand. "Let me know if I can be any help to you, all right? You're a Mugwump, you know, but a damn good one."

Bass trusted Darley as the commissioner. He was a Texan who had married a Chickasaw, so it made sense why the Eastern District of Texas in Paris had given him the post of this secondary court and jail. "Chokma'shki," Bass said, thanking him.

He walked past Eddie without speaking to him or anyone else as he continued through the humidity and stench of the courthouse halls. He paused at the last door. The wind hummed at the seam of sunlight beneath it but whistled elsewhere outside as he pulled his neckerchief over his face and fit his hat on tight.

◆ ◆ ◆

They returned to the trail that led back to Calvin, and within an hour the wind and dust began to simmer, so Bass and Eddie stopped to share a can of salmon and let their horses drink from a narrow bend of the Washita River. After pouring out a pound of oats for each horse, Bass eased down on the bank with the can and the opener.

Eddie kicked at the sunburned weeds along the bank. "Where you reckon Bennie at?" he asked.

"There're two places I know he'd think to go hide and wait for me, and that's Pea Ridge and Younger's Bend. Course, he heard you talk about Younger's Bend."

"Jesse's cave, maybe?"

"Well," Bass said, piercing the can with the fish's bottom jaw, "was Jesse's, all right, but Belle's a time or two, and Rufus Buck, Dalton boys, and probably a hundred Confederate deserters. And hundreds of Osage before them."

"And Pea Ridge? No caves at Pea Ridge, is there?"

"No," Bass said, "but there's mountains to hide on and hog peanuts to eat when there ain't nothing else."

Eddie kept walking and kicking, swinging his right leg straight as a pendulum, and the cast-iron fish kept leaping in Bass's hand and biting the can. "Who don't make a mistake hiding in that cave?" Bass asked. "It's a lot closer than Pea Ridge, so let's start with it 'cause Bennie know about it 'cause I showed it to him once."

"Yeah, could be," said Eddie, pausing his legs but not turning to look behind him. "But what if he don't want you to find him and went straight to Arkansas or God knows somewheres else?"

Bass dropped the can opener in his coat pocket and bent the lid back. "Well, Eddie," he said, taking up his spoon, "we'll check Pea Ridge and any other places once we check Younger's Bend. I expect my son to be awful damn scared. He'll wanna talk, so he'll hide and stay put, waiting for me to get to him. That's what my heart saying."

"Gotta listen to that." Eddie swung his legs back in action at more weeds. "I'd shore eat me a snake instead of any canned food if I find one. Shore will."

Bass clinked his teeth on his spoon and dug into the can for another spoonful of salmon before chewing, and he chewed a long time before swallowing. He probed the wad of meat with his tongue, again and again, to break it up and feel for bones. The last time he ate salmon, he ate too quickly, and a bone thin as a needle got lodged in his throat all day.

"Huh," Bass said, swallowing, then clearing his throat. He wouldn't let this stop turn into something longer. "Eat this, and let's get."

◆ ◆ ◆

After they ran a couple of miles farther east, Bass slowed Hammer so that he could speak to Eddie. "See that?"

"See what?" Eddie's head swept left and right.

Bass refrained from pointing. "On the ridge. That rider a mile or so yonder."

Eddie looked to the southeast where a Chickasaw village and ranch lay at the end of a deeply rutted road. A green-and-brown ridge rose with the curvature of a rainbow beyond it, and a sorrel was taking its rider in the same direction as Hammer and Flycatcher took them. "What about him?"

"Just watch."

Eddie watched, and so did Bass, then Bass saw it again: how the rider glinted.

"See that?" Bass asked.

"Yeah. A telescope?"

"Or field glasses," said Bass. "He ain't admiring the Big Dipper this afternoon, and I don't see nary a uprising."

"A scout?"

"Think so. Let's watch him."

The man on the sorrel kept pace with them over the next few miles, and every few minutes there came a glint until the ridge descended into flat land. By then a glint came from a hilltop from the northeast.

After crossing into the Choctaw Nation, Bass and Eddie waded across Little Sandy Creek and approached the old Shawnee Trail. The town of Allen, named for Deputy Bill McCall's son, rested on the trail just north of them, and the trail just south of them crossed the Middle Boggy River, making this a good spot to hem a body. That likely explained the horn of dust, braided from many sources kicking it up, that appeared on the other side of the rise ahead. Eddie kept turning his head to look at Bass and get an answer about what they should do as if confronting whoever it was wasn't an option, but Bass kept his eyes fixed on the swirling dust above the crest line.

"Be all right," Bass said.

Once they topped the hill, they could see who rushed to meet them. Crossing the broad Texas Cattle Trail rode a five-man posse on well-fed horses closely following a pack of bloodhounds on the scent, with noses and ears down and tails up, while a supply wagon dragged in the rear.

"They ain't hunting Bennie," Eddie said. "They hunting us!"

"Be all right," Bass said, slowing Hammer to a stop. Eddie and Flycatcher did the same.

The bloodhounds advanced in a wild, howling tangle, wagging tails as they bared teeth and slobbered. They circled Bass and Eddie, and the five men circled the dogs. Then the two men behind Bass and Eddie dismounted to yell at the dogs to hush, and they began rounding them up on ropes. The supply wagon eventually caught up with the rest of the party, and when it stopped, the final strand of the cornucopia blew past.

"Y'all lost?" Bass asked.

None of the men sitting on their horses uttered a word. The oldest one of the posse showed his age with his outdated buckskin clothes and gray Rip Van Winkle beard. He was also the tallest of the posse, as tall in his saddle as Bass. He kept his eyes on Bass while the others glanced back and forth at the two men in their party dragging the hound pack away to the supply wagon. Bass hardly had to shift his eyes from the old-timer to see what the dog men were doing. Each was stooping to pick up a hound, and that set the entire pack to cowering. Then one by one the men began slinging the bloodhounds into the wagon.

Once the men returned to their horses, the old-timer spoke with a twang that marked him from Appalachia. "Our dogs tell us that you men are Deputies Bass Reeves and Edwin Reed."

"That's right," Bass said, "but you didn't need no dogs to tell you that. Hell, you coulda just asked." He turned to Eddie. "Wouldn't you a told him who you was if he'd just asked?"

Eddie nodded. "Go by *Eddie*, though. Call me *Eddie*. Be sure to tell your hounds."

"Oh, I know exactly which scoundrel you are," the old-timer said. "Once a thief always a thief. Runs in the family, don't it?"

The other men sniggered.

"Hey," Bass said in a resonant voice that quietened the posse, "help my noggin follow why a body like you would hound-dog the law."

"They must be outlaws," Eddie said.

Bass turned to Eddie, then back to the old-timer. "You boys outlaws?"

The men sniggered again, and this time the old-timer joined them. "Well," he said, pushing the wide brim of his hat up to his hairline, allowing Bass and Eddie to see how blue his eyes were. As blue as the blue quartz in the Ouachita Mountains. As blue as his paint's right blue eye. "I wouldn't trust a thief or the killer's lying, murdering father to do this job."

"Your opinion a me don't matter," Bass stated, unmoved. "As for my son, we just picked up a warrant in Pauls Valley 'cause we aim to catch him and turn him in. Father or no father, doing what's right. Letting the court decide if he guilty or not. Not you."

"Aim to see to it he escapes, you mean?" the old-timer said. "If so, we might just be right there to catch you, or, shit, kill you and him both when you try."

Eddie turned to see Bass's reaction, but Bass remained still as a rock, what he told himself to be.

The old-timer took in a long breath and stretched his back and neck straight, causing his saddle to creak as he made himself taller.

Bass listened to the hounds whine and whimper from being shut up in the supply wagon. He was barely managing to ignore the repeating drum music of his Colts—the five quick beats he could fire with either hand in one easy measure.

"Instead," the old-timer said, "how about you lead us to him? I give you my word we'll take him in alive. How's that? Ain't that a fair deal?"

Bass moved his eyes across each of the three men he could see without completely turning away from the old-timer. He moved so much more slowly than the melody that cranked on its own in the back of his mind. "Do you boys want me to arrest y'all for imped-ing a investigation?"

"We allowed to investigate, make a citizen's arrest if we want," the old-timer declared. "You know that." He crossed his arms, and Bass crossed his. "Where you recommend we commence?"

Bass laughed. "Anywhere but where he obviously ain't. You don't see him here, do you? But before you move it along, I tell you what. I don't mind kicking off a boot first, if you don't, and we'll just see for truth whose feet bigger. Wanna see who the liar among us be?" He leaned forward, eyeing the old-timer.

The old-timer didn't budge, but his men were watchful he might.

"Be fine you don't respect me and Eddie here," Bass said. "Free country, right? Like how I don't respect old-timer fugitive slave trackers or Indian butchers. 'Bear the infirmities of the weak,' said Paul." Bass laid a hand on Hammer's neck and stroked her hard, smooth muscles. "You think 'cause you was a Texas Ranger once means you somebody here in Indian Territory? Shit! Don't take no dogs to tell me who the fuck you is, *Bigfoot Wallace!*"

The old-timer's blue eyes pinched tight as he scrambled to dismount. "Goddammit," he grumbled along with a string of other cuss words as he hobbled closer to Bass. As if fatigued, or as if rarely in his life he'd set foot on land, the old-timer dropped to the ground and instantly began working to disengage a boot whose heel resembled a doorstop.

"Watch it, Bigfoot!" Bass blurted. "Gonna get that dandy fringe all dirty."

"Come on, n——!" the old-timer said, throwing off his boot. "I never shied away from a provocation. Let's go! Let's see what you got!"

"All right," Bass agreed. He climbed down and motioned for Eddie to stay put.

The old-timer sat on a shelf of crunchy dust with his legs stretched out in front of him, bearing one ghostly big foot indeed. Bass settled down on the hot dust across from him.

"You ain't the first son of a bitch to try me," the old-timer spat, dotting the dust.

"Five dollars Bigfoot bigger than your man's foot," a young posseman on an amber stallion hollered to Eddie, who must've answered without speaking because Bass didn't hear a thing but sniggers and the muttering of the old-timer as Bass reached for his right boot and heaved it clear.

"Come on, put her up," the old-timer said.

Bass tugged off his sock and stretched out, pressing his foot against the old-timer's ghost foot whose toenails were gnarly as snail shells, though twice the size, but Bass's toes did top the old-timer's.

"There, there!" the old-timer said with excitement.

"There where?" Bass asked. "You know you can't count them dragon claws."

"Can too!"

"There," Bass said, pointing, not touching, "your foot ends where you see that dead-looking flesh."

The old-timer's lower jaw dropped, and every one of his teeth was marbled brown, yellow, and black and rounded and holed like creek pebbles. "Who says?"

"I say, and I'm the law in these parts." Bass bent his leg to pull his sock back on.

"That's some hog shit!" The old-timer stood and scooped up his boot.

"*You're* some hog shit!" Bass scoffed. "Growing your toenails out to make your foot look bigger!" Bass laughed and pulled on his boot.

"Hog shit," the red-faced old-timer muttered as he stomped his foot back into his boot.

Eddie giggled. Bass liked hearing him that way. "Pay up!" Eddie called.

The posseman on the amber stallion farted as he slid to the ground holding a Winchester slide-action rifle around its octagonal barrel. "Suit yourself," he said, fighting to squeeze a hand into his tight denim pocket. "Consider this a loan 'cause I always win my wagers back."

Bass pointed at the old-timer, who was swatting his dusty trousers with his hat. "I bet you ain't never really cut the head off no Mexican bandit neither. Headless horseman!" Bass laughed. "You probably just gave the poor soul a sorry haircut!"

The old-timer stilled his hat. "You don't know what you're saying, who you're fucking with."

Bass hauled himself back onto Hammer. He saw Eddie had his money and was tucking it into a pocket of his striped trousers. "Big Lie Wallace and you others," Bass said, starting far to the left of the old-timer and sweeping his arm all the way to the right, pointing across the whole scowling lot, "know I will kill every last one of you if you give me any more reason to."

Bass clicked his tongue, and Hammer leaped ahead, breaking past the old-timer and then the supply wagon—the hounds erupting into a boil.

Eddie raced to catch up, and Bass caught him grinning.

"What?" Bass asked.

"Never heard you talk like that, boss." He couldn't stop grinning.

Bass shook his head. "Never had to."

11

A Devil

This time Bass and Eddie galloped off the trails. They crossed fenced land by jumping leaning posts and sagging wire and following a northeastward diagonal, which Bass saw in his mind as an arrow. If the arrow sailed through a herd of white-faced Herefords, Bass and Eddie rode through them, and if it sailed through or over other herds and things, groves and trickle creeks, for nearly two hours Bass and Eddie did just that—sailing parallel with the Canadian River to their left but straighter even than it. But after passing Calvin to the south and nearing Indianola, they moored up in the shade on the knobby knees of a bald cypress and each opened a can of deviled ham.

Bass loved a bald cypress. The Seminoles he'd lived among as a fugitive slave had been the first to teach him the value of the eternal wood. His lingering admiration for the tree led him to notice a bagworm sack on the lowest branch. It was small and brown like a young pinecone or a miniature bald cypress itself that hung upside down among the God-green needles. He then noticed another sack on another branch, and that led him to see the entire tree was decked with the boogers.

Eddie smacked his lips, but, like anything else eventually, he stopped smacking his lips, and wouldn't Jennie be happy about that if she were here in her old state of mind and body? Bass listened to him swallow as delicately as a frog, and he thought about pointing out the bagworm sacks, but Eddie spoke first.

"Why you reckon they put a devil on ham cans?" Eddie licked his lips and teeth. "Make any sense to you?"

Bass remembered wondering that very question before but not what he'd ever decided. He lowered his head to look at what remained in his can. He shook his head and scraped together his last bite.

"Ain't the worst grub," Eddie said. "Ain't devil bad."

Bass smiled. "How does not a hair grow on your face except above your lip?"

"Shoot," Eddie grinned and tossed his can into the sun's glare. Then it struck Bass what he'd decided.

"Maybe 'cause the devil's everywhere? Not just in ham cans. *Even* in ham cans. Ham don't matter." Bass stood up with his weight tilted much more on his right leg, his right boot, as the solid but not unforgiving cubit of earth between those bald cypress knees showed a bit of give. "A dang good message for when a body stops to eat."

"Dang if it ain't," Eddie said, pushing himself up from all fours, "but I'm still partial to the ham."

"I guess." Bass strolled to Hammer, who was nibbling a sprout of grass, and lifted the dark slack reins from the smooth curve of her bowed neck. Against that even gray, the leather looked cracked like the skin on the back of his mother's hands. Or like that of his own. He spread his fingers apart to stretch the cracks. "Let's sail a little more the way we going," he said.

"Then south?" Eddie's saddle creaked from his mounting weight. Flycatcher blew, then Hammer blew and twitched.

"Uh-huh." Bass nodded, sitting tall to ease his lower back. "No reason to change." He tugged Hammer away from the bald cypress. "Be a good idea to have a lamp or two."

"And tobacco!"

"Course, that too," Bass agreed. "And maybe a shovel."

"Shovel?"

"How this hunt's going, I expect we'll need to bury a slew a men."

"For real?"

"For real," Bass said and clicked his tongue.

His mind, full of vague and distant frets for Bennie, began to calm once they fell back to following the arrow, seeing no glints from any side and not a hide or hair of a single bounty hunter. They sailed a little closer to Indianola and all the lake swamps beyond it as if they might go searching for Bennie in that unhospitable briar patch or, even farther, in Muskogee or Fort Gibson along the Arkansas River. Not that Bass intended to proceed close enough to Indianola to meet another congregation of white men. Soon, at the next crossroads, he'd turn the arrow south for a race to reach McAlester.

But Bass decided against turning or even slowing at the crossroads. For Eddie's sake he pointed to the sky, then gave Hammer his heels to urge her faster over the crossroads because the three buzzards he watched drift ahead in a wide rotation now compelled him forward. The landscape was changing rapidly now. Now it was the plume of dust ahead of the buzzards that Bass spied, then it was the wagon ahead of that dust as if the wagon, loaded with vegetables for the Indianola market, pulled a plow. A log, or something like a log, was tied to the wagon and bobbing along the road behind it, creating quite a stir.

Bass rode up beside the driver, a Choctaw wearing a straw hat and showing fear to see him. Bass shouted *yokohpa* and showed his badge. The driver didn't reach for his rifle and didn't hesitate to brake.

Bass slowed Hammer faster than the wagon slowed, so it rolled ahead. Now Bass was riding alongside Eddie to his left while cabbages, onions, and bushels of peas passed to his right—cabbages mainly. Bass continued to slow, and now Eddie and the wagon drifted in front as Bass followed the rope back to the thing within the thinning and unraveling plume of dust that the buzzards wanted.

Bass pulled his neckerchief over his mouth and nose and waited with his eyes closed for all the dust from the wagon and horses and thing to settle.

"Well, looky there, boss," Eddie said. "Before, During, and After have come joined us for dinner!"

Bass opened his eyes and could feel them bulging to comprehend what Eddie saw—the buzzards falling from the sky like autumn leaves the size of elephant ears—but also what Eddie couldn't see from where he sat—the buzzards lighting about a noosed corpse. It was the noose, first, that Bass's eyes settled upon, then the Negro's sheared-short lamb's wool.

He jumped to the ground, landing hard on both boots, and under the jarring, his left leg gave, but *oh, Lord*, he stayed upright and stomped closer to the boy that had no face and no clothes or skin on his torso and no flesh on his arms or legs. The bones had been completely dragged clean of cover and the bones were missing bones. There were no hands and no feet. The only clothes that still clung were the shredded shirtsleeves.

Bass kneeled and watched his hands rip away a shirtsleeve. He tugged his neckerchief free of his mouth, then spat into his hand. He took a breath and held it as he made mud of the dust on the boy's shoulder, where there should have been skin left, kept like a secret. When he wiped the mud away and saw skin too dark to be Bennie's, he released his breath, thinking, *Dear Lord, thank you, Jesus.* He could focus his eyes now on the boy's raw head and the cheekbones and jaws below. The boy was a freedman. A Choctaw freedman was his guess.

"Not Bennie, is it?" Eddie asked, approaching.

Bass stood with a jolt and strode past Eddie, seeing little else but the driver's shape on his seat, his boots swinging below it, while the sun hung there on the other side. Onions passed bushels of peas, and cabbages passed onions. The driver's boots kept swinging, and the straw hat sat tilted against the sun. The driver was too silent for this moment.

Bass couldn't think of the right words in Choctaw so he quit trying. "Who you got noosed? Why you got noosed? What the fuck!" The driver swung his boots again, and Bass grabbed one and heaved it back, up, and away over his shoulder to make the light driver fly off his seat.

The driver flapped his arms as he dropped through the air, and the impact of his back against the ground popped his straw hat loose. Bass stood over him, watching the driver gasp like a fish and then cough. The driver squirmed, arching his back but holding his stomach in a fit of coughing. Bass was ready to stomp him, but he waited for the little man to start breathing regularly and answer a damn question.

"Katimi ho? You hear me? Answer me. Hattak lusa mvt?"

The driver sat up, cleared his throat, and nodded. "Hattak lusa mvt," he said, admitting the man was Black, a freedman.

"Chahta?" Bass asked, and the driver continued nodding, squeezing his eyes shut. He heaved and coughed again but began to breathe without trouble. Bass kicked the driver's leg to remind him he was waiting.

The driver sat up, but without opening his eyes he explained in his language that he'd found the man dead in the road with the rope around his neck, his trousers pulled down, and, words failing him, he flattened a hand and chopped at his lap to indicate what there were probably no words for in Choctaw. He shook his head, saying he couldn't have put the body with the vegetables, so he'd tied the lynched man to his wagon. He said after he sold his vegetables in Indianola he'd planned to speak to the Lighthorse police.

"Why didn't he just leave him in the road and go get help?" Eddie asked, but if the driver understood English, he pretended he didn't.

Bass gave the driver time to answer, and Bass inexplicably recalled a straw hat rolling like a wagon wheel. He'd been a boy, or a young man rather, just learning he had a natural gift with guns. George Reeves's father, William Reeves, Bass's first master, had fixed a straw hat to a birch tree for target practice. It had been the first truly happy moment Bass had ever shared with a man as white as a straw hat.

"They thought it was Bennie, didn't they?" Eddie asked. "But why drop him in the road? Why not try to collect for him?"

Bass gazed at the driver, who sat hatless and blind in a stubborn pose, appearing to fear all manner of hell would rain upon him if he proved alive.

"Somebody must a told 'em it wasn't Bennie." Bass was tempted to pour out the Choctaw's vegetables to make room for the corpse but instead kicked the driver again. "You gotta man to bury. Pisa! Wakaya!" he called out, telling him, "Look! Stand up!" Bass turned to Eddie, who looked as helpless as the driver, only standing and seeing instead of sitting and not seeing. "Fuck it," Bass said, turning away and thrusting a hand into his coat pocket. "Ain't enough of him now to claim anyway." He slipped out his knife, then he went to the rope and sawed it until it fell from the wagon with a thump of dust.

The buzzards were feasting, and Bass didn't see any reason to stop them. At his saddle rider he removed his coin purse. He didn't want to, but maybe he ought. He kicked dirt as he stepped up to the driver. "Huh," Bass grunted and tossed two dollars onto his lap.

The driver plucked the coins up and squinted at them.

"Knew that'd wake him," Eddie said.

"Let's get," Bass said.

12

Smoke

The afternoon sun continued to burn through their clothes as the deputies rode down into McAlester. Bass regretted that he and Eddie had never had adequate time to prepare their hunt for Bennie. With a little more time, they could have traded their horses or stopped to disguise themselves—incredulously, not for his son's benefit. But maybe they could yet. Bass instructed Eddie to hide his badge, and Bass rode with his head down, shaded by the black brim of his Stetson. Maybe before leaving town they could at least pick up new hats and shave their mustaches—something Bass hadn't done for any reason in more than thirty years. Appearing as himself, even when part of a plan, had never left him feeling very comfortable or sure among those who bustled, and few towns bustled like McAlester, fueled by the nearby coal fields.

Entering the town from the north, alongside the Katy rails, was a long slide into Main as if the entropy of creation could be precisely measured here in depth with every bed stick and horse step to what gradually felt today as the lowest place on earth, where a still river or sea should have bedded instead of buildings. A double colonnade of storefronts on Choctaw Avenue appeared as black with coal soot as dominoes: Busby Hotel, Lamar's Livery, Restaurant, E & O Fruit Stand, Barber, Drugs, Furnishings, Confectionery, and RC's Feed on the south side faced the new All Saints Hospital, Hale-Halsell Grocery Co., Butcher, Tailor, Harness & Stove, Gibbs Cigar Store, Opera House, and J.J. McAlester Mercantile Co. on the north side. As for the wide avenue itself, it reeked to high heaven. Traffic rolled or hoofed by with a reliably friendly word or nod, but, dear Lord, how everyone slopped through or dropped more live-stock mud as they went, keeping the worst of it forever fresh with a godforsaken fuss of flies.

Eddie tipped his head and hat toward Gibbs Cigar Store.

"After," Bass said. He wanted to get his order in first at J.J. McAlester, which apparently was doing a lot of business today, given there was no room at their hitching posts. Bass and Eddie tied up instead in front of the opera house and used the edge of the boardwalk to scrape the bulk of the muck from their boots, then stomped next door to loosen the rest.

"So," Eddie said, opening his arms wide, "this is where the great can opener discovery came to pass?"

Bass chuckled. "Right here." He wanted to keep his hat brim low but raised it slightly to determine if there was anyone inside he recognized.

Miners of all races who worked J.J. McAlester's coal fields patronized the store to use their line of credit. A few of them were here today, stooped and plodding and still covered in coal dust, dimly eyeballing denim trousers and gloves.

An altogether different sort of customer—a young, thin white man in a plaid suit who sported a fine pair of fox-red mutton chops—was asking the clerk in overalls if he could order sheet music for his students.

The clerk hunched a shoulder. "Can try," he mumbled, talking around the pencil clamped between his teeth. He propped a boot on a keg of nails and set a ledger on his knee.

Bass slowed, feigning interest in a game of checkers, a deck of cards. "Gemütlich, the bootlick!" Bass heard George Reeves sing from the caves of his memory. If Bass had ever retrieved or tied his master's boots with a hint of a smile whenever the morning sun or the no-sense war or the moldy hardtack or the master's infantile manner warranted it, Master Reeves would give Bass a lash of his tongue.

"The composer," the customer said, pausing to enunciate clearly, "is Czerny, Carl Czerny."

The clerk studied the customer as if he were deciding what to say about the piano teacher's sideburns, which grew to his shirt collar. He removed the pencil from his mouth and tapped the air with its lead point. "He Cherokee?"

The customer dismissed the notion with a toss of his hand. "His name sounds more Cherokee than it looks." He spelled the name for the clerk and then added, "'The School of Velocity.' See if you can find that for me. It's an opus I hear will whip a child into Listz before you know it." He craned his head to see what the clerk was writing in his ledger. "You're close," he said, then spelled "school" for the clerk and then "velocity."

Bass moseyed on but remembered Jennie in perfect health at her piano. He wished he knew if her mistress, Rachel Reeves, had used "The School of Velocity" to teach her how to play. Jennie's long fingers could stretch a whole octave with ease and really dance across those black-and-white ballroom tiles.

Bass turned onto a path with stands of shovels, picks, and axes. "Pardon," he said and stepped aside to allow a pretty, painted white woman to pass. She kept her eyes lowered as she carried a copper coal scuttle in front of her. It hung from her wrists in the same manner as her purse. He caught her woody trail of ambergris and took a deeper breath to taste the musky spice as he reached for a shovel. He doubted he'd have the luxury of time to bury anyone, but a shovel was good for moving rock. He handed it to Eddie, then saw, beside the picks, a wooden crate with words he recognized burned onto its lid: "The Giant Powder Company" and "dynamite."

Bass raised the lid and removed a single stick as fat as a cigar. He felt the heft of it. The nitroglycerin mixed with sawdust and rolled with butcher paper didn't seem to weigh more than a half-pound. The price was scrawled in pencil across the front of the crate: fifty cents a pound, which seemed a little high, like everything else in this store. Bass consulted Eddie. "One should do us, right?"

Eddie jutted his chin. "There's two of us, though."

"Yeah," Bass said. He reached for another stick, and Eddie grinned, revealing the dimples on his right cheek. Bass wanted to be certain they had whatever they'd need. Not that he'd ever found himself in a position to need dynamite, but he'd watched railroad men and miners use it dozens of times to clear the slightest bump in the road. He started to close the crate but stopped himself. He slipped the sticks into his left coat pocket and reached into the crate again to pry open the tin can of blasting caps. He would sure need those. He plucked up a pair by their fuses, which ran to gunpowder charges the size of crickets, and tucked them into his right coat pocket.

"Gotta keep them separate, you know," Bass said, hoping to teach the boy something. He shut the crate. "Now them lamps." He looked away to survey the room. No one seemed to be minding him and Eddie, and that was good. The miners were still milling around like dark ghosts, while the young teacher had gone on his way. The clerk, now behind the counter, was standing in a peculiar pose. He'd hung one of his arms through a strap of his overalls, letting his hand rest against the bib, while his hand held what appeared to be the stump of a pickle.

The perfumed woman walked nervously toward the counter, her floral dress washing to and fro with irregularity. Bass watched her set the coal scuttle on the counter without a word. That's when Eddie tapped Bass on the arm and angled the shovel ahead, pointing at the end of the path they were already on.

Bass turned and there they were: lamps with hangers crowded on a shelf. "Eagle-eye Eddie," he said and reached for the shovel in Eddie's hand. "Now's a good time, I reckon, for you to go on and get us tobacco. You know what I want."

Eddie bit his bottom lip as if to prevent a smile, then moved his feet to leave.

Bass clutched his coat to stay him, and Eddie raised his head. Beneath his hat's faded brown brim his dark eyes looked alert.

"Pick us new hats first," Bass muttered. "Ones we'd never want."

"How about an ugly coat to match?"

"Ponchos a good idea." Bass looked around, but no one seemed to pay them any mind. "Don't say nothing you got to, you know."

"And don't turn my back to a door or linger in a doorway?" Eddie winked and strolled away, smooth as a fish through water, toward a table near the open doors that was stacked with hats. The miners no longer milled among the assortment of clothes but were now bunched in line with their arms full behind the fragrant woman. Then two Negro cowboys strode in with spurs clanging, passing Eddie trying on a white hat, and two white cowboys entered after them. The store was as busy as a train station.

Bass held the shovel under one arm, collected two lamps by their wire hangers, and joined the line behind the miners. The woman had already left the store, but her perfume hung around like a hook.

Bass rocked this way and that until he was standing in line sideways so that his back was turned neither to the store's open doors nor the clerk at the counter. He could watch both pairs of cowboys this way as they appeared to roam the store without pause or purpose. He shifted his attention to Eddie walking up with ponchos and two white hats. Eddie handed him the larger of the two hats—it hardly had any body to it—and the ponchos were the most threadbare things Bass had ever seen. The fabric wasn't wool or alpaca but thin cotton only a little thicker than muslin. Bass shrugged but also nodded.

"Leaving them here," Eddie said and laid the bundle at the end of the counter out of the way before strolling out.

One by one, the miners left the line to bunch up to the side until the last miner unloaded his arms and then reloaded them. The clerk had glanced in Bass's direction a time or two while helping the miners, but his scrutiny had always been limited to what Bass was buying. And that didn't change when Bass stepped up to the counter. He set the lamps down first and then the shovel before withdrawing the sticks of dynamite from his pocket. A tuft of curly brown chest hair sprouted from the fork of the clerk's stained shirt.

"I need oil for these, and I'm getting those hats and ponchos yonder," Bass said.

"Gimme a minute," the clerk said, carrying the lamps to a room behind the counter.

Bass turned to look behind him as if he might expect Eddie to return any moment, and he found the cowboys had stopped roaming. The pairs had wandered apart and now stood at opposite ends of the store, each with an open stance angled in his direction. They appeared frozen with fear or intent as if they were at a wake or merely waiting for a signal to raise their weapons and fire.

The clerk's footfalls returned before Bass noticed him at the counter with a lamp hanging from each hand. Bass watched the oil sway as the clerk slid the lamps onto the counter. The clerk removed his pencil from behind his ear and wrote numbers in his ledger. He worked slowly, then cocked his eyebrows. "You got caps for them?"

"I do." Bass collected the sticks of dynamite and tucked them back into his left coat pocket.

"Two?"

"Two," Bass confirmed. He turned as if to scour the store. "I do hope I ain't forgetting nothing, though. Lot's here." Feeling enclosed, he recalled what Geronimo had told him at Fort Sill.

Both pairs of cowboys stood perfectly still, or not perfectly still; they were talking but talking low. "Don't forget," he heard Geronimo say and Zi yeh translate. Both of them, the Apache and then the English, with the music of an echo.

"Mind if I ask what you blowing?" said the clerk.

Bass turned back to answer. The clerk was looking him in the eyes for the first time and leaning on one leg.

Bass shook his head and sighed with a whistle. "I got one pickle of a stump that snapped my shovel like a twig."

The clerk's eyes glazed over and then he lowered them to the ledger. "Better you than me."

"Nope, better *you*," Bass chuckled, wiping his hands on his coat and then letting them hang but with his elbows hitched to keep his hands floating next to his six-shooters. He glanced again at the cowboys—at the white ones, the Negro ones—when a shotgun

thundered outside. All four cowboys startled, ducking and spinning toward the open doors, while the clerk leaped away from the
counter as if to hide in the rear room. As Bass gauged the blast or
his memory of the blast, he realized the shotgun hadn't actually
thundered outside, not where every living thing seemed to scream,
grunt, or whinny among heavy footfalls—not right outside. It had
gone off away—but closer than far—as if behind nearby walls. Then
another shotgun blast ripped through the air, identical to the first.
The shrieks and stamps outside sped up and got louder as if they
all agreed someone was getting shot twice.

Bass found his hands gripping his Colts as he shuffled his feet to
the doors to look out. He couldn't decide where the fire was coming from, if from the west, from Gibbs Cigar Store, but everyone
outside suddenly appeared to think so, now fleeing to the east past
his eyes and the open doors.

Bass halted his boots before they struck the boardwalk, deciding
instead to dart a dogleg around the stacked hats to the window. He
brushed the curtain aside and saw men crouched behind horses with
pistols and rifles out—onetwothreefourfivesix of them on this side
of the avenue and the other, and all were aiming at the French-style
doorway of J.J. McAlester as if all six, maybe more, were waiting
to ambush him as he ran out for Eddie. "Eddie," he allowed himself to whisper.

Bass turned to the door closest to him, propped open by a black
iron, and kicked the iron aside, which sent the door clattering against
the frame. When gunfire didn't riddle it, he leaped across the remaining doorway, kicked aside the second iron, and flung that door
closed. He turned to face the store, to see the clerk peering out the
back room, whereas the cowboys were holding their ground with
drawn revolvers. "Get in the back," Bass told them.

The cowboys didn't move.

"I'm the law so do what I tell you. I got this. Go on."

The cowboys budged but only slightly.

"Move it!" he shouted.

The cowboys moved faster now, so he looked for something with weight, like the long solid table that shirts and trousers sat folded on. He bounded behind it, keeping his Colts out, and shoved the table with the heels of his hands, scraping and barking the table across the floor as clothes fell, until it slammed as a brace against the doors.

"Marshal Reeves, you're gonna have to come out cheer!" a goose-strong voice croaked from the avenue. He sounded as though he had a sore throat but didn't mind shredding it further by yelling. "Got questions for you to answer. You know about what."

Bass dismissed the notion of lighting dynamite.

"Well?" the man continued to yell. "All we want to do with you is talk."

Bass could hear Geronimo chopping his words. *I should have never surrendered.*

"You played marshal long enough!" the man shouted. His head must have been round because the words he spewed sounded fatty and like they were cranked out of a meat grinder.

"Ain't a marshal," Bass yelled.

"Course," the man shouted back. "N—— can't be no marshal like he can't be no Texas Ranger. Please excuse my error, *deputy.*"

Bass suspected this man was John Armstrong, the Ranger who'd captured John Wesley Hardin on a train in Pensacola, not far from where Geronimo had been held prisoner. The selfsame one who'd tricked Bass for a hundred dollars. He knew Armstrong, and he knew him to have a fat head.

He eyed the store, but where could a body hide in such a box, with only one way in or out? The room in the back was merely a place to be cornered. He heard Geronimo again and remembered his stiff fingertips roving over his woolly hair when Bass saw everything here to make what he needed.

He loped away, up the path of tools, and holstered a Colt to grab an ax. He struck out for the store's west side wall, but, passing the counter, he spotted the hats Eddie had picked out. Bass holstered his other Colt to throw off his Stetson and eyeballed the larger of the two white hats as he held it in midair. It would never last as long as a Stetson. The felt was thinner, softer, lighter, and would surely be cooler, but it was so damn white! He eyeballed the hat, like a hellish tooth-colored mushroom in his hands. "Fuck it!" he said and mashed the hat on his head.

He rushed to where he was going, to an oval braided rug that hung on a pine-plank wall, displaying scraps of about every color there was. He tugged it to the floor and rapped the wall with the blunt end of the ax, again and again, finding where there was a stud and where there wasn't.

"We come to talk to you man to man," the man outside yelled. "Reckon you can handle that?"

Bass felt the weight of the ax in his hands. It felt insignificant, as delicate as a spine, one that had been cleaned away from all the meat and guts and was just deep down a mechanical thing of things barely connected, like cogs and wheels that were locked but could break like glass. He planted his feet.

"Man to man?" Bass asked.

"Man to man!" the man shouted back.

"Gotta back up first!" Bass hollered. "Gotta gimme room to walk out!"

He waited a moment until the men outside would surely be talking, then he reared the ax back for a good swing and split a foot-wide pine plank down to the floor. He whipped his head toward the front of the store and studied the light at the windows and below the doors and listened, but the bounty hunters weren't ready yet to force their way in. They were holding back for some reason, maybe to appear civil to the town. His second swing broke the plank free.

"Well, you coming?" the man asked.

"Well," Bass hollered, "you gotta back it up more than that. I'm waiting. Ain't in a hurry." He plunged the ax into the next board. "Go on, back it up!"

Once that second board was down, he commenced kicking the boards out that were nailed to the other side of the wall in the business next door.

"We hear you knocking around, barring the door with whatnot, like we can't shoot our way past it and drag you the fuck out cheer, boy! Don't make us!" The man and his men laughed.

"Or maybe," countered Bass, laughing, "I'll shoot my way out first and kill every last one a you mushroom-skin motherfuckers!"

"Oh's, that so, is it? And maybe we might just torch the place. We ain't gotta go in."

"Don't back it up then!" yelled Bass. "Y'all keep them tater heads out where I can see 'em. Sure as shit I'll blast 'em. I love a tater hunt! I'll pick off most a you."

A hushed stirring commenced outside as pairs of boots shuffled closer or farther away.

Bass remembered the lamps and made a move to hurry back to the counter when he saw one of the Negro cowboys peeking out from the back room. From a look of concern, the cowboy appeared younger now. He could've been Bennie's age.

"Hand me one of them lamps, will you, son?" Bass wouldn't need both. He didn't actually need either, but he wanted those men outside to know where he was going. Otherwise later, if they didn't follow after him, he'd have no idea where they could be.

The cowboy caught the lamp's hanger with a hooked finger and then stopped and motioned at the shovel.

Bass shook his head, and the cowboy clanged his spurs around the counter as the other Negro cowboy showed his face. They were both as dark as Bass used to wish and pray his own skin would be, as dark as Jennie's was—so dark that God's grace could always shine from it but more from a mirrored thing than a blinding thing. Like from deep water, not snow. Wouldn't that be something of a reminder to always have light on you, like some moon glow?

"You got room now. We give you room!" the man hollered from the avenue. "You coming out or not?"

Bass watched the windows and doors, and when nothing changed, he turned to the cowboy holding out the lamp. Bass took it, then looked at the doors again.

"You, who I'm talking to," Bass shouted. "Is you Armstrong?"

"*John B.* Armstrong!"

"The one who always wears a hat on a slant 'cause his head so big?"

"You ain't still mad I pulled the wool over your eyes on a horse trade, is you, boy?" He laughed. "Yeah, you know me!"

"Yeah, I know you got John Wesley Hardin only 'cause the boy's pistol hung up in his suspenders. I best warn you I never been much on suspenders."

A pistol fired, and a window crashed, making the cowboy crouch.

"Consider that your warning, n——!" Armstrong yelled.

"Shit," said Bass. "I'll be sure to tell J.J. McAlester hisself who the one shot up his storefront!" He reached his arm through the hole in the wall and stood the ax against the opposite side. Then he squeezed through the hole and entered the black room of the opera house, too early in the day to be in use but already echoing his movements as if his presence had been expected. Once, when he was a boy and Auntie Totty was showing off a dress she'd sewn for Mistress Reeves, she turned his attention to the garment's underside. "See. Gotta make the selvage smile, too," she'd said, though she wasn't smiling. "Begin and end everything you do, Bass, like everything showing."

Bass spun to look at the cowboy, framed by the wall's jagged edges. "Hang that rug back, will you, son? May buy me a minute or two."

The cowboy pealed his dry lips apart. "Yessir," he said. He stretched his arm through the hole, and Bass took the lamp from him. "Say, you Bass Reeves?" the cowboy stammered.

"I am," Bass said. "'Preciate you." He lowered to collect the ax and was surprised to find, after turning around, that the hole had let in enough light for his eyes to make out the rows of empty wooden chairs set up for a performance. So he took off running, but the bullet in his left thigh was a seed that would forever germinate pain. He clenched his jaws and his grip on the ax, and he was panting when he reached the other side of the opera house. He clattered the lamp and ax on some chairs and fumbled with his fire tin to find a match and light the wick before the rug went back up and covered the hole, but the cowboy was quicker.

Outside, Armstrong emptied his lungs for Bass to hurry up.

Bass, at last, held a match roaring to life. He lit the wick with it and turned the wheel, and finally he was hurling the ax again to open another hole.

"Your partner ain't talking, but maybe you will," Armstrong shouted. "I'm gonna count to ten and you better come out and talk, or we finding something to do with this here Cherokee. I *think* he Cherokee. Your deputy Cherokee, right? Don't look Choctaw to me, and that ain't good for his rights here in McAlester."

Bass wrenched and kicked the splintered planks down, and swirling shafts of yellowish twilight poured into the opera house with a heavy scent of tobacco and gunpowder. He withdrew a Colt and peered inside Gibbs Cigar Store. He saw no one left or right through a lingering cloud of smoke and dust, so he stepped through the wall with the lamp, then blew into the chimney to put the light out. He looked left again, across a bloodless floor toward the front of the store, and through the red lettering on the plate-glass window, he saw a man on the boardwalk standing behind a porch post with a shotgun braced across his forearm and aimed in the direction of J.J. McAlester's.

"Five!" Armstrong yelled, his voice carrying through town. "I'm bound to killed my allotment of Injuns in my life. Don't you make me kill another blasted one, Bass Reeves! Not for some no-account coward woman-killer! Shit, *six*!"

Bass turned to scout the rear of the store. Three whisky barrels—a fifty-three gallon and two thirties—stood together as a table and seats, and behind them hung a black velvet curtain that closed off a back room.

"Eddie?" he whispered. "You there?" He glanced over his shoulder, but the man's aim outside remained fixed on McAlester's.

"Seven!" Armstrong counted.

Bass stepped easy around the barrels. "Eddie?" he repeated, and that's when Eddie appeared, sprawled on the floor in the shadows of the barrels. The horseshoe nails Bass had used once to patch Eddie's bootheels, that's what Bass saw first, and then Eddie's striped trousers and his blood, pooled out from his gut. Eddie lay belly down in it, though his face and head didn't show, not with the edge of the curtain resting across his neck.

"Eddie," Bass muttered. His chest clenched. He stepped over the cloud-shaped pool of blood and ripped the curtain aside to reveal Eddie's dark disheveled hair, his dead-open eyes, and those dimples of his one last time.

"Eight! And I ain't talking about supper even if I am getting awfully damn hungry." Men guffawed or cackled up and down the avenue. "You hear me, Bass Reeves? I know you do."

Bass bent a knee and laid a palm on the back of Eddie's head. "Lord, please take this sweet boy if you haven't." He felt the fineness of his hair, like that of his girls when they were little.

"Nine!" Armstrong hollered. "Let me reach ten, and your partner's the first one we open up. Or hang. Maybe burn. Maybe in that very damn order. We got all day to play, but we ain't waiting all day for you to come out, now."

Bass rose slowly but without pain, and, clutching the velvet, he jerked the curtain off its rod. Hooks clattered as he unfurled the cloth with both hands and let it float down over Eddie. He faced the front of the store, clenching his teeth. When he passed the hole in the wall, he picked up his lamp, pulled his hat brim low, and strode toward the door.

"Ten," called Armstrong, and his crew began hooting and howling and firing weapons into the air now that the time had finally arrived. Bass turned the doorknob and walked out. The shooter on the boardwalk in front of him was grinning but not shooting in celebration. He was waiting to shoot and apparently hadn't heard Bass open the door and approach him, so Bass set the lamp down first before buffaloing him with one good wallop of his Colt. As the man crumpled, Bass caught the shotgun.

Still no one had noticed him. It was as if his skin really was invisible. So Bass leaped off the boardwalk carrying the shotgun in his left hand and the Colt in his right.

"You hear that, Bass Reeves?" Armstrong shrieked from behind a wagon parked in front of the confectionery on the opposite side of the avenue.

Bass jogged across the smelly sludge with a ducked head to appear afraid of being shot. A few heads turned but then turned away again. Maybe it was more than his skin. Maybe they believed a man wearing a white hat was someone who couldn't be taken seriously. When he reached the other side, he slowed and straightened and strolled right up to Armstrong himself, who was slouched against a wagon wheel, his hat sure enough sitting at a tilt on his round head.

"The next shot you hear, boy, is for your partner!" Armstrong hollered in the opposite direction with a Winchester held across his chest. "Then we're coming in! Won't be no deals after that!"

"Damn right for my partner," Bass said behind him.

Armstrong's head rotated owl-like. "What the hell?" he grumbled, squinting. He raised his eyes to Bass's guns, then his eyes and freckled cheeks and mustache, longer and frayed at the ends like a busted rope but just as thick as Armstrong's. Armstrong appeared to focus on Bass's bad-tempered grimace when Armstrong's eyes bulged with recognition. Grunting, Armstrong swiveled, trying to level his rifle. Bass chose the shotgun and squeezed the trigger, blasting the ranger's head and hat against the wagon.

Bass threw the shotgun to the dirt and drew his other Colt as he spun to find two shooters posting up to the right of him on the boardwalk and a third across the avenue, crouched between horses. All three were trying to steady their aim but firing too soon and missing and getting blown back by Bass's Colts. He fired in rapid succession, right-left-right, and looked for more coming, but those who remained of Armstrong's crew now scattered for cover.

"I'll keep killing if you keep pointing them weapons," Bass shouted, spinning to check on those he'd shot and those he hadn't. "Y'all hear me?" He searched rooftops and windows and both ways along the avenue. The shooter stretched out between the horses was the only one he'd hit who was still moving, and he was squirming, digging ruts in the road with his bootheels while the piebald and bay stamped and whinnied and bucked around him until their reins came untied from the post and they galloped away. The shooter's hands held only his own bleeding belly, so Bass looked past him to J.J. McAlester's doors opening, the left and then the right.

The Negro cowboys poked their heads and pistols out. "Need help?" asked the one who'd helped Bass with the lamp.

Bass motioned with a Colt for them to join him. Help would quickly end this, allowing him to push on. He doubted he had much time left to find Bennie.

The cowboys opened the doors wider and stepped out, then the white ones followed. The last of the crew hiding behind horses in front of McAlester's clambered into view and onto their mounts and rode hard out of town for their lives.

13

The Washout

In these modern times, it would take no more than a matter of minutes for word of the events in McAlester to spread throughout the territory after the initial telegraphs were sent to the federal court in Paris, the Choctaw Lighthorse Police, and Doctor Jesse's office in McGee. The wires would then tap dance for hours between any number of federal and tribal municipal offices, train stations, banks, and newspapers. What was uncertain was how long it would take rogue bounty hunters like Bigfoot to learn of those reports, which would certainly name Deputy Reeves as a participant. There couldn't have been a single eyewitness that hadn't observed Bass leave the scene with two horses and a lantern. All that was left for anyone unfamiliar with the Choctaw Nation to inquire about was the location of the nearest cave, and there would be no confusion on that point since there was only the one.

Hammer meanwhile hammered Bass eastward to it, with Flycatcher in tow. Bass thought it might kill her to run her so hard, but this was good, straight running, where he'd make the best time. When she began to shorten her stride and rock, wanting to quit, he kicked her even though he'd never kicked her, and the loyal mare gave him several more miles before giving up again, short of Wilburton. At Mail Creek he let her rest. That's what he'd decided to call the narrow spillway from Moshulatubbee Lake after he'd seen the Butterfield Overland Mail coach stop there years ago to water the team.

While Hammer and Eddie's buckskin gelding bent for water, Bass poured the last of the oats onto the ground. The evening sky purpled and pinked as he cut the tow rope, swapped the saddles, and hung the lantern around the stock of his rifle. Then he mounted Flycatcher, who immediately pulled on the reins to keep eating, to delay another run. To show the gelding he was in control, Bass tugged the reins so hard his fists hit his chest, which reared Flycatcher up on two hooves, whinnying and thrashing his head. "Heigh-ho!" Bass shouted to wake him up. Then with a stiff neck, Bass kicked him into a gallop.

He didn't like to abandon a living thing. He'd done it once to save and free himself, and it had pained him his entire life. Now he prayed he'd save and free his son. He prayed in song, even though he didn't sing aloud, as he watched the shadows for the foot of the Sans Bois Mountains jutting out. That was how he imagined Florida looked: like a foot slipped into the ocean. Finally, almost to Wilburton, he rounded the foot of the Sans Bois Mountains—though calling the land Florida—where he began his northward climb through black walnut, redbud, and longleaf pine, knowing from memory but also noting their fleeting contours.

He was filled with the Holy Ghost, so he thanked the Lord for filling him. Then in his thoughts, he sang:

Filled, filled, like a shoe be filled,
My soul be magnifying you, Lord,
This uphill climb be the love for a son,
My arms be yours, your might be mine,
We'll scatter the proud, we'll lift the meek,
As a team we'll do every magnificent thing,
So no cause to wait to praise you, Father,
You done blessed me, filled me good,
Look at my socks, take a look at my shoes,
I be filled like today be Christmas Day!

Maybe Bennie was in his tight spot at that moment, singing his own hymn and dreaming he heard these drumming hooves. Bass smiled, wanting to believe that must be true, then noted a hint of dust on his tongue. He looked ahead, above the road and the trees that hid the next bend. The thinnest veil appeared to cover the darkening sky, appearing to funnel from a chimney not far away—from those trees and stars to these trees and stars—but racing closer.

He slowed Flycatcher to a canter, and the chimney drifted farther away until the dust veil disappeared. Whoever was ahead of him was riding in the same direction, so he sped Flycatcher to catch up. When the veil reappeared, so did the hint on his tongue, but the dust quickly thickened above and in his mouth, and he found the chimney before him, before the next bend, and it was slow and heavy and barrel-shaped in the road and loud as a wagon. *The wagon,* he realized, and the bloodhounds he couldn't see in the dark and behind the dust trail must have seen him because their hornlike throats bawled and bellowed.

Bass rarely tried to meet fast with faster. At his age it made better sense for him to rely instead on his smarts, to find an option that made good sense in the moment, and right now good sense told him he couldn't allow the hounds to sniff out his son. So as he whipped the reins and rode up along the left side of the wagon, he unholstered a Colt and stretched out his arm as if to touch the rear wheel. He fired three times at the hub, then wrenched Flycatcher off the road before the wagon collapsed behind them with a piercing crunch of wood.

The driver cussed and the bloodhounds yelped as the wagon spilled them onto the road. Bass looked back one last time before Flycatcher darted into the trees.

If Bigfoot's posse was on the road ahead of the wagon, they would now be turning around to investigate the gunfire and wreckage, but Flycatcher was breaking too much underbrush for Bass to hear if any horses followed in pursuit. It was safer to assume they were.

Most of the trees were old enough to crowd out vegetation, but navigating under a moonless sky was not easy. Bass crouched, but a black walnut branch was sometimes too low and stout for him to

bully past, and he had to reroute Flycatcher westward when turning northward was what they needed to do to rejoin the road. The
cave was no more than a couple of miles to the northeast.

Bass expected to run up on another spillway but couldn't recall
exactly how it wound. Eventually he and Flycatcher outran the
thickest clusters of black walnut and found better space among the
pines to turn northward and run faster. After about a mile, he began
to right them to the northeast, and the tree cover fell away and a
horseshoe bend of the spillway suddenly lay before them, broad
as the Red River. They wouldn't have to cross it, but he tugged the
reins and held his breath.

Voices and horse thunder seemed to scatter and pulse from all
directions except the way of the water. The posse wasn't near yet
but was approaching and converging on him. He held his breath
again and prayed he'd hear he was mistaken. But that sounded blas-
phemous for him to say, so he corrected himself, praying he was
right—right in everything he right now thought. The clearing and
the stars shimmering on the water offered depth to the original
contours of the trees and the impressions of the ground, but it all
proved to be a different form of flat, with nowhere for him to hide,
with or without a horse.

In the bluff beneath them was a washout where Flycatcher could
step down to ford the spillway, but, no, there wasn't time for that,
and Flycatcher was too winded, panting. Bass could send Flycatcher
alone across the spillway as a ruse, but he couldn't be certain Flycatcher would go. The fatigued and frightened gelding might return
and root him out.

Bass twisted in the saddle to search out the best position to defend.
The pines would prove too difficult for him to climb and would provide no cover anyway. He turned back to the water and surveyed
the bluff—the washout—which appeared large enough for him.

Hoarse whispers carried, then distinct words coalesced.

"Where you?"

"Thisaway!"

"Here!"

Bass understood enclosures, it was true, so when the thought occurred to him—or the command—to leap down into a hole the size of a grave and grab the reins to lead Flycatcher down over him as if the horse were nothing but a mound of fresh dirt, he listened because God tended to speak to him at times like these.

Bass reached for the lantern and tucked it into the deepest crevice at the center of the dry washout, then unsheathed his rifle and fixed it lengthwise. He'd crawl in beside it. Remembering his hat, he grabbed and flung it, and it settled on the water—the color of a sail on a sea. Then he thought better of keeping the lantern. He bent down for it and hung the hanger around the saddle horn, then wrapped the reins around a wrist. He looked into Flycatcher's panicked eyes, bulging large as eggs. Bass had no choice. He heaved a deep breath to give himself strength and hauled the gelding down with him as he tucked his boots into the hole. Flycatcher was stubborn, still up on his hind legs, until Bass yanked the awful weight of the horse directly over the top of him. Flycatcher whinnied and thrashed to stand back up, but Bass had wrangled his Bowie knife from his coat pocket and plunged it just beneath the horse's throatlatch. He waggled it violently to ensure severing the jugular and carotid and windpipe, but it was hard labor to cut through so much young muscle.

Bass strained to hold the horse down as the blood boiled over his hands and down his sleeves. He squeezed his eyes and lips closed, refusing to breathe, holding on, while Flycatcher squirmed and snorted, panted, gurgled, and kicked. If the posse had been calling out, had been riding or stepping up close, Bass couldn't know.

Bass slid the knife free but kept a fast grip. Strands of mane fell across his face. He wiggled his toes, then tried to wiggle each foot, but the solid weight of the horse sufficiently covered them. His eyes fluttered open, but the washout was pitch black and he could only hear his heart in this bath of blood. He allowed himself to place his empty hand against Flycatcher's smooth coat and slowly took a shallow breath, then closed his eyes again and prayed. *As a team we'll do every magnificent thing*, he repeated.

A cough a vague distance away silenced his prayer. Because it was loud enough for him to hear, it could have come from the bluff above him, like Bass could reach through the abyss of dead horse and touch the tips of the man's boots.

He and that man who was bound to be white could have been looking right at each other. It had been like this his entire life, with the other not seeing him. As if, foreign as death, Bass had become invisible merely by being born. As if a horse had stood between him and every white man every day of his life. *Almost* every white man. Far too many of them. Too close to all of them. Maybe to some sometimes he'd been something, but rarely human. A man with memories and dreams who had once been a baby. A sacred thing with his own fate. No, the white man had to give him a fate and keep trying to give him one and make it stick. He'd been a boy to them, that was for sure. When he was a baby, he was a boy, and when he became a man, he was still a boy. And he was still a boy to them now. He would be a boy for the rest of his life on earth. Never a man or a father who could love his babies or declining darling wife or aging mama or poor wife's cousin who'd learned to put everyone first. He loved them all, and his love for his grand-mammy and granddaddy and auntie and Eddie and Judge Parker, every body and thing he'd ever loved, dead or alive, like every horse and dog and comforting morsel, was real inside him, yet, like its shadow or soul or maybe its body even, its *real* body, he somehow kept it all with him and nursed it and could never lose it. Maybe that was how it was for any loving soul no matter the color. There it was; he felt it: love for each loved one balled inside him like seeds or taters, or pearls if they could clench, heat up, and ache in a dark place like this, as a bullet could. But he didn't want to be seen today. Not now by that white man who coughed. Not nary yet. He did not like to dwell.

He strained to hear, or he believed he did. He had strained that storming December night in 1890, too, when so close on Bob Doz-ier's trail, after so many years, he was ambushed a second time. It was Bass's final ride on his old sorrel Strawberry, following tracks no more than an hour or two old on the muddy, wooded slopes of the Cherokee Hills. Bass was praying he'd reach Dozier before the rain filled or washed them away. And then they met.

Dozier's shot had missed but had cut the air near his ear, prompting Bass to hop out of his saddle. They traded pistol fire from behind trees until Bass threw his shoulder backward as if hit and spun, losing his hat and falling to his chest on the sopping ground. While the wind whistled through the cold rain needling his neck and head, he had strained to hear Dozier's approaching movements, if there were any. He waited like this but between explosions of thunder. He waited and strained like this.

And then Dozier belly-laughed to break his own silence just as he'd done years earlier when he'd drunkenly ambushed Bass asleep in his camp. A flash of lightning made the black Seminole skin of Dozier's tilted face white. The next time lightning flashed, Dozier was already four or five steps closer and away from the protection of a tree. Though not as loud, he was still laughing—laughing as he'd promised Bass he'd laugh—as he ambled through mud.

When Dozier had learned Bass was tracking him, he let it be known. Only two days earlier, he'd posted a warning to taunt and spook Bass in an attempt to shake him off his trail. On the back of a wanted poster nailed outside of the post office in Tahlequah, Dozier had pencil-scratched, "I will laff the last laff Bazz Reez." His name appeared below in capital letters for no one to miss: BOB DOZIER, the prominent farmer-turned-infamous-ringleader who robbed banks, stagecoaches, and stores and held up high-stakes poker games and stole horses and cattle and ambushed cattle buyers, jewelers, and travelers throughout all parts of the Cherokee Nation.

"Stop and drop your gun," Bass ordered, suddenly lifting his head.

Dozier stilled his legs and quit laughing. He was as frozen in place as a tree. Despite the darkness, though, Bass could see the shine of Dozier's enlarged eyes. Then Dozier dropped to his knees, swinging his firearm in front of him, but Bass's aim was already fixed above Dozier's buttons and his pistol but below his face—at his uncovered neck because Bass didn't like looking at a body's eyes when he pulled a trigger and because, well, a neck shot was the mark of a marksman.

"Think he killed to hush him?" a man asked, his voice muted beyond the washout.

"I reckon," another man sort of squawked. This one could have been Bigfoot.

The words didn't fully reach Bass. It was as if they were uttered in another room and drifted to him from above, through a transom.

"His hat."

"I see it."

"What else you see?"

Bass waited for the one who sounded like Bigfoot to answer.

"I see he took his rifle but left his lantern."

"I guess he was so fast to run he plumb forgot to grab it."

"I guess you better stop guessing."

A long silence followed, so Bass began to wonder how long he should wait before trying to climb out of his horse hole. Slimed with blood, it would not be easy.

"Maybe 'cause it's busted."

"Shit, he coulda made a busted lantern useful if it was useful. His boy ain't hiding in no cave."

"Why else he come all this way?"

"What if he left that there 'cause he's decoying us? The cave already been checked once, and he wants us to check it again? Shit, but we hadn't checked this way yet. Why don't you swim down the creek and see if you can't catch him?"

"Shit, I'll follow it."

A snigger followed by a thump on the ground and the cracking of a stick sounded near.

"I'll go up, and you down a ways and then let's cross. 'Member, shoot to kill this'un. We'll worry about making the law work for us later, hear me?"

Bass waited to hear the other one respond, but there was no such clarity. No more thumps or sticks were cracking. He could've been biding his time inside a cellar to check on the ruin from a twister.

After one passed in the Chickasaw Nation one fall, he'd found a cow in the fork of a tree. He'd followed its dreadful, mournful mooing across a meadow and through a wood and across another meadow to a small grove of soapberry trees. They were nearly stripped of all their yellow leaflets, and the ground was lathered here and there with their broken nuts, and there she was—a looming thing, solid black as if a shard of space had fallen from the sky. Bass went back to his prisoner wagon for his axe and chopped a limb to free her, but she broke a leg from the fall. She broke ribs, too, he would discover later after he'd shot her and started a fire. By the time he'd cut back the hide and opened her up and found she was with calf, her owner showed up with two sons to inspect their property. Without hesitation, the Chickasaw man and his sons pitched in to carve and cook and eat what they could.

He began to fear it would be too late for Bennie if he waited any longer, so he squirmed his hips and legs out from under the sagging barrel of Flycatcher's body, then struggled to his knees, dragging the rifle with him, the knife still in his fist. He thrust a shoulder against the gelding's neck to nudge it over and blood oozed over his head as he squeezed past, rising on hardened legs until he lost his footing and dropped hard on his knees. He panted and tried again, digging his heels into the mud and rising on his weak, aching knees until his legs quivered like loose guitar strings. He emptied his hands of the rifle and knife on the dirt of the bluff and clawed himself out.

He held his breath a moment longer, lying silent with his eyes still shut. Hearing nothing but the night animals, he allowed himself to then fill his lungs. There didn't appear to be anyone in the night but him, no one here and no one coming. He wiped his hands on the inside of his coat. Now he could reach into his trouser pocket for his handkerchief and wipe the blood from his eyes. When at last he opened them, the night's darkness no longer seemed much dark.

14

Snuff

Bass searched the blood-black shadows with a stooped back until eventually he found his knife by the hilt's silvery zigzag shape beside the gelding's twisted tongue, spilled long as entrails.

His left leg throbbed at the bullet as he bent lower to pick up the knife. He wiped the blade and then the handle on his handkerchief before sheathing the knife inside his coat pocket. Then he bent down again for his rifle. He wiped the trigger and hammer and pushed blood away in rivulets from the receiver. He'd need to reload his weapons when he had a moment far away from this clearing, so he paused by his saddle rider to fill his trouser pockets with .45s and .45 Governments for his Colts and Winchester. Then he reached for the lantern, which had come unhooked from the saddle horn and sat cracked against Flycatcher's belly.

His eyes followed the men's footprints as they moved from where he stood, going in opposite directions along the water. He held the rifle angled downward in the crook of an arm to drain the barrel of blood while the lantern's wire hanger hung across his fingers. Though he strained to hear human calls or brush crunching beyond croaking frogs and the common gyring night racket of birds and insects, he could hear nothing else, leaving him feeling half-helpless until he'd unholstered a Colt in a cross draw. Now with both hands useful, he felt balanced enough to climb the bluff.

The pines made for quick tromping. And from what Bass could discern from the heady fragrance of sap and the occasional collection box he bumped into and the squares of barkless trunk he saw meagerly reflecting starlight, most of the trees had been hacked.

The fragrance was actually clearing his head and lungs, invigorating him. Boiling the sap into tar or pitch could serve so many uses. He'd harvested longleaf pine sap back in the day for Master Reeves, George's father, who would sell it to a merchant who would then sell it to the navy for sealing ships, though there was always some leftover to make rosin for lighting a quick fire or for melting a dab to seal and heal a cut.

Every fifty to hundred yards, Bass would stop to catch his breath and listen out. While reloading his weapons, he heard wolf pups howl and a mountain lion cry like a woman screaming from a nearby perch, but no bloodhounds. None yet. The ground inched higher and harder; he noticed that too. Before long there was as much rock as dirt beneath his boots, and the pines began to thin, so he was watchful for them to fall away soon. He was close.

The cave sat on the mountaintop as if it were a monument to mountaintops. He'd seen newspaper pictures of the U.S. Capitol, and he thought the shape of the cave resembled its dome, though without all the fuss.

Bennie had been serving as his posseman when Bass had shown him the cave. That had been in 1891 after his posseman Floyd Wilson had stopped taking the work if it meant roaming long periods of time away from the Cherokee Nation. Floyd had become friends with Clem Rogers, a successful cattleman and Cherokee senator, who had convinced Floyd that Claremore would make a nice home for his family. For two years until Eddie joined him in 1893, Bass had no steady posseman. He went out alone, hired a friend or family member who was looking to pick up a little extra cash, or teamed up with another deputy. He often based his decision on how risky the work appeared to be or how big the haul was. His last resort was to lean on one of his sons to read subpoenas to him in camp and guard prisoners and help with the cooking. Being the oldest, Robert had been the first to serve as Bass's posseman. Newland came next. Then Bennie, once he'd turned eighteen. Edgar too. Every robust, healthy boy with a robust, healthy soul in him at some time was bound to go crazy to explore Indian Territory. They had all begun at too young of an age, begging their father to take them on an adventurous hunt for bad men—his sons as well as his daughters—but Bennie had been the worst at it, even threatening once to follow him if Bass dared say no. Bennie pretended to be joking, but Bass knew better.

In 1891 Bennie's craving for heroism had become too great for Bass to ignore, so he decided it was time to expose his son to heroism's perilous consequences. Ignorance was the parent of fear, but Bass deemed a voyage or two would have to be enough for each son to learn what their daddy's work away from home entailed and to agree a life of it wasn't suitable for young men of their character. Sure, raw freedom among nature's elements and mysteries could be alluring, as well as meeting the most interesting Americans a body could ever imagine—those reared on the Trail of Tears or in the Scottish Highlands or on Nantucket Island, some good and some evil but most in between. But in Indian Territory there was also death and a boatload of it. Sometimes it seemed to Bass there were the forsaken and there were the dead, and no one else. Those who thought differently simply hadn't lived long enough for their minds to change.

It was at the end of May. They had just arrested William Right in the Creek Nation for clubbing his son to death—a sickly thirteen-year-old. After feeding his horses, Right had walked to the nearest Lighthorse agency and turned himself in. The situation left Bennie shaken. He and Bass talked about it at the cave a few days later while Right remained chained in the prisoner wagon with two other suspected murderers—also white men—whom Bass had arrested for killing John Irvin, a Negro who had been found in Blue Creek with a bullet in his head only days after the two white men, supposedly his friends, had threatened his life. The white men found themselves in Bass's wagon because they couldn't give him an alibi for the time the crime had been committed. One of the suspects would later argue that the fact that Irvin's wife had called upon him to check on her missing husband was evidence the widow trusted him, and therefore the court should as well. Convinced by such logic, the U.S. commissioner decided to forego indictments, which led the *Fort Smith Weekly Elevator* to take the opportunity to discredit Bass not only for arresting law-abiding citizens but also for hauling them like animals in his wagon all over the countryside for almost a month. Now it was George Reeves who was discrediting him. Bass could see the direction the nation was going. As he made the West safer for settlers, the West was becoming whiter like the East and less safe for everyone else. Discrediting him was a means of discrediting all Black folk, to justify finding new ways to put the irons back on them. More and more were taking their shot.

Bass and Bennie had entered the cave with a torch Bass had lit with rosin. Without speaking, they had wound through a tunnel until they eventually found the first of two chambers. Bennie quickly raised his head because the room was gray instead of black due to a small bronze shaft of light that melted down from a corner opening in the barn-tall ceiling. The hole was big enough for a man to squeeze through—even a man of Bass's size—but Bennie didn't appear to grasp its importance or see all there was to see. So Bass told him to look again. That was when Bennie realized that what he had perceived to be a crack running from the opening and continuing along the cave wall was actually a rope. Bennie laughed as he hurried to it and took the rope in his hands and tested its strength.

"Have at it," Bass said.

Bennie grinned and immediately started to climb the rope. He was a strong young man despite inheriting his mother's small frame. He was agile and quick and fiercely competitive. He went up, stuck his head through the portal, and came down with no trouble. He laughed again, enjoying himself. "Come on," Bass told him. "There's another room I want you to see."

The hole in the ceiling of the second chamber was closer to the center, so the rope hung down visibly. This time Bennie casually walked to it, its frayed end dangling less than a cubit from the flat limestone floor, like the floor in either jail cell in Fort Smith. Bennie reached out a hand, a finger, and touched it.

Bass silently watched as he held the torch, its shadows dancing from his breath.

Bennie looked up again, then down for some reason, and he stomped his feet as if testing the strength of the floor, as though he might knock a hole in it and discover another chamber was below that one.

"Would you a done it?" Bennie asked.

"Done what?"

Bennie looked up from the floor in Bass's vague direction. "What that man out there done. For me or any of us?"

Bass pushed his hat back to let the cooler air of the cave cool his head. "That would be one pregnant lesson I wouldn't want."

Bennie reached up and gave the rope a quick tug as though he expected a bell to ring. "What if I wanted you to?"

"Well," Bass said, "I'd have to try everything else first, you know? What if you weren't dying after all? What if there was some new elixir you could take? You always gotta let the Lord work his plan." He remembered Bennie lowering his face again, and he remembered shaking his head. "I just don't know, son. I understand the man's thinking. I wouldn't want a body to suffer neither, especially my son or any a my baby girls, but there's a lot to try first, to wait on, to reckon with, you know?"

"But if all that was behind you, would you if I wanted you to?" Bennie raised his head high, stood straighter, and they gazed into the bottomless rooms of each other's eyes until their souls felt released into that timeless cave where the inside was outside as the outside was inside. It was as if they were fearfully and lovingly clinging on to survive, like how they did father and son a lifetime ago in deep spring water when it was the boy's time to learn to swim.

Eventually Bass pulled himself away and turned, saying, "I just don't wanna find out."

◆ ◆ ◆

When Bass saw the woods thinning, the edge of them directly before him, and the steep incline of the mountaintop just beyond the edge, he stopped to lean against a pine to rest his legs. Once he'd stopped panting and could hold his breath, he listened to the yonder barks and clucks of restless black-crowned night herons and, in between them, when there was nothing else, the wind pushing steadily past him. Perhaps it was the earth's turning he heard and felt, almost a whistle it was so steady, steadier than common wind. Either the posse was too far away to make a sound he could hear, or he was simply above their sounds, a place where they could not reach but were not at all far away.

Hiking over rock with a bullet in his leg and blood in his boots was no easy charge. If it weren't for the earth pressing him onward, he would have lingered until his legs had quit throbbing. He would have stretched out on the ground to mop the blood from his boots and sprinkled dirt in them to keep his feet dry. The Lord knew he needed more rest but told him and the earth to keep moving. He was almost there, almost to him.

So Bass shoved himself off the pine and was passing the last tree with one heel in the clearing when he saw silver boulders and the side of the mountaintop ahead of him, and he hesitated to watch not just for white shapes but perched yellow ones ready to spring. A narrow path also lay ahead; he just couldn't see it going both left and right around the boulders and rising upward to the mouth of the cave. If he took the path to the right, he would pass the natural stone corral where Bennie could have hidden his horses—his own black one and Dell Weems's liver chestnut—and, beyond it, the crevices in the mountainside where a body could tuck. Going left was the faster way to the top, where he prayed his son wouldn't be, so Bass would go left in case his son was there in the cave and in case he wasn't.

When he saw no threat ahead, he strode on.

"Stop yourself right there," a bearish voice hollered. "Stop, I tell you!"

Bass halted but repositioned his stance to have solid footing. "Ain't moving," he said, eying the boulders. A man's voice—deep but young—had come from their direction, one Bass didn't recognize.

"Empty those hands. All of it! And your gun belt too. Take it off."

"I'm the law."

"I know that, old man. Do what I say, I tell you."

Bass lowered slowly to lay the rifle, the lamp, and the Colt on the ground. "You could hang for this."

"Shut it!" the young man said with a quiver of nerves in his voice, which began to sound vaguely familiar to Bass. Then the young man fired a .22 rifle—but not at him—like a cluck of the tongue toward the sky, hardly louder than those night herons. He pumped his grip and fired again quickly without aim before the first casing had finished clinking against boulders. A glint of the barrel showed where the shooter crouched, low to the ground and peering at him from between two boulders.

Bass raised his hands, hopeful the young buck would eventually distract himself trying to determine if the others had heard his signal and were coming. Bass wouldn't have much time before someone arrived.

"Your belt! You heard me; drop it!" Boots scuffed against rock as the young man rose. His indistinct face glowed now like a picture—a moving picture—of a face hung in air. His jaws worked a wad of tobacco as if he were starved and had thoughts of swallowing it.

"Go easy," Bass said, lowering his hands to reach for his buckle. "Ain't looking for no shootout with you."

The young man chewed as if he were full of pressure and then just as quickly his jaws stopped and he spat. His movement gave Bass another glimpse of the rifle, its octagonal barrel. "Hurry up!"

Once Bass let his belt drop, the young man stepped away from the boulders with his jaws again in motion, which made Bass wish he had tobacco. Tobacco sure sounded good right about now.

"Mind if I join you?" Bass asked.

"What? Shut it, old man, and come sit it right here, away from your guns, you hear?"

Bass stretched a long step over his belt and everything else, then started to ease down.

"More!" the young man grunted.

So Bass eased back up and took another long step and could now make out the young man's face from the shadows.

"Good God, that blood all over you?" the young man asked. "Whose, by God?"

"Mine," Bass said weakly. "All mine. Got hit, and it wouldn't quit. Can I sit now? I shore need to sit now."

"I told you to, didn't I?"

Bass lowered to the ground with a groan. So this was the young man with the 1890 slide-action Winchester and the amber stallion. The one who'd farted and lost five dollars to Eddie for thinking Bigfoot's foot was bigger. The one who always won his wagers back.

"Does your daddy know you run off with his rifle?" asked Bass.

"Hell, what you mean? This'un mine!"

"Most young'uns like the nut-cracking clickety-clack of a lever action. Pretty fun, I gotta say. That slide-action nice, though, if you like the feel a that corncob grip. You like the feel a that corncob, do you?"

"Shut it, right now!" He held the rifle on Bass.

"Don't feel like talking no way." Bass released a breath with a groan. "Can I least have myself a snuff?" When the young man didn't immediately answer, Bass continued, "I'm going for my snuff tin. Just in my coat pocket."

"You might be dying, might not, but you sure be dead if you try something or don't shut it."

"Can't be killed twicet," Bass said. He reached into his coat pocket and slowly withdrew his fire-starter tin. He held it up and turned it over to show the young man, letting the can flash in the starlight like a squirming fish. Then he set it on the ground in front of him, lifted the lid, and placed the lid beside the tin. "I 'preciate this."

The sight of the truth—that the tin was a tin and not a pistol—must have eased the young man's nerves because he leaned back against one of the boulders and let the barrel of his rifle tip toward the ground.

Bass could scarcely make out the strips of charred sackcloth and the wood of matchsticks. He had a piece of steel and flint in the can, too, half-submerged in the rosin powder, but he only wanted the rosin. He sank the tips of his thumb and forefinger deep into it for a good pinch and placed the pinch in the cup of his other hand. The wind pushed but didn't bull. *Don't bull*, he told it. Then he reached for another pinch of rosin. And then another. "I like to light mine," he said.

"You do what, old man?"

"I used to sniff it, you know, or pack it in my cheek, but my Cherokee friend taught me to light it. You let it burn, and you breathe the smoke in like a cigar but way better. Wakes a groggy head in an instant, really clears it."

"Don't burn your hand?"

"Well, not no more." Bass brushed his fingertips together over his palm to knock every speck of powder off before reaching for a match. "Wanna try?"

"Shit, no." The young man pushed away from the boulder and stepped closer. He sniggered. "But I'll watch you make a fool of yourself."

"You must learn to swallow before you cough. That's something my Cherokee friend would say," Bass told him, but it was not true. That was something Bass had said after a silence several times to Eddie when they were up late and drowsy before a fire or on the porch in Calvin drinking, and Eddie had never failed to chuckle, even that first time. Bass always had chuckled with him. He had to. Truth sometimes was a secret because it sounded like a joke.

"Must learn to swallow before you cough? What's that supposed to mean, old man?"

Bass struck the match off a tooth and watched the blaze ball down. "I was hoping you could tell me," he said. Once the flame had grown tall again, he tucked the match between the middle fingers on the hand with the rosin. Bass glanced up at the young man, at his eyes wide with anticipation, at his mustache and sideburns, at the moles spattered across his neck, and at his eyes again, dark blue or green or gray. Bass felt the heat of the flame sinking closer to his skin, so he smiled at the young man before turning to look at his palm, and then he flung his hand up—not straight up, but up and out. When the rosin flew through the flame, it ignited so much like gunpowder, roaring into a plume of fire that engulfed the young man's head and arms, his entire upper body.

He shrieked and stumbled backward, dropping his rifle and flailing at the fire swirling about him while Bass rose and followed him. By the time the young man realized he wasn't actually on fire and that the fire had already vanished into smoke, Bass beat him down quickly and watched him crumple to his knees.

Furious that this anguished young man must have searched through Eddie's clothes for his God-Almighty five dollars while Eddie lay dying or dead on the floor in Gibbs Cigar Store, Bass caught his head by his stringy hair, braced the boy's skull against the ball of his left knee, and proceeded to strike him in the jaw fist after fist until his knuckles stung from the young man's sideways teeth or splintered jawbone cutting through his cheek. As if an echo from each strike, Bass's left thigh stung from where that gunslinger in Keokuk Falls had lodged his hellfire pearl.

Bass told himself to stop before he knocked the young man's head clean off, so he released him, letting the young man finish falling flat. Bass sucked in a long breath and stood straight, his blood raging. He listened out, then strapped on his gun belt and holstered his Colt, then collected his fire tin and his rifle and the young man's rifle and the lamp, then took off running, no longer feeling a thing beyond what he heard and what he saw.

15

Hello

Bass wasn't running for his own freedom, but he was. The image of Jennie sitting up in bed in the slave quarters was real in front of him. She was darker than the darkness of the cabin and was around him now—as dark as the wet bark of a blackjack except for the moonlit gravestone of her nightshirt. She'd been too ill to run away with him. The fear charging through him was just as real as knowing that he would never see her again, that she would die before his return. Yet he could've also been running to her as he ran to the cave and the cave's Jennie tree of infinite embodiment—darkness so airy and fragile yet ringed with strength that was her strength and with onward-flowing tendril webs and far-searching branches just as blackness could be and always had been and always would be. Again and again, internally and externally, and so lovely. Yet there was pain, a family of it. And there always would be.

He heard them coming. He heard their calls and snorting horses climbing the mountain and striking their shoes on stone. He couldn't have them searching. He needed them knowing where he was. So when he reached the ridge and saw the mouth of the cave, the steps of broken stones leading to it, and the pass that stretched from the steps almost to him, he dropped the rifles and slid a hand into his coat pocket for his fire tin.

"Marlin," the men called, and the men questioned. Their sounds appeared to circle until the men must have found the one called Marlin because then they got quiet until they got loud again, cussing about the condition Bass had left him in. "Bass Reeves!" one of them roared with an Appalachian twang. Bigfoot.

Bass lit the lantern and could see now that most of the oil had leaked through the cracks in the glass reservoir. He turned the wheel to raise the wick, and the flame grew brighter. He wouldn't need it to burn long.

The men hadn't spotted the light or they'd be racing to him, so Bass set the lamp on a level rock and clasped his hands to make his flute.

"Stay put," he whistled. "Keep quiet." Bass had taught his son—all his young'uns—the Kickapoo flute. Whistling a handful of messages to each other out of the clear blue sky had become a family tradition. "Come to me," Bass would whistle to set off a chain of hide-and-seek games, usually after he'd staged a ruse or two by stuffing pillows under a blanket, positioning his boots beneath his bed, leaving a door open if it had been closed, or closing a door if it had been open. He'd even hear the older ones advising the younger ones, "Stay put. Keep quiet."

"Stay put," Bass whistled again as loud as he could sound his flute over so many other night noises. "Keep quiet. Keep quiet. Stay put." Again and again he whistled until he heard the bounty hunters saying, "There. There he is. Where? There! There at the cave. The cave!" Their voices were jumbled low and far away, but they rose together and flew past him like a flock of birds.

Bass hung the lantern around his wrist and grabbed the two rifles. When he stood, an errant bullet struck a nearby rock before the blast of the pistol could echo off the mountain. The men hollered as they charged on foot. If he posted up and picked one or two off, the others would scatter, so he climbed down from the ridge to the pass and hurried for the cave.

Bennie had laughed when he'd entered the cave in 1891 and found himself drenched in its blackness. Then, delighted by how the cave lengthened his laugh, he hollered *hello* before learning he needn't holler to achieve the rich magnified resonance of a church. The next time he spoke the word in a common manner and then he whispered it. Then he whispered it again and again, each time more hushed than before. Eventually he decided to say simply *hell* and discovered that the cave would finish the word for him. Bennie laughed about that, and so did Bass as they trod through the tunnels.

"Bennie?" Bass called now into the winding entrails beyond the lantern's glow. When there was no answer from his son, he churned his legs as fast as the cave bends and his knee bends allowed—the light flashing and dimming storm-like from the swinging lantern. If the men outside continued to holler or fire weapons, he couldn't hear any of it. In here it was just Bass and the cave talking. "Bennie?" he'd ask, testing his hunch, and each time he was relieved to hear no answer but the cave's. Bennie had listened, by God. He'd heard him. Bass had told all his young'uns never to hide in the first place people would think to look. And not in the second one either. He'd taught them ways to outsmart a tracker so that they understood an inkling of their daddy's life as a fugitive, not only as a lawman, though he found himself perturbed, questioning his judgment.

When Bass reached the first chamber, he slid to a stop and set the lantern on the floor. He debated as he caught his breath how he'd carry the rifles up, then realized he didn't have to himself. He reached for the rope to thread it through the eye of the lever of his own rifle and through the trigger guard of the young man's. He thought ahead that he'd tie a clove hitch knot when his concern mounted that the rope wasn't where it always had hung along the wall. He stretched his arms high and wide, not trusting his eyesight or the lantern light against the crinkle-crankle wall. He patted the limestone and swung at the air all around him, but nowhere was there a rope hanging from the ceiling hole. There was nothing for him to find, he decided, but a trap.

Bass held his breath to listen beyond his heartbeat. He heard no one coming, nothing. He reached for the lantern and clutched the rifles into one arm. Maybe Bigfoot hadn't found the other chamber and hadn't removed the other rope. He released his breath with a cough and a gasp, and his boots rasped against the gritty floor as he shuffled to run, so he couldn't have been certain what birdsong he'd heard just now—if that was what he'd heard—so he stopped again to listen.

"Come to me," the Kickapoo flute sang.

Bass again stepped beneath the hole, but it was too dark outside, way up there, to see anything more. "Son?" he asked.

When the rope dropped from the sky, it was as if God himself had answered because it was how God had always spoken to him whenever he was outside of a dream—always with a deed and not a word.

Bass grasped the rope and threaded it through the rifles how he'd planned, then tied his clove hitch. He was ready, so he gripped the rope above his head with his left hand before realizing he couldn't leave the lantern for the bounty hunters to use against him. He kicked the lamp into a burst of light and rattling glass shards and blind blackness, then took a breath. He hadn't attempted to climb like this in many years, and he'd always done it best when barefoot so that he could also grip the rope with his feet, but that wasn't an option tonight. He had to go. He had to hurry. The Lord had never given him anything he couldn't handle, so Bass lunged high with his right hand, clung, and heaved himself up, then clamped the rope between the fork of his boots so that he was pushing up against the rope as much as pulling himself up. He reached and reached again and again, milking the rope and rising and standing without pain even, but the men were coming. The cave walls muted them, so they could've been close.

When Bass's eyes rose above the opening, he expected to see Bennie's bright face and freckles and porkpie hat and his arms stretching to help him up. But there was nothing stretched but the rope itself, as taut as wood around a boulder. And there was no face but the boulder's face. The men below continued to make noise but were prudent, slow moving, or lost, going in circles. Bass fought himself out by clawing at sandy rock and then clambering mole cricket-like on his elbows until he was, at last, sitting on the cave's dome ceiling and reeling up the clattering rifles.

Once he'd untied the knot and held his Winchester across his lap, he searched the edges of the boulder, large enough for his son to hide behind and peek from. There were other smaller boulders and a tree up here, and there were stars, so many stars, like sand in soil. His eyes returned to the boulder and the rope wrapped around it, snug as a belt.

"Bennie," he called softly, gazing into the heart of that boulder and seeing his scared, beautiful boy. "I gotta take you in, but you know that. I ain't gonna let these bounty hunters have their way, and I'll testify. I will. I'll tell how you come to me about you and Castella and how I failed you. I didn't guide you to no place better than this, so that's on me too." He glanced back at the hole. He had time yet to speak his peace. He turned again to the boulder and searched the edges, praying his boy would step out. "I can see to it the judge take pity, and that what's left of my name after all this will keep you off the gallows. You still my flesh and blood. I love you, son, but you fucked up. Castella deserved better, and you owed her that. You owed her that, no matter what."

Voices intensified below, so Bass turned from the boulder to look down through the hole. He watched as light edged into the chamber. He waited, and a man emerged bearing a torch. Three others inched behind him into the room. They turned their heads and pistols in all directions, even briefly up at Bass, but knowing they couldn't see him in the shadows from that distance, he held still and focused on the tall one in buckskin clothes.

When glass crunched under their boots, Bigfoot stopped and squatted to study the broken lantern. He grunted at the others and pointed at the cavern floor. The posse backed away as the torchbearer lowered the burning branch to illuminate the broken lantern and its glittering lake. Bigfoot stood up, then pointed upward. Not at Bass, not at the hole, but at the ceiling directly above the lantern, four or five cubits away. The torchbearer raised the branch high above his head, and Bigfoot pushed his hat back and rolled his head and bearded face in a circle to scan the entire circumference of the chamber's ceiling before lowering his head to eye his crew.

"Let's watch out leaving," Bass heard him say.

The men retreated as cautiously as they had appeared, with Bigfoot the last to leave the chamber. When the room went black again,

Bass turned from the hole and found Bennie fully revealed, standing beside the boulder and wearing his porkpie hat. From his slumped shoulders he looked scared, but in the face he was also beautiful.

The incessant barking of black-crowned night herons seemed to die down to make room for what at first sounded like a mournful steamboat whistle, but Bass knew it was the hounds howling much closer than before.

"Where's your hat?" Bennie asked.

Bass smiled at the sound of his voice. "Traded it." Then he remembered the bounty hunters below. "Did you pull the other rope up?"

"Yessir."

Bass nodded. "You got your horses in the stone corral?"

Bennie shook his head. "Hid in the woods."

"Good. We might be able to end this right now. Might not. I'm gonna try." He dipped his hands into his coat pockets and withdrew the two sticks of dynamite and the blasting caps with mice-like tails. His son's eyes opened wide. "Get ready to lead us to them horses," Bass told him. "I'm about to blow this cave to hell."

Bass pushed the caps into the ends of the sticks, then reached for his fire tin—the closest thing to a partner he had left. Poor Eddie and Floyd, and Judge Parker was on his way, and each and every Strawberry, and wherever Hammer was, and too many sons finding trouble, and now Bennie, soon-to-be spending the rest of his life in prison—if not Bennie's life, Bass's. He lifted the lid and fished for a match. He looked up at Bennie, who was in his twenties, but he could've passed for a teen. "Huh," he said, nodding at the .22 Winchester beside him. "Take it, but don't use it unless you absolutely got to, understand?"

Bennie lowered his eyes in submission, from shame, so Bass closed his can, put it away, then struck his match. He cupped the flame to protect it from the earth's pressing, believing wind, then eased the fuses to it, and when they caught, they caught like bacon grease will catch and sizzle. Bass delayed none, tossing one of the sticks into the hole in front of him. Then he moved to push himself up, and Bennie leaped to his father's side to help. They collected the rifles and rushed to the other hole, which already glowed from a torch below. Bass tossed in the second stick.

"Run, run!" the men below yelled, and their voices rang out like a droning brood of cicadas as Bass and Bennie took off themselves, together, leaping. To anyone watching below, they would have appeared to be holding hands, holding something, or tethered by something, bumped up like a natural pair and leaping in unison from the dome to a flat-topped boulder below and then to another that they hung down and dropped from before being obscured by more boulders and trees whenever the dynamite exploded like a two-syllable word, like two peas in a pod, before the dome collapsed.

PART THREE

1898

16

The Treeing Walker-Mountain Cur

The treeing walker-mountain cur had lost its scent for sleep and food and water as an inevitability of all black things in accordance with the contrary essence of the hungering hiding n——, George understood now. Of course, he did now, with divine clarity. So, of course, the cur being black would prove a hider, a plotter, a deceiver, a drooler, and if he'd proved vigilant, placing himself elastically beneath himself to become less a master and more an overseer, George would've foreseen the end and not let his kind dominion let a wagging persuade. Of course, he should've known the mutt would eventually topple the ends of his nature by becoming a lowly rooting thing, waiting for him below the porch, where it had always before—as a steady disguise—simply slept or woke slowly from, dragging stretched limbs into the light and curling a submissive tongue. And he should've, of course, known, stepping outside as Rachel's roses perfumed the morning and as he was adjusting his hat and taking the back steps to the ground he'd owned for a half-century, that the frothy devil would, at last, unhole itself to charge and chomp. Not even Rachel remembered how the dog they called Tick had come to live with them. Years ago it had wandered or followed up from somewhere as black as sleep, covered with ticks, and now it was dead, and now, goddammit, George, himself, was dying too.

The floor was no longer their bedroom floor but his hole floor and a roof to Rachel, who could hide safely from the plotting slave inside the hole inside the cur inside of him that wanted to break out, not to bite her, but to split her, to rip her down to her skin that was no hole and no sleep and no shade, to both split and own her how a king and master and colonel of his mountain could yet in this country, by God. She was too far down from him, but hearing him yet, he knew. "You hear me down there? You hear me, Rachel, goddammit!"

He dropped to his old knees and old strewn clothes and pounded the floor until the chamber pot rattled in its hole inside its cabinet and his old fists stabbed with the pain of his toothed leg, and Rachel called up through the floorboards or the seams of the shutters and the curtains, screaming, crying, "Oh, honey, stop. I hear you!"

He squirmed his sweating belly and penis and thighs against the hard naked wood and pressed his nose against it. "You've got to get the book to him," he hollered and licked the fissures in the floor. "Got to get it to him, you hear me? Read it to him there at his door or give it to Winnie or Jennie, but make sure they read it, and make sure that thieving, murdering, perjuring, illiterate Black nothing knows that his miraculous unbirth was my doing more than Samuel's. You'll do that, won't you? Tell me, Rachel, goddammit!"

"I'll do it, I told you. I'll do it, you hear me, so stop, oh Lord, will you stop!"

If only George could stop like that treeing walker-mountain cur stopped to snatch up his hat after he kicked and punched it and hobbled inside to his study to fetch his Winchester because his Colt Dragoon was a hole like anything stolen was. That was the thing: Tick had stopped—actually stopped—for his hat that had been tossed in the tussle and was lying like a dead bird on the porch, and he snatched it up as if its master's head was still inside it, maybe thought it was, then escaped like a n—— back to its hole before the master could get back outside. That was the thing. That it stopped so much like Bass himself who didn't kill dogs but knelt low like one and testified to it. Just to show he could.

George's head rang with the hurt of his leg, and it began to spin, so he closed his eyes to slow the spinning, but he was falling through the air from it. To unbarb the whole knotted spinning wire of himself, he tried to suck in a deep breath but didn't have the suck in him. He'd vomit again or try—he knew that—and he wept water, anticipating the spasms, a choking that could take his head clean off. But he wouldn't return like a dog to its vomit if he did. Not even to mop it up or sling it aside.

And the n—— was without form, and void, George muttered, attempting to still himself with his old Confederate rye recital; and n—— was upon the face of the n——. And the Spirit of God moved upon the face of the n——. And God said, "Let there be white," and there was white. And God saw the white, that it was good. And God divided the white from the n—— and the day from the n——, sleep from white and work from shade—prepossessing and good in its place, after its kind—but shade of any shade moving upon the white was a n—— creeping beyond its borders, a multiplying beast and blight demanding infinite division and infinite fight, a film on the eyes that commenced an insidious unbecoming, a subtractive saturation and n——ization of the moral organ as if to delete creation one white creation at a time.

Officers of the Eleventh would laugh mightily around the nightly poker-rye-and-carrying-on table, but that only covered up the hole whose edge the toes of his boots were constantly edging. He'd laughed to laugh with them but resented their oblivion to the darkness not even they were awake or white enough to feel was brimming.

A hole was indeed a hungering hole, a n—— without form with a spade in its belly that dug itself as deep as the self, with hole lips like n—— lips stammering that it wasn't. By God it lay there as if within reach like it really lay there, begging him in his own image to step up to it and believe it would stay and be true and he could fill it when sleep was a Winnie or Jennie of shade and nothing more.

George opened his eyes to the mahogany block of the chamber pot cabinet and pressed an ear to the floor to quiet the air, but he was panting and couldn't stop. He slipped an arm underneath him—as if inside himself—to again feel what white felt like in a hole, then the floor shook, and he was still enough and silent enough to hear the muffled boom below as if from a fallen body.

"Rachel?" George's voice cracked. He squeezed his fists, believing he could climb free of his hole if she would just present herself once more. If she was her old, free self and only verified they were alone or even not and then left but would return to her old, naked, free white self, too, when she heard his old self trying to climb free this time through the seams of the curtains and shutters and rose-scent waves and cattle lows blowing from the boxcars running north of them near the river.

"Rachel?" he called, earning an echo. "Rachel!" he said while he could.

◆ ◆ ◆

She was too shaken to speak right away or stand straight on the warped boards of the porch. She slammed the door to shut George out, then fell apart, clinging to him.

Bass had expected their meeting to be the only pleasantry he could glean from the insufferable peck of blight that encountering George again was sure to be, but he wouldn't have predicted a reunion with Mrs. Reeves to be this warm. It was as if she'd spent all the intervening years willfully forgetting she had ever been a plantation mistress married to a slave master, and today the notion must have met her with electric urgency that what people like Bass had been to her family was nothing short of that, *family*, for what else could logically explain the intensity of her attachment?

Seeing the boards of that once-majestic mansion stacked up the same way, but not exactly the same, now peeling and leaning and rotting and warping from years of rain and sun as those same years had grayed Mrs. Reeves's hair and yellowed the white background of her dress and made a disheveled buttonbush sprout in the low spot in the yard between the porch and the road, while she convulsed against his lapels and her spotted hands squeezed his sleeves, he didn't quite feel himself. Holding George's wife how he'd never held a white woman before didn't help. For much too long he hadn't held any woman close, only his mother. At least no one was here or going by who could look on in judgment and rob her—or him—of this small comfort on this hot September day. "He's so sick! Out of his mind, Bass," Mrs. Reeves said, her words gushing but chopped as her whole body choked and drummed from agony and sorrow. "I can't bear it!"

When a deputy in Paris, Texas, received word from a lawyer in Pottsboro that George Reeves had contracted rabies from his own dog, he telephoned the commissioner in Pauls Valley, who in turn forwarded a telegram to the Choctaw Agency in Calvin, and a Lighthorseman new to the job delivered the message to Bass's cabin on the Canadian River. Bass, though, hadn't been home—if that was what the cabin that was now empty of Eddie's and Bennie's company had been to him. The Lighthorseman returned the next day and again the day after that, which was when Bass finally appeared on his porch to greet him after spending a few days fishing and hunting with his old friend Joseph Stigler, a widower himself who had served as a deputy in Fort Smith in the early eighties. Stigler was the postmaster of a cow town originally named Newman for the resident doctor but later renamed Stigler for the postmaster because Newman, which was forty-five miles southwest of Muskogee, sounded too much like Norman, which was eighteen miles southeast of Oklahoma City, and that created too much confusion for the Post Office Department. It had been Stigler who had provided what Bass had deemed his and Bennie's best hope for sanctuary two years ago after their furious ride from the cave in the Choctaw Nation. First they hid in Stigler's barn for a few hours of rest and then, after washing off in a cow pond, Stigler ferried them in his covered wagon to the courthouse in Paris. Bass had always told his friend he should be rich from playing his fiddle and harmonica for the entertainment of presidents and kings the world over, so it tickled Bass beyond measure that he'd devised a way for Stigler to collect George Reeves's reward and at least be rich.

Bass had once seen the young Lighthorse policeman riding his sorrel barefoot about town, his boots tied together and slung around the pommel, but they hadn't spoken long enough for the policeman to know the famed deputy couldn't read. When the Lighthorseman leaned over his saddle to give him the telegram, Bass, weary from being a taker on his fishing trip, crossed his arms.

"Can you read, young man?"

"Yessir."

"Good, 'cause I can't or won't. The words on that paper will say as much to me as a corpse. Hell, less."

It wasn't the news the Lighthorseman would read but the admission that Bass had uttered from his own lips that he recalled while consoling Mrs. Reeves on the warped porch of that scaly mansion in Pottsboro, Texas, the one place in the world he'd prayed he'd never see the sight of again. Maybe he shouldn't have been stubborn all his free life, refusing to learn the white man's language only because the white man had refused to teach it to him all his enslaved life. A body couldn't very well live a life and also plan for it, but relying on the Lord to forever provide him a reader by his side, at home and everywhere else, wasn't exactly living. He'd been wrong about something else, and what his lived life had taught him was that a lawman and a father had no business being both. Holding Mrs. Reeves, he remembered holding Bennie after his trial and again before his shackled son boarded the train to Fort Leavenworth to begin serving his life sentence. Bennie had crumbled, too, crying like he never had as a boy, crying so like this poor white woman who wasn't poor at all, falling absolutely apart.

"I'm proud of you, Bass," Mrs. Reeves had collected herself to say in a single breath. "What you've done with your life." She pulled a handkerchief from a sleeve and dabbed her eyes. "It's amazing. I wouldn't dare say that in front of George."

"Expect not."

She sniffled as she pulled away. "You must be here to pay your respects."

"Yes, ma'am, thought I ought," Bass said, looking at her, and he was aware he was looking at her. It was so easy. But then she shut her eyes as if to say it wasn't so easy for her, and she gave her head a quick shake.

"He's been obsessed with a book. This was before the bite. He keeps telling me, insisting, I make you aware of it, make sure that you see it."

"I know about it. I've seen it. Samuel Harman's book you talking about, right? *Hell on the Border*?"

She nodded and looked away and heaved a sigh. She was twisting her handkerchief as if to wring it dry.

Stigler had been the one just days ago to show the book to Bass. He had gone to his saddle, produced it from his saddle rider, and rounded their campfire as solemn as a bailiff, carrying it with both hands in front of him. Samuel's book, though, had been heavier than any bible and longer even than *Moby-Dick*. All Bass knew was that the book was devoted to recording the life and times of Judge Parker and his Fort Smith court, the lawmen and the outlaws, and that, in the course of his research, Samuel hadn't spoken to Bass once about any of the thousands of arrests he had made or dozens of shootouts he'd survived in over twenty years as a deputy. His friend had read the story to him about Jimmy Casharago, who proved to be one curious character but not the least bit real, not like the man Bass had known.

In *Hell on the Border*, Cash was no more than a fried fish. That was what Bass believed the stories in newspapers and books tended to serve: a meal, with folks like Bass being what was tossed with the guts during preparation. A story writer counted up the crop rows and could tell you what type of pea was growing and how much rainfall it needed per season and what part of the world that type of pea had come from and all that, but the writer missed the truth of the way a thing was—unless the story writer was Herman Melville. That man turned over every stone to tell a story. But most accounts Bass had ever heard had a hollow plan that didn't remotely approach the treacherous thing that life was. Sure, it would have a nice flavor smoked or roasted in, and it might fill a body up for a time, but a meal wasn't the same as life or even truth.

So Bass hadn't been the least bit surprised that Samuel had left Bass out of Jimmy Casharago's story and out of Belle Starr's story and therefore out of Eddie's and so forth. Or that Samuel had decided to leave stories out altogether, the ones about the Coldiron brothers, Frank Buck and the Bruner brothers, Jim Webb, Chub Moore,

Yah-kee, Tom Story, Bob Dozier—so many—perhaps because those stories would have provoked readers to wonder more about the lawman than the outlaws, and they'd want to know his name. Those fish, cleaned or not, would have come alive as a school and consumed the whole forsaken wreck and made *Hell on the Border* a Negro book, and Samuel had never been the sort of white man to allow that.

Stigler, on the other hand, had been mad as hops. "History is biblical," he fussed. "It's sacred, or should be." Then to burn away his frustration, he snatched up his fiddle and bow as if a bow and arrow and began to stalk, began to sew, began to saw. Bass loved to watch him play.

Bass held his battered tin coffee cup with the tips of his fingers and watched the steam rise and the smoke from the campfire ascend in silver feathers the color of Stigler's bone-straight hair. His feet were beginning to toast inside his boots. He might soon kick them off. He sipped the coffee, and his eyes drifted shut. Stigler's fiddle made the prettiest and saddest music Bass had heard since Jennie would sit at her piano teasing her favorite Bach concerto with so few notes stretched over so much silence. She'd trickle here and trickle there when he least expected a trickle and then brooding chords would swell.

"Bass, come on join me," Stigler said. He'd always enjoyed Bass's songs, but Bass didn't have the heart to dream up words for one. He chose instead to hum and enjoyed the humming. He drifted along, humming for a while, then he popped his lips to break it up and clicked his tongue, imagining frogs riding horses in the rain. He clapped his hands and slapped his legs, and Stigler's fiddle made him want to hoot, so he hooted and then hummed when he wasn't hooting and popping and clicking and clapping and slapping and then, with his hands, till the end, he whistled.

◆ ◆ ◆

"Tell me, Bass, I need to know," Mrs. Reeves said. "How's Jennie?"

His old houndstooth coat hung heavy on his shoulders. "Jennie's gone, ma'am. No longer in pain. She had it bad. Been two years now." To be polite, he held his hands in front of him to hide his pistols.

Mrs. Reeves was shaking her head. She reached out and touched his arm. "God bless her. She was such a good soul." She gazed off toward the buttonbush and its red seed balls.

"Thank you, ma'am. She was that." He couldn't miss Jennie now without missing Judge Parker, since both had fallen within weeks of each other mere months after Casharago's hanging in 1896. First Jennie and then Judge; Bass had been in town for neither. Like that and like that, he'd been ambushed. Each one had already been buried whenever he learned their time had come and gone. It was the saddest miracle of all to lose a loved one and feel nothing from the passing.

"Like a sister to me or best friend," Mrs. Reeves said. "I just loved her. I really did. I really did." He watched her eyes fill for Jennie, then they shifted briefly to his. "Go speak to him through the door. The door needs to stay locked. Rub is up there keeping watch." She shuffled backward to a rocker and eased into it. "I'll plant myself here so I can have just one more moment of peace."

"Yes, ma'am." Bass stepped toward the door and held the brass knob as he peered through the fan-shaped transom window into the foyer, which seemed much smaller than he recalled, making the darkened staircase also seem much closer to the door, a throat to the mouth.

The knob felt loose and rattled as it turned, and the hinges whined until he stood inside, removing his hat and shutting the door behind him. The dank, unstirred air in the house was pungent as vomit.

A thump of a head or a heel or an elbow struck the floor upstairs. When Bass reached the staircase, he stopped to listen.

"Rub," George repeatedly muttered above. "Rub, I know you hear me. I know you're there."

Bass took the steps but stopped on the landing.

"Go get her," George said. "I'm telling you, go get her and bring her to me. Bring her to us, Rub."

Bass climbed the remaining steps and watched Rub's round head turn in his direction to see him rise from the well. Rub sat in an upholstered chair in the hallway beside a closed door. He sat bowed as if from a stomachache. His skin was the darkest color in the house.

"Rub, is it time? Is she back? Rub, you know what to do, don't you? You understand, don't you, Rub?" George's words sounded wet, heavy, and slow as if George had secreted them.

Bass approached without a word. Rub tilted his head to see him, showing his scarred cheek, but he was also silent.

"Rub? Rub?" George begged.

"Yessir?" Rub said.

"Who is it? Who's there?"

"You been talking enough about him I guess he done heard."

Bass shook his head. "What're you still doing here like this, Rub? The War Between the States long been over."

Rub glared at him. "Getting paid. *You* getting paid to be here?"

"Who's there, goddammit?" George asked. "I want to know who. *Who*?"

"Bass Reeves, sir," Rub answered.

"Bass?" The name was a whisper. "*Bass* is here, now?" George began to pant. "You hear me, Bass?" His voice was gathering strength even as he huffed. "Bass, you goddamned hungering hiding n——, unhole yourself this instant!"

"George," Bass spoke calmly, "you always showed when I was at my lowest."

"Because you were always at your lowest."

Rub snickered.

Bass sucked in a deep breath, then swallowed, then he shut his eyes and clasped his hands and hat together in front of him. He had come to say this, so he did: "The Lord is my shepherd; I shall not want." He liked how his voice filled the hallway, though George pounded the floor and raged for Bass to end his prayer.

As Bass recited the Twenty-Third Psalm, he recalled a story about General Nathan Bedford Forrest and his brother William that Judge Parker had told him on their first meeting in January 1875, after

Judge had ridden through the snow from Fort Smith to Van Buren to recruit Bass as one of his deputies. With the audacity of his older brother, William had ridden his mount into the lobby of a Memphis hotel that served as General Grant's headquarters after the fall of Vicksburg. William had spun his horse in a circle beneath a chandelier and brandished his sword while letting out a rebel yell to panic the enemy before riding back out. Judge had told him that story to emphasize the importance of surprise. "Bass, if you're bold enough, catch people off guard, they'll lose their mind. Every officer in that hotel would have sworn on my bible that the rider was Nathan Bedford, so that's how the story was told. People still believe that account because people tend to see and remember what they want or what they fear, what makes the best story, not what's actually in front of them."

Bass's imagination drifted to those early years as a deputy in the territory when he relied on the psalm to quiet his mind and nerves or stay awake. He'd recite the psalm for hours while riding Strawberry through dust and rain and over rocks and clover. There had always been a moment during his recitation, his meditation, when he realized he was floating between states, between past and present, between ground and sky, between wakefulness and sleep, and it seemed then he was levitating, that his precious sorrel was the Lord and the Lord was a cloud and that cloud was carrying him.

When he reached the end of the psalm in the upstairs hallway of George Reeves's mansion, that moment and feeling returned. He was aware that he was above Rub sitting and George crawling, and he decided to begin another prayer, one specific to George and his damnation. "Lord," he said, "you led me to George Robertson Reeves and his father and family a long, long time ago, so that, I figure, I would grow strong and wise in every way and meet Jennie and have all our beautiful young'uns, which I love you for. Not doubting you none or nothing, but you and I both know George was already dog-bit way back when, so I expect by now, behind this door, he's sprouting a damn tail."

Rub guffawed.

"Yes," George exclaimed, "a tail!"

"I ain't foolishly trying no more to lead him up your gangway, Lord, but I do pray that when this son of a bitch kicks the bucket—"

"Whoa, now!" George said while Rub continued to laugh.

"—his dog-man nose will someway sniff his way dancing there to you in the land a things beautiful, things amazing, things a bunch dang sweeter than the foul fart air in this falling-down cabin of a old-master mansion and that dog-man nose of his will finally rouse his cold dead heart that's neither dog or man, just stone."

"Enough about my nose and heart, Zip Coon," George muttered, his old voice as creaky as two dry sticks rubbed together. "Tell me more about my tail. My *tail*."

"It'd shore be a miracle a grace if you found him worthy, Lord," Bass continued, "but maybe this rabid dog-man can squirm hisself closer. Closer enough. He shore might if you throwed in $25,000 to make up for the generous reward he give my good friend Joe Stigler."

George spat beneath the door. "Choke that motherfucker, Rub, and split him open. I'll lap his fucking blood, I'm goddamn thirsty enough. Do it, Rub, you hear me?" he snarled and slurred. "Then Rachel, fetch Rachel."

"Amen," Bass added and opened his eyes. Rub was hanging his head and burying his face in his meaty hands as if he were tired, as if he were praying, as if he'd finally had enough of the man they'd once called their master.

"Oh, Lord," George said, panting, "how you must hate me with all your Christian heart. You don't love your enemy, do you, you hater skinned with darkness? Admit it."

Bass leaned closer to the door and pressed a palm against it. "Course I hate you. 'Cause I hate evil. I'm a man, but just a man, George. I ain't trying to be God out here."

George cackled and the door vibrated. "You're dying, Bass Reeves, and you don't even know it. I have, at last, vanquished you. You're a ghost no Lord of yours can save. One day from now, you'll be limping along, and suddenly, Bass, you'll realize you don't remember a goddamned thing. You'll look around, grasping at straws, but there won't be memory of you anywhere. No book of remembrance. Nothing. Invisible as the hole you're in, the hole you are—to the law, to the nation, and to your own hole young'uns. And I see it; I swear to you I see it so clearly now. They'll cast you where holes are cast, in a pathetic potter's field, because you had to sell everything of value you ever stole. Guns, horses, houses. Then your hole young'uns will sell off what worthless shit you did have. It may not be written but now it's spoken: you'll be broke again as a fucking slave, a fucking mule, *my* fucking mule, motherfucker. And then, *poof*, gone."

Bass licked his mustache from the corners of his mouth. "If that so, George," he said, "that's all right. A tail ain't bad to have or be like, true, true, but as much as sometimes I'd like to be something else, George, I'm a man. I ain't ever forgot I had to fight you to be one, and as a man, I gotta celebrate a hole. Breath to breath, dust to dust, you know?" He lowered his hand from the door and patted Rub on his rounded back, then stepped away.

George shouted and thrashed against the floor as Bass coursed through the shadows of the stairwell and the pale shafts of window light as he crossed the foyer. George was shredding his throat with cries, then Bass was standing once again on the warped porch boards in front of a closed door and smiling at Mrs. Reeves, sweetly sleeping in her rocker.

PART FOUR

1909

17

The Beat, the Bag, and the Boy— So Bright

His body moved with the grace of a clock, from bed to floor and door to door, as if rigor mortis were already setting in.

For decades, whenever he was home, wherever home was, Bass had kept his bamboo cane in his trunk of disguises. After his injury in Keokuk Falls, he began to hang it with his hat on a coat hook on the hall tree by the front door, both in Calvin and then here in Muskogee, using it only when he ventured out. Now he kept his walking stick close even after removing his guns. Where he went, it went in his left hand, his own constant body servant, in case his head started swimming so fast he might fall without it. Dizziness and the nausea and vomiting it could lead to were so far the worst of it, worse than the stomachaches or the swelling of his feet and legs and eyelids. If he stopped throughout the day to rest and eat plenty of fruit, he could keep the dizziness and sweat at bay, and though his piss might be cloudy, it wouldn't be bloody.

In the beginning he learned the value of routine. When he walked his beat in Muskogee's Negro District, he followed the same route with as few deviations as possible. He turned left from the boardinghouse on the north side of Howard Street and headed into the sunrise to meet the boy on Altamont. He'd lived on that street before he remarried, back when he was a federal officer appointed to the Northern District, with Muskogee as its court seat, with a jurisdiction consisting of the Cherokee, Creek, and Seminole Nations. Sometimes after a rainstorm had flooded the roads, Bass remembered Muskogee for what it had been when he'd first arrived in the area in 1862 as a fugitive. It was a waterlogged canebrake known as the Three Forks due to the nearby convergence of the Arkansas, Verdigris, and Neosho rivers. Like so many other swaths of Indian Territory, the bottomland had gone unmolested by white men. But then came the 1870s and the grading and bedsticks of the Missouri, Kansas and Texas Railway: the first railroad to enter the territory that formed a wishbone connecting Kansas and Missouri to the beeves in Texas. Rail camps gave birth to overnight towns along its southbound spine, attracting thousands of investors, immigrant workers, squatters, peddlers, and outlaws. A decade before the French began assembling the Statue of Liberty on Bedloe's Island, American engineers had stitched across the nation's heartland an altogether different embodiment of ingenuity and liberty—that cautionary demarcation between law and lawlessness and the haves and have-nots, known first as the Dead Line but then increasingly, more affectionately, the Katy. From a conflagration of rival opportunities, Muskogee had risen on that heart scar like a boil—if a boil could become a callus and then a fist. Muskogee was now the second largest city in the state, with a thriving colored population that Bass was proud to serve even if the pay was a hell of a lot shorter than the walk.

The morning glow began to hump up ahead of the sun, like the rounded back of one fatigued old man struggling to rise under the weighted cover of another long, restless night of war dreams and George dreams and cussing. When Bass reached Altamont Street and turned south, the sun had not yet cleared the rooftops, which was typical for a few minutes after six. He liked his right hand to be free when people approached or passed in wagons, but this was Altamont. He knew the ones he saw: the washerwomen at the Silver Steam Laundry, the kitchen help at Turner Hotel, the day laborers who trekked eastward to find work at Vitrified Brick Company, Muskogee Canning Company, and Chapman's Lumber, and they knew Bass. They exchanged their usual greetings without slowing, and off those younger, healthier Oklahomans went, scissoring their legs to avoid being late. Sometimes he saw the newspapermen for the *Muskogee Cimeter* in their suits and polished shoes, but not this morning yet.

Bass went easy over the ruts to cross the street, holding his satchel away for balance in his right hand while he leaned into the cane. Bass wore a badge on his coat's lapel and carried a Smith & Wesson New Century .44 on his right hip and a whistle in his right coat pocket, but he'd never once carried the club that the police department had issued him, just as he'd never worn a uniform with the thimble-shaped hat because only white officers received those. For the Negro police who could only arrest other Negroes, Chief Kimsey overlooked protocol. "That don't mean you can go lone wolf and wear anything you please," he'd said, eyeballing Bass before allowing his eyes to sail across the three other newly hired Negro policemen standing in his office on the evening of November 15, 1907. Statehood wouldn't go into effect until the next day, uniting Indian and Oklahoma Territories as the forty-sixth state, yet the indication was already clear that Jim Crow would become the law of the land. "The suits you're wearing are respectable enough," Chief Kimsey said. "Wear them."

From the window behind the chief and the chief's desk, Bass watched hat brims and coat tails and bell skirts of the Negro men and women congregating across North Third outside Hinton Theatre lift and ruffle from the wind as a maroon Ford Model N glided by. Bass was sixty-nine, still working and still wearing his houndstooth coat and trousers and plaid bowtie, the first suit he'd ever owned, nearly thirty-five years old itself.

"Y'all will get your badges in the morning," Chief Kimsey told the men, and his eyes settled on Bass again. "You're to display them over your heart. No secret business to police work. Your people need to know y'all one of us."

"Our people will name their firstborn sons after us and sing songs in our honor, ain't that right?" Bass looked to the others as they agreed.

"Wouldn't that miracle be nice," said Chief Kimsey, absently tugging the end of a sideburn of graying red hair.

"Chief," said Paul Smith, whom Bass had known to be reliable with a rifle after they served earlier in the year together as deputies when Paul had distinguished himself in a gunfight with a secret order of black anarchists squatting in a house on North Fourth Street. "We get extra pay for felonies?"

Chief Kimsey quit tugging his sideburn. "Look, there won't be rewards for allowing crime to run over hills and dales. I ain't expecting y'all to work miracles like you're baby Jesus and the three kings from Orient Are, but be good and fair to them, by God, and most will be good and fair back. That'll be your reward."

"Mine'll know me by my bag," Bass declared.

"Your bag?" Chief Kimsey looked low on either side of Bass, as did the three other policemen. Although Bass's right arm hung straight, his hand made an open, empty cage while his other hand clutched only his cane.

"That's right," Bass said. "I got a satchel a guns and a boy to tote it."

◆ ◆ ◆

Bass admired the stone and brick of Dunbar School for colored children, which to him was as glorious as a courthouse. Then he came to his old residence and stopped. He wondered what tasty meat those who now lived there had eaten the night before. Unlike the boardinghouse he owned on Howard, he had rented a room here and lived with three other families. He and the boy's parents had been good friends. Since Art had been a butcher on North Main, each night he returned home with cuts of meat for his wife, Sheri, to cook for the next night's supper—usually ham hocks, chicken necks, or chitterlings, though sometimes bacon, beef shanks, or short ribs, and there was usually enough in Art's sack to share with everyone in the house. The owner kept their rent low for that reason, and for that reason, Art and Sheri would probably never live elsewhere.

Before the weather had turned colder, the boy waited for him on the stoop. Bass wouldn't have to stop walking. The boy would hop up and appear next to him, and Bass would hold out the bag and he would take it. Nowadays the boy waited just inside the front door.

Bass stopped but never took the trouble to climb the steps to knock. He moved the satchel to his left hand so he could reach into his pocket and blow his whistle, but not forcefully enough to wake every dog in the Negro District. But the door didn't immediately open. The boy kept him waiting today.

"Rise and shine!" Bass tipped his hat. "Morning, Miss Celeste," he said to those passing on the sidewalk. Then the front door opened.

"Bass!" said Art, stepping outside without a hat or coat, and Bass feared the boy was sick and wouldn't be working today of all days. Sheri followed Art and then the boy appeared behind her, wearing his coat and tweed hookdown cap.

Art met Bass on the street and shook his hand, then Sheri took the steps down and gave him a hug.

"How you faring this morning, Bass?" she asked.

Bass listened to his body. He was sore and swollen and throbbing all over. The spinning got faster when he thought about it. His sweet baby girl Lula, with the biggest and cutest buck teeth, had been only twenty-one when her heart had given out during an epileptic seizure in 1899. "I feel better moving," he said.

"We love you," Sheri said as her hand caressed his back. "God bless you."

"God bless y'all." Bass stepped away because her circling hand was making him nauseous.

"We'll come by every Sunday to check on you," Art said.

"Do that," Bass said, and the boy caught up and took the satchel.

They were as far south as Market Street and waiting for men on horseback to go by before Bass spoke again. "I never told you about Henry on the plantation in Texas."

"Nah, sir. Don't believe so."

"Well, he was a good boy, brave as Isaac." He could see Henry running by the blur of Central Baptist Church, churning his legs as if he were taking off in a hurry right now on Market and disappearing into the dogleg turn onto North Fourth. "He took two lashes of the whip because Master George wanted to show me how cruel a man he was. Henry was your age, about ten, and dying to prove hisself."

"I'm twelve, Mister Bazz," the boy said.

Bass nodded. "Course you are now. And you ain't never been a yammering weak mouth neither. Almost a man."

When they crossed, Bass felt pride in his church for having heat and electric light. But Reverend Hobson should have never been selling liquor to pay off church debt. It didn't matter the reverend had been the one to baptize Bass three years earlier. The law was the law.

"Henry, you know why the law's the law?"

"Way to heaven, Mama says," the boy answered.

"True, but the law ain't always the way to heaven. Plessy versus Ferguson." His stomach and feet hurt, and the wind on his face spun the church too fast around him. Until he could sit for a moment in the churchyard, talking helped. "To show Negroes got control of ourselves," he said, trying to focus on the tip of his cane and the placement of his shoes. He could slip them off easily, but he missed the ruggedness of boots. He stared down, watching. *Portland cement*, he thought, *what a thing*! "To stave off every bad thing they say," he continued as he reached the bench under the golden leaves and dangly seed pods of a honey locust. He took a few even breaths. "We got spirit but ain't wild. Got brains and hearts and souls big as theirs. Lots a times bigger. You know why?"

The boy looked his way.

"Pride," said Bass. "Course, we get the taint a pride too, but white people something else how they teach their young'uns to be proud when we make a dang effort to teach it outta ours. Big difference."

"Yessir," the boy said. He chose not to sit, instead giving his attention to the ground. It was how Eddie would have done at any age if there were sticks resembling snakes or snakes resembling sticks. Some had thorns on them that looked like fangs and forked tongues.

"I know you heard me talk about Judge Parker, but I don't believe I ever told you how he passed."

"Nah, sir. Don't recall."

"Bright's disease. On a day in November like today."

The boy was quiet, nudging a stick with the toe of his shoe. Bass leaned the cane against his leg, reached into his coat pocket for an apple, and took a bite.

Bass closed his eyes as he chewed. Once he'd swallowed, he opened them again. "Judge was good as God makes a man," he said. "Bright's cut him down in three months. I already had it one." He took another bite of the apple and shut his eyes again.

Once he'd chewed and swallowed the core, Bass pushed up. "All right," he said, "I'm feeling more myself now."

They walked past the rows of homes along North Fourth, and Bass's people came outside to greet him with a wave or shout, or they ran up to him to bring him fruit or say a prayer. Some were dressed, others half-dressed. Bass knew most by name. This stretch of his beat would be the part of his job he'd miss most if a body could miss a thing in heaven. Routine could kill a deputy, but a policeman needed to embrace it because his people needed something or someone to depend on to put their minds at ease. So he became their sun or moon, a season in the day. He was Bass Reeves from the old days, and he was coming round the bend, slower now and huffing with his cane and boy and bag, but coming. He was there working for them like a sorrel, a gun, a clock, a train, an automobile, a trolley. They would miss him too.

At Columbus Avenue, the southernmost border of his beat, Bass and the boy took an alley eastward to reach North Third and walked along another row of homes. Bass joined Eearl Love on his porch and ate two plums while the ninety-six-year-old great-great-grandfather gummed tobacco and gazed away with pearly blind eyes as he and Bass shared their oldest memories. The Creek freedman hummed a song his mother had hummed to him while she worked. Bass remembered his mother working, too, and he remembered the slave quarters filling up with Uncle Moseley's songs, the shadows of the bodies breathing around him, and how the dark log cabin with its breezy seams could become a cage of light on a clear night with a full moon. Then Bass turned to the boy sitting on the porch steps listening, not saying a word as he fidgeted with a loose button on his coat. "What about you, son? What's your oldest memory?"

The boy looked over his shoulder into the sun and squinted. "*Pow . . . pow.* Was too young to know what that was. Just knew something that loud and scary couldn't be good. My daddy told me years later what I heard was my uncle firing birdshot into the woods to scare off a white man who wanted to kill him for stealing something he didn't steal."

Bass knew the rest of the story from Art, so he didn't pry. Eearl must have guessed it.

The next time Bass needed to stop to slow his spins was at the police department when he sat in Chief Kimsey's office to hear his daily update.

"I got nothing but good news one more time for you, Bass!"

"Glory be," Bass said.

"Two years!" Chief Kimsey slapped his desk. "That's unheard of. Two years of peace!"

Bass smiled. He kept his eyes shut, but even the darkness spun. He licked the persimmon juice from his fingers and then wiped his hand on his trousers.

"I'll come by in a day or two to pick up your badge and .44. No need for you to walk all the way down here again, all right?"

"Appreciate you," Bass said.

The chief gripped Bass's shoulder before retreating to his desk. "Son, you've learned from the best, so you come back and see me in a few years if you decide to work for us regular."

"Yessir, chief!" the boy said. It was the most jubilant Bass remembered the boy sounding. Bass opened his eyes and found the boy grinning at him as if he'd been waiting for Bass to witness his joy before it vanished.

"You okay, Mister Bazz?"

Bass took a deep breath and pushed himself to his feet and cane. He patted the boy's head. "Right as rain. Let's go finish our work."

◆ ◆ ◆

There were two jails, right and left of a walkway. One held white men and was almost always near full capacity—at twenty-five—while the other jail rarely held more than two or three Negroes who had been arrested in beats other than Bass's. Today there were no Negro prisoners, so each cell held ten or so white prisoners. To keep the peace the jailers would spread them out when they could, a strategy that rarely worked among the free in the nation, so it rarely worked here.

Bass liked to look in on the prisoners after his update to get to know the faces of those who perpetually stayed in trouble in case they wandered into his beat. So he'd gone—what a blessing—two full years as a policeman without a single one of his people committing a crime, not even a misdemeanor.

From the jail, Bass and the boy walked east on Denison Avenue, then south on North Second. A southbound train screeched its brakes and blew its steam whistle two blocks farther east of them. When they crossed Court Street and then West Broadway, they could see the Katy slowing and then stopping, with passengers crowding the windows. At North Second and West Broadway stood the Homestead Building, the tallest building Bass had ever seen. Eight stories of white stone and red brick and as many windows as five or six passenger trains. The courthouse was on the third floor, though Bass had no intention of going up. He simply wanted to stand on the sidewalk once more at its base while gazing straight up the side of the high-rise into the heavens. He stumbled from dizziness and laughed as the boy braced him.

"Never saw nothing this tall in Chicago or Detroit. Course that was, what, close to thirty years ago," Bass said.

The boy smiled.

"Feeling hungry yet?" Bass asked.

The boy hunched his shoulders. "Startin'."

After checking in at each of the businesses on the first floor, stores that sold books and jewelry, clothing, groceries, confections, and drugs, they took a seat on the stools at the counter of the drug store because in the Negro District they still could. Bass sipped coffee and ordered buttered toast to go with his plums, while the boy drank a Coca-Cola and ate a lunch plate of sausage links and grits.

"Did you know a whale sometime is white? Did you know that?"

The boy stopped chewing and shook his head as his fork hovered over his plate.

"In school you learn a whole bunch a things like that." Bass wrapped a hand around his coffee cup. "You know the Statue a Liberty up in New York?"

The boy shook his head again as he siphoned cola through a paper straw. He swallowed and swallowed again. "Ain't never been anywheres else," he said.

"No, but you heard of it?"

"Nah, sir," he said, so Bass explained what it was, then set his cup down to reach into the pocket of his trousers for his coin purse. He found a penny and held it up.

"The Statue a Liberty was brown once like this here because it's made a copper too. Nowadays the statue's green, they say, from being outside so long. You see, color don't mean a thing whether we talking about a statue, a whale, or a hungry boy."

The boy was listening so Bass continued, "Years ago a white man called Herman Melville wrote a book about a big old white whale name *Moby-Dick*. Sailors were afraid of it out in the deepest sea because it was different. Didn't matter most of them was white too. It was *different*, hear me?"

The boy nodded and bobbed his head thoughtfully, slower, as if his mind had drifted off to the deepest sea and he was happy about it. Then he stretched his neck over his plate for another taste of cola.

"Always know if you're different," Bass said, snapping his coin purse closed and laying it on the counter between his plate and hat, "and know what makes you different. So you know how others are looking at you. So you can always watch yourself around them people. Be different but watch yourself. Follow the rules when the rules are good, and speak up if they bad, but be different in your head and body by being smart and strong and patient 'cause with patience comes good judgment. Being good and not evil. Being kind and not selfish. That's different. Be different."

"Yessir, Mister Bazz."

Bass patted the boy's arm and said a silent prayer for his own sons, and he named them all, on earth and in heaven, and when he named them he named Bennie first because Bennie's good behavior at Leavenworth gave Bass hope that the boy could one day walk free again. Hope for a pardon occurred to him frequently.

Once Bass stood with his coin purse open, the maid stepped up on the other side of the counter. "Not today, Mister Bazz," she said. "On us."

"You sure? Both?"

The dark-skinned maid nodded with a warm smile that reminded him of Jennie and Eddie—of Eddie's dimples. "We'll miss you, Mr. Reeves! Y'all be blessed."

"You, too, young lady." Bass and the boy collected their hats. Outside they put them on and watched a trolley pass on Broadway.

"Deputy Bazz!" someone yelled from the back of the streetcar—a man waving, wearing a straw boater hat and a bowtie.

Bass raised a hand to whomever it was. He tried in vain to fix his eyes and recall, but he let himself think instead of Theodore Roosevelt standing on the back of a railroad car in 1905 as the newly inaugurated president traveled through Indian Territory, stopping to give the same fifteen-minute speech in Vinita, Muskogee, McAlester, Atoka, and Durant. Roosevelt would grip the black iron railing with his left hand while leaning over it and swinging his right fist like a club as he bellowed to thousands, thanking them for their votes and promising unified statehood.

Roosevelt had bellowed better than any man Bass had ever heard. Bass liked him, at least the man he'd met and hunted wolves with the following week in Big Pasture, Oklahoma Territory. Bass enjoyed Roosevelt's stories and jokes and hearty laughter, but he absolutely detested his ignorant notions about Indians. If Quanah Parker hadn't agreed to join the hunting party, Bass doubted he would have gone. What Bass had never debated was his answer to the U.S. Secret Service when they telephoned him in Marshal Bennett's office. Bass had been a deputy then for the Northern District. Wishing to avoid the mistakes the Secret Service had made with William McKinley four years earlier, the calm, clear voice in Washington asked Bass— through hundreds of miles of copper cables—if the president could rely on him and his expertise to watch for potential assassins and help keep the crowds from mobbing his train. Bass cleared his throat and said, speaking up, "I be proud to, yessir."

"Until you change it, the law's the law," Bass told the boy as they crossed Broadway, and the sun warmed his shoulders. Horse hooves sounded all about him, but he only heard the horn of an automobile on another street. "One day before you know it, you'll be hearing aeroplanes overhead."

"That be something, wouldn't it?"

"Well, maybe. Watch they don't shoot at you."

Bass and the boy stopped at the edge of the sidewalk to scrape the mud from their shoes. "You know President Roosevelt gave a order that all Indian men had to have their hair cut? Believe that?"

"No! Why, Mister Bazz?"

"Humble 'em. Nobody but white folk can have pride in their people, you know?"

"Didn't want 'em being different?"

"That's right. That's why statehood made Indians honorary white folk. You see what it is? Just bribery. Don't have to ride on the back of a trolley. Can eat and sit anywheres, but they gotta give up their long hair and being Indians." Bass lifted his cane and pointed ahead of them on North Second. "Barbershops ain't just barbershops no more. Nothing, son, be only what it seem. *Everything* always something else." He approached the glass door of the bank on the corner. His reflection looked tall enough and almost thin enough to be his granddaddy, Sugar, while the boy could be him. Bass raised his cane to his mouth as if to bite it. My Lord, how Sugar walked a beat with his stalk of sugar cane in the front and back of Bass's mind. He watched himself smile, then lowered his cane to the cement pavement. "You know, son, I done waited so long to see my granddaddy and grandmammy, I almost can't wait to die. Hand to God, death ain't just death no more neither."

"Nah, sir, it ain't," the boy said. He stuck his tongue out at himself in the glass, so Bass stuck his out too. Then both—all four—were laughing.

◆ ◆ ◆

After speaking to the banker and tellers, Bass and the boy proceeded to the pool hall, the photography shop, and the long row of barbershops, restaurants, and tailors on both sides of North Second. Bass's swollen feet and eyelids were beginning to hurt equal to what he suffered from the spins. It was that time of day, when cats slept and flowers wilted. At the undertaker's parlor near Denison Avenue, Bass needed to sit. While the boy went off with Mr. Dandridge to peek at the latest corpse he was dressing, Bass slid out of his shoes and enjoyed his quiet time in the low electric light and comfortable tapestry armchair but then disrupted it himself as he bit into an apple. Two pears were all the fruit he had left in his pockets. He liked pears, but he wished he had more apples. He loved apples. His daughter Sallie loved the color red. He did too. How he loved a sorrel.

Eventually Bass caught his breath, the spinning ceased, and the throbbing in his feet and eyelids eased to a flutter. The boy returned, and the two began walking westward along Denison. When Bass had been hired, he'd chosen to work the day shift because he'd wanted to know his people, actually make his people *his people*. The primary duty of the night shift was checking that shop doors were locked. "I won't police doors," he'd told Chief Kimsey.

They turned south on North Fourth and stopped for another rest at Turner Hotel where, in the kitchen, Bass traded his pears for apples before looping back to Denison by going north on North Third. When they reached Court Avenue, they stopped to watch white people file out of Hinton Theatre, a telltale sign that the colored folks were still inside sweltering in the clover-shaped balconies, which were so close to the heat-trapping dome that everyone in the district had been jokingly calling their designated seating section n—— heaven. It didn't matter that it was now November and the sun was dropping. Men and boys exited with soaked shirts and their coats slung over their forearms, and women and girls were swiveling their hand fans nonstop. Despite it all, they were smiling and giggling, having enjoyed the touring music and magic show, and they were relishing not only the outside air but also the simple fact that they were alive with each other. Bass loved his people.

At the boardinghouse up ahead and across the street, a group of men milled outside with bottles, where a group of men always milled to watch the sunset after work and get drunk.

Hearing running footfalls on the sidewalk behind him, Bass spun and placed his back against a storefront window to see who was in such a hurry.

A young man in a dapper suit and a fedora with a pheasant feather flying from its band began to laugh as he crossed North Third in long strides. "Hey, Franky!" he called, and Franky stepped away from the group in front of the boardinghouse to greet him and share his bottle.

Bass's heart was beating fast, and he was too dizzy to move beyond lowering his hand from his holster.

"You okay, Mister Bazz?" the boy asked.

Bass shut his eyes and continued to lean against the storefront window and hold his cane. He opened his right palm and pressed it against the cold glass.

"You know, Mister Bazz, I'm gonna keep my word and go back to school starting tomorrow."

Bass opened his eyes. They felt puffy, and he wanted to rub them, but he knew he shouldn't. He and the boy looked at each other for a moment without blinking. "That's terrific, son. So glad to hear it. Your mama and daddy will shore be happy."

The boy smiled, and Bass took a long, slow breath and pushed forward. After a few steps Bass waved to Franky and the others.

"Hey, hey!" Franky said, slapping his dapper friend on the arm. "Don't let his cane or hundred-year-old mustache or midget sidekicker fool you none. That man with the satchel is a bear. He arrested his own son."

"Own son?" the dapper one chuckled. "Not much of a family man?"

"Even arrested his own preacher!" Franky added, and the group of men cackled.

"They all thieves," the dapper one said.

"That man a legend!" crowed Franky, pointing at Bass. "Marshal Bass Reez limping right there from a bullet he took in a gunfight."

"Only a deputy," Bass clarified.

"He once killed a whole lynching party of bounty hunters with a stick of dynamite. That be true, don't it?"

"Not the whole party," Bass said. "And it took two sticks."

The men either bent over or bent back and howled.

"Was in self-defense," Bass attempted to explain.

"Hey," said Franky, "how many guns you carrying right now?"

Bass raised his hand. "Night, gentlemen. Y'all behave."

"Yessir," "Night," "Night, Deputy Reez," one said after another.

◆ ◆ ◆

At Commercial Avenue, Bass and the boy turned eastward, crossing North Second and then North Main as they walked to the Katy station. On the platform on the northbound side of the station house, families of all races sat on benches in the humming and flickering glow of electric light with bunched or stacked luggage, trunks, and crates. A Negro woman and a Creek woman sat on blankets displaying baked and smoked snacks for sale. A train originating in New Orleans was expected to arrive in half an hour.

Rivulets of sweat coursed from the band of Bass's hat, down his temples and neck and back and underneath his arms. He wanted to speak to Van Lynn, the stationmaster, but Bass couldn't bring himself to turn to the station house window or lift a hand. Bass gazed straight ahead at everything spinning in front of him with unfocused eyes, needing to sit first after their long walk here before greeting Van Lynn or anyone else. Bass liked saying his name, Van

Lynn; he was an interesting white fellow from Philadelphia who'd grown up on trains after running away from home.

The boy grabbed a hold of Bass's sleeve to let him know he was moving in a good direction. If not, the boy would tug his sleeve. A young colored man sitting alone on the periphery stood up from a bench. "Sir, here. Make yourself comfortable," he said, rising and stepping aside with a blooming plant in his arms.

"Thank you, sir," the boy said.

Bass remained standing for a moment before taking baby steps to turn himself around. His left leg ached as he bent down to sit. He closed his eyes and took short, even breaths. The boy heaved the bag onto the bench with a clatter at Bass's side before taking a seat.

Bass leaned his cane against his leg and removed his hat, and the sweat trapped on his head poured freely over his brow and eyelids. He reached into his pocket for his handkerchief and wiped his face and head and neck. He balled the handkerchief in his fist, then used it to wipe one of his apples.

"Starting to feel better, Mister Bazz?"

He chewed and savored the juice. "Startin'."

A high-pitched cry like a mountain lion's ripped the air, and Bass's eyes flashed open while his right hand moved inside his coat. But then the cry melted into a woman's laugh. Bass began to breathe again. Sometimes he woke Winnie with his dreams and his cussing, and she would lushly coo to him as the pillowy touch of her arms and breasts and waist and thighs cradled him with God's generous love. "It's all right, baby," she'd say. "Don't you worry none. Winnie be here, baby. Winnie here."

"When are *we* ever gonna be made honorary white people?" the boy asked.

Bass swallowed. "Good question, son."

The boy swung his legs below the bench. "What *times* mean?" he asked.

"What you mean, *times*?" Bass took another bite of his apple.

"Like two times two?"

Bass paused his chewing. "That's math."

"What it have to do with time?"

"Don't know, son. You needs to find out. But it mean something like *of them*. Two times two is two a them twos, which add up to four."

"Huh. Same as two plus two?"

"That's right."

"Yessir."

Bass took a deep breath. He sure hoped to find a letter waiting at home for him. To hear from Bennie or Sallie or Alice was one of the few blessings left for him to enjoy. None of his young'uns but those three ever wrote a letter. He loved to hear Winnie read one. He'd ask her to read it over and over to him in bed until Bass could recite it after they put out the light. Now that his mama was staying with them to help Winnie tend to him while his ailing carried him to glory, she'd be up to see him return, rocking and knitting or sewing and wanting to hear a letter read over and over too.

People seated nearby gasped at something amazing like a letter, so Bass opened his eyes to see it. But he discovered armed bandits with red neckerchiefs pulled over their faces. In the blur of his shifting vision, he counted three of them scattered across the platform. Then he spotted a fourth at the stationhouse, pointing steel at Van Lynn on the other side of his ticket window.

"This is a stickup!" The bandit in the center of the platform held up an empty twenty-five-pound sugar sack, and hands among the passengers went up. "Don't think of reaching for any guns if you wanna live to make your train. We're gonna come around, and you're to put your money in quick."

Bass looked to the other bandits, also holding up sugar sacks. The closest one stood about fifteen feet away but was turned elsewhere, so Bass reached for the satchel and hauled it onto his lap. Then he reached out once more and patted the boy's leg.

"Be okay," Bass said. He unpinned his badge and tucked it into his breast pocket, then slid his New Century free of its holster. He held it behind the satchel.

"Hurry up," hollered the closest bandit, who was moving even closer, going down the outer ring of benches, shoving the sack or the muzzle of a .38 Special in passengers' faces, barking for them to hurry.

Two or three women here and there pleaded with the bandits or their husbands. The bandit holding a pistol on Van Lynn seemed calm but then swayed, bobbing his head as if he were dancing, and then his pistol bucked with fire and a bang, followed by crashing glass and a dying wail. Passengers jumped and screamed, and a baby cried.

"He ran for it!" the bandit explained, terrified by what he'd done. "He . . . he was going for his gun or something. I had to shoot him."

"Who's next? Who the fuck's next?" asked the bandit standing in the center of the platform. He was the tallest of the four, or seemed so, and he seemed and sounded white and like a ringleader, and now he was turning and pointing his six-shooter at the train passengers seated around him.

None of the bandits sounded familiar to Bass's ears beyond how all bandits spoke to strike fear, but the three he'd heard all sounded white. The one on the yonder side of the platform was too far away for him to judge.

Bass took another bite of his apple and shut his eyes to slow the platform. He willed himself not to think about Van Lynn and Van Lynn's family. He willed himself to think only about his apple.

"Look at this old n——! Must be nice to have no worries during a holdup. Sitting here eating a fucking apple."

Bass opened his swollen eyelids. The bandit stood about three cubits away and was aiming his Smith & Wesson .38 Special between Bass's eyes, but the bandit's own brown ones were shifty and enlarged from fear.

"What the fuck're you doing?" The bandit pressed him to take his sugar sack. "Give me your money, old man, and eat your damn apple some other fucking time. Hurry up!"

Bass let go of the apple before he could eat his favorite part. He strained to focus through the spins until there was just the one bandit standing in front of him and shaking his sack. Bass blocked out all other racket. It was just him and this one bandit.

"Know what," the bandit said, pulling away the sack and pushing it at a gentleman on the bench in front of them. "Put your shit in it," he insisted then turned back to Bass. He stepped closer, reaching for his satchel, but Bass held onto it.

"N——, let go!"

"Just clothes and a bite to eat for me and my boy."

"What's going on?" the ringleader asked. He was far enough away and so was the bandit who'd shot Van Lynn and the one who'd always been far enough away, yonder over heads and hats like rows of cabbages, some like tumbleweeds, some like small houses, like a city stretched around those hot-tempered high-rises. Bass could focus on this one.

"Give it!"

When the bandit reached again for the satchel, Bass shoved it off his lap and all the pistols he'd collected over his life—twelve of them—spilled into a clanking pile.

"What the hell?" the bandit said, gawking at the lot.

Bass stretched forward and stripped the bandit's .38 out of his hand. "You're under arrest," he said, keeping his New Century .44 low to his lap as he now did the .38.

"Under arrest?"

"What the hell's going on over there?" The ringleader wove through the crowd to investigate.

Bass kept both pistols low to his lap so that none of the other bandits could see them until the ringleader was close enough. Then Bass raised one for him.

The ringleader froze. He stilled his legs and arms and the pistol that he pointed elsewhere.

"You under arrest, too, so drop that six-shooter to save your life."

"Under arrest?"

"N——s can't do that anymore," the first bandit croaked.

The ringleader shook his head. "It's a new day."

The spins were dying down, and Bass was feeling blessed. "You feeling blessed," Bass asked the ringleader, "or forsaken? Or maybe dead already? You seem like a ghost of every white man I ever killed."

"You don't even have a badge. Look, I know the law," the ring-leader barked, jouncing his head with each word as if he thought he might stab Bass with his neckerchief-covered chin. "A n——can't arrest us!"

"You right about that," Bass said. "But this really wrong n—— can shoot you the fuck dead. Or I can hold this here six-shooter on you till a white policeman come. You pick."

"What the fuck's going on there, Skip?" the yonder one shouted.

"There four of us, you crazy ass," the first bandit said. "You can't hold a pistol or even two on all us."

The other two bandits roved closer from the station house and the yonder side but kept their distance, looking over and back at the passengers surrounding them and waving their pistols back and forth, confused as chickens.

"Wait," said the ringleader, gazing at the pile of pistols on the platform then looking up at Bass, "these yours?"

"Well, I reckon they yours," said Bass, "if you brave enough to pick 'em up."

"Are you that deputy?" The ringleader's shoulders sank as if he'd hitched them up all along to make himself seem taller. "Are you that n—— *Bass Reeves*?"

"You heard a me?" Bass asked.

The bandit ringleader shook his head. "You really exist?"

Bass grinned. "I ain't just whistling Dixie."

The ringleader's white hands went limp, and the pistol dropped with a thud against the platform. Then he raised both hands above his head.

"What the fuck're you doing?" asked the first bandit.

"What the fuck, Skip?" yelled the yonder one.

"Jesus, the old n——'s Bass Reeves," the ringleader called out. He bent to his knees.

Bass turned to the first one and pointed the .38 at the platform in front of him. "You too. Down."

"What the fuck? This is fucked!"

"Down," Bass ordered, and the platform tilted and spun, and the bandit who'd shot Van Lynn bled into the first one, but then the one behind the other took off running. Bass forced himself up without his cane to see above the crop of heads and aimed his New Century. The bandit who'd shot Van Lynn was in midair, leaping off the platform and losing his hat to the darkness beyond the halo of light when Bass held his breath and fired. The bandit's head exploded more like a cantaloupe than a cabbage.

White women shrieked as Bass turned to the first bandit with the .38 still trained on him. Then he eyed the yonder bandit, sighting him in a fog with his .44. Then he eyed the ringleader, down on his belly, before returning to the first one, still not down. "That satisfy you I can kill you, fool? Down, dammit! Two years, fuck."

This time the bandit dropped to his hands and knees and spread out.

Bass shifted his attention back to the yonder side, but the bandit was no longer there.

He reached to find the boy to force him down when a pistol cracked and the bullet splintered the bench behind them. Bass fell to his knees as he pushed the boy onto the pile of pistols. Screams amid shouts and the pounding of boots erupted across the platform.

"Stay put," Bass told the boy. He couldn't see beyond the murk, but he rotated his head left toward the first bandit as though he could see him, then he rotated right toward the ringleader for the same reason. Believing he might vomit, he prayed in the way he'd long grown accustomed. That prayer of his in times of need that needed no words and felt entirely dreamlike as if he were suddenly under silent water yet, like a fish, was fearless and fast, acting and reacting according to the instincts of faith—when the shepherd of the Lord was working within him like an engine, like a heart, a lung, a liver, which knew for him what he must do, where he must go, how and when and, of course, why. Why was a given.

At the end of his patience, Bass raised his head, and from a current of brown and gray murk, a burgundy triangle appeared where the ringleader lay, and then a white teardrop hovered yonder, passing and vanishing, and then from where the first bandit lay appeared another burgundy triangle, floating—then it took off like a cardinal in flight. Bass raised both pistols, tracking the cardinal, which seemed to stop it. "I'll shoot," he said.

"No need," the first bandit said, and the triangle lowered back to the floor.

Bass checked on the ringleader, and when he saw the triangle, he turned to see what could be coming at him from behind. He saw no triangle, no burgundy, only browns and grays blackened on the edges.

Bass surveyed the murk back to the ringleader and the first bandit, to their floor-level burgundy neckerchiefs undulating or appearing to, then surveyed the murk back in the other direction, not with haste but with faith. *He leadeth me. He leadeth me.*

"Don't shoot. Please don't harm her," a man begged somewhere to Bass's right, beyond the ringleader.

"Back away. Just back the fuck away," the yonder bandit shouted from the same spot.

"Bass!" the woman screamed. "Bass, help me!"

Bass stretched his neck and found the burgundy triangle of the yonder one and strained to focus on what was around it, to see more than blur and blotch and blight. He took a deep breath and held it, but he lost patience again and huffed. He braced himself against the bench and struggled to stand.

"I'll shoot her. I'll shoot her dead," the yonder bandit warned. "And I don't give a damn who you are. Best back away or I'll shoot you too."

The bandit's triangle turned and thinned and nearly disappeared, becoming merely a line, straight as a mast. Bass raised his .44 and waited for his hands to steady. He waited for the triangle to turn again and show its burgundy face, that sail shape of centuries-old spilled blood that covered a vicious hole that seemed to exist on white men solely to take and take and bark and bite to impugn the dignity of Negroes forever.

"You too! Back away, I tell you," the yonder bandit shouted.

"Let her go," a man pleaded.

"Yonder bandit!" yelled Bass. When the bandit turned, the line became a triangle again—a heavenly target—and Bass pulled his trigger as the bandit pulled his. Bass's .44 covered the sound of the bandit's .38, but Bass saw the .38 spew white fire like bubbles and felt the bullet whiz past his ear, its wake like a breath. All he saw of the triangle was that it was there, then it was there with a polka dot, then it fell to the ground like a leaf.

"You okay, Mister Bazz?"

The woman's sobs were muffled by a tender embrace. There was no sound like it. Bass turned too quickly to check on the other two bandits and lost his balance and vision and uncontrollably vomited.

Bazz.

A man's head the size of a cannonball struck Bass in the chest, blowing him off his feet, and his back bounced against a wall or a floor. The grunting . . . the grunting up against him was like a rooting hog, and the hands around his throat all came suddenly. Bass opened his eyes, and a scarlet neckerchief hung in them. He was sprawled on his back without breath and couldn't cough. Now the bandit was strangling him or was determined to.

Bazz.

He blinked, and he heard it—actually heard it this time—the boy calling him, "Bazz!"

Bass struck the bandit's arms and attempted to pull them away, but they were too strong, so he swung a fist, and the bandit's head turned sideways, but the bandit's grip held firm.

"You ain't shit," the bandit spit out.

Bass understood now this was the first one—the ornery one—he was striking in the jaw. When the bandit's grip finally opened, Bass threw the bandit's weight aside and clambered on top of him. He thought if he could hold the bandit's wrists down, he would cuff him. The bandit's hands were small and weak, but not his arms. It would be faster to choke him out.

Bass's reach easily stretched past the reach of the bandit's arms, but before he could wrap his hands around his throat, the bandit clasped Bass's throat, and Bass let him only because that allowed Bass to grab his. This time he could wrap his hands around the bandit's throat and interlock his fingers. He watched the bandit's brown eyes stare into his. It would be so easy to break his neck that Bass decided to break his neck. The bandit's grip was loosening already as the bandit gagged and stared like he might cry. His face was turning dark red above his neckerchief.

Bass could let go and cuff him first, but he had no more patience and quickly turned to check on the boy.

The other bandit, the ringleader, was no longer on his belly but up on his knees and had taken Jim Webb's Remington from the pile of pistols while the boy stood behind him, needing both hands to cock the trigger back and steady the long barrel of George Reeves's Colt Dragoon aimed at the back of the bandit's head.

"Don't do it, Skip," the boy told him, "or I's gone blow yo motherfuckin' head off."

Bass and the ringleader eyed each other as if that were their secret signal to hold in their laughter until after the church of this final sequence of shame, when the ringleader let go of the revolver and dropped his chin and when Bass relaxed his grip on the sorry bandit's throat. But Bass couldn't help himself.

While the first bandit bucked for air and coughed as if popcorn kernels were stuck in his throat, Bass rocked back on the bandit's legs and laughed until it hurt to laugh. Then he cuffed him and laughed some more.

It would be a long night after a long day, waiting for white officers to appear. Giving statements. Consoling passengers. Shaking hands. By then the train had arrived, blowing its whistle and smoke, but now there were no passengers for it. They had all gone home. Yet out of the blue, Bass would start laughing again. A fit of laughter felt so much better than a disease.

Bass continued to laugh all the way to Altamont Street. By then the sun was rising and the boy was explaining to his parents how he'd captured an outlaw named Skip. When he repeated what he'd said to the bandit, Art and Sheri flushed as red in the face as white people, but once they looked into each other's eyes the way Bass and Jennie had done so many times before, they knew there was nothing to say or do but laugh. The boy grinned in amazement from his newfound freedom and, of course, launched into the story again. Their laughter continued to grow, rising an octave among the morning workers, until Bass, leaning on his cane, needed to sit on the boardinghouse stoop.

He opened his satchel and withdrew the 1860 Colt Dragoon, with its ivory handle and ornate nickel plate. "This pistol got a long, important history," he explained to the boy but also to Art and Sheri. "Was the first thing I ever felt free enough to take what I saw I was owed, and it'll be the last thing I give 'cause it ain't mine no more to keep." He gripped the handle tight, feeling it good. "This here saved me twice." Bass inhaled a long, calm breath as if he were enjoying a cigar, while Art and Sheri looked on with sorrowful faces. The boy was still grinning, though. He couldn't *not* grin, or maybe Bass's world was spinning more than he could perceive. "I'm saying I want you to have it, son," he said. "It's yours. You owed it now . . . if your mama and daddy agree."

Art and Sheri nodded. "Go on," said Art.

So Bass held out his hand, palm up, fingers closed on top, and let it bloom. The boy's weightless fingers lifted the Dragoon away with the precision of a doctor. "Y'all need to know," Bass said, "he can't never fire it. It ain't reliable no more. That Colt Dragoon the only pistol—the *onliest* one—he coulda taken outta my bag that weren't loaded." Bass smiled at the boy admiring the gun. "Shit don't work. Hadn't in years. Just a showpiece."

Once Bass started to laugh again, he didn't want to quit. Even after he said goodbye and good morning to his friends on Altamont and was walking home alone. Even after he opened his door and welcomed Winnie's arms and waved away Pearlalee's concern for his torn and sullied suit. Even after he hung up his hat—but not his cane—and set his satchel down. Even after they led him to a bowl

2. Muskogee Police. Courtesy Daniel F. Littlefield Collection, Sequoyah National Research Center.

of apples on the kitchen table and began to titter and teeter in their chairs at his inexplicable laughter. Especially then.

Yet Bass couldn't wait to tell them why he couldn't stop laughing or why he didn't want to stop, even if they might not fully grasp what he had to tell. It wouldn't be the same for them. It couldn't be. Though his blessings were many throughout his long life, they were never actually his to own. They were God-given and intended, like the fishes, for the multitude. The story of his life as he lived and saw it, which was how anybody saw it who had ever lived it with him, was to the contrary more like something like his mustache: something uniquely his and no one else's.

Acknowledgments

I am especially indebted to the following:

Art T. Burton, for being my big brother—the locomotive, fire-box, stoker, and water tender—in everything Bass Reeves. You're the son of a Pullman porter. Of course you are.

Ernest Marsh, for being my friend in everything Bass Reeves, our "god uncle."

Orange Rex, for buying a ledger of death certificates at a thrift store and discovering for all of us where Bass Reeves was buried: Harding Memorial Cemetery in Muskogee, Oklahoma.

Shironbutterfly Thomas Ray and Oscar Dean Ray Sr., for bestowing upon me the Bass Reeves Legacy Preservation Trailblazer Award at the 2022 Bass & Belle Wild West Film Fest.

Booksellers Debbie and Alan Foliart of Chapters on Main Bookstore and Coffee Shop in Van Buren, Arkansas; Roxanne Laney of Arts & Letters Bookstore in Granbury, Texas; and Patricia Mansfield of TCU Campus Store in Fort Worth, Texas; for always keeping the light on for me.

Western History Collections at the University of Oklahoma, for sending me a PDF of Richard Fronterhouse's thesis *Bass Reeves: The Forgotten Lawman*, and for answering all my questions.

Jennie Buchanan and Caroline Speir, for being such welcoming executive directors of the Museum of the Western Prairie in Altus, Oklahoma, and the Fort Smith Museum of History in Fort Smith, Arkansas, respectively.

Mayor George McGill, for your passion for Fort Smith's history and the city's most famous son.

Diana King and your second cousin Huston Glenn, for generously sharing the details of what Robber's Cave was like when Huston was a child playing in it (before the detonation of its ceiling).

Steve Yates, for inspiring me with your dynamite story in that wondrous old cave in Kimpel Hall, and for always helping me any time I call.

Owen Eubanks, for telling me about the time you took your daddy's (my granddaddy's) trick to a junior college speech class and demonstrated the pyrotechnics of longleaf pine rosin, for telling me again in minute detail, and then for demonstrating it off your back porch for me and the kids one summer evening.

My son Josh Carra, for leaning on me, night after night on our smoky summer deck as I approached the end. *Are you sure you can't take it higher, Stan?* you seemed to say with every knowing look and word, until I'd raised my game for the final time.

My other son, Owen, and my daughters, Shania and Emme, for inspiring every sweet part of every sweet character. There's not much sweetness in this book, but what is here is yours.

Stanley Thompson, my brother, for always happily lending an ear to a line.

Judy Coppage, for being an extraordinary agent and bibliophile. (Hi, Sydney! It's Sidney.)

Chad Feehan, the showrunner for the Paramount+ miniseries *Lawmen: Bass Reeves,* for finding my books and trusting me to be a creative consultant.

David Oyelowo, for embracing my books, for hungering every detail, insight, and hunch I could share on and off the page, and for resurrecting Bass Reeves for the world.

The entire staff at Bison Books, for believing in Bass Reeves, me, and the trilogy from the very beginning, when there was just one book for you to accept, guide, and cover with classic Bass Reeves attention and skill.

Printed in the USA
CPSIA information can be obtained
at www.ICGtesting.com
LVHW050849050823
753980LV00002B/2